JENKINS

CONFEDERATE BLOCKADE RUNNER

EMILY HILL

A.V. Harrison Publishing
Copyright ©2010
Emily S. Hill
All rights reserved.

Library of Congress
TXu 1-523137461

FOR NOAH AND NATALIE

A NOTE ON HISTORICAL REFERENCES

The two articles from *The Baltimore Sun* used in this novel, "Release of Rebel Prisoners from Fort Warren" and "Col. Cyprian T. Jenkins, An old Baltimorean, Dies in the State" appear as originally published, and are reprinted with permission, all rights reserved by *The Baltimore Sun.*

The content of all other newspaper articles, obituaries, and telegraphs is fictional, but attributed to newspapers in print 'in the day'.

MAP

GULF COAST:
CEDAR KEYS TO TAMPA BAY, FLORIDA.
REPRINTED WITH PERMISSION OF
JEFF MILLER, HISTORIAN
NEW PORT RICHEY, FLORIDA.

Table of Contents

xxi   A Note on Historical References

1	Massacre at Green Swamp	1
2	Reminiscing on Baltimore	4
3	Jenkins Lane	9
4	Gainesville	24
5	Vermont ~ Mrs. Colburn's Story	34
6	Fort Brooke	47
7	Hernando	58
8	Fair Haven	68
9	West Point	75
10	Jacksonville	91
11	Bay Port	110
12	Rose Hill	128
13	An Invitation	146
14	Kildall's Reading Room	149
15	Eliza Unrequited	154

TABLE OF CONTENTS

16	A Suitor Heads to Vermont	173
17	The Randall's of Baltimore	180
18	A Fair Haven Wedding	185
19	War	198
20	Betrayal	213
21	Capture	223
22	The Reverend's Folly	236
23	Bay Port Shelling	252
24	Thirty-Five Men	261
25	Yulee's Landing	269
26	Greenwood Cemetery	276
27	Author's Notes	279
28	The Rest Of The Story	285
29	C.T. Jenkins Obituary	287
30	References	290
	Study Guide	292

Massacre at Green Swamp

"Yah! Yah!" "Yee-haw!" Desperate cries, meant to spur on their beasts, punctuate the air as Newburne's Company of Mounted Rifles ride toward the blockhouse on the edge of Green Swamp. A group of settlers are waiting in desperation, trying to hold out against a Seminole war party that have then surrounded.

The horses of Newburne's Company gallop hard toward the river, as the riders hold onto hope that they can cross the turbulent currents in time. It is the second day of a three-day ride. Hooves pound the hot Florida sand, kicking up fleas and burrs. The men, volunteers and militia members, have been driving their animals relentlessly since sunrise. It was cooler when they started out, much cooler. Now, mid-day, their clothes stick to them in the humid air, the sun bakes the backs of their necks, and the muscles of their shoulders burn from holding the reins of the charging steeds.

C.T. Jenkins, a twenty-four year old from Baltimore, is among the riders. Jenkins, a volunteer in Newburne's Company, has jockeyed his mount one-third of the way back from the lead horse, setting a hard pace as the Company of men charge through the harsh landscape.

By sunset fifteen horsemen pace the banks of the Hillsboro River, desperate to cross the next morning, not knowing what lies in store for them on the other side.

Waiting for Newburne's Company are eleven settlers, some injured, all of them starving; some even starving to death. The air in the blockhouse is rank;

hanging so heavy the settler's breathing is labored. For days there has been no wind, only the humid veil of a Florida summer.

The defeated settlers sit crumpled next to each other along the walls of the blockhouse. The men peer vacantly across the darkened room at the womenfolk who are sheltering in the blockhouse with them. Their eyes flicker bright in the darkened room as they blink or shift their position.

An hour earlier the settlers where charged by a Creek tribe which overwhelmed them with an onslaught of shrieks, their horses whinnying. The surviving settlers have made it out of the chaos and into the silence of the blockhouse that could easily become their tomb. The door is bolted from the inside. Dead calm stretches through each day, past each sunset, and late into each night for days on end. Even the whoops and war cries from the war party have died down. There is no food, no water, but there is hope. Settlers have been known to survive a fortnight under such conditions.

Two men lay just outside the entrance to the blockhouse; now carcasses, their dried blood smeared over grotesque death masks. The expressions of pain and horror are frozen on the victims' faces. It hadn't taken long, after being scalped alive, for the men to die.

A third carcass hangs, staked to a pine tree; one stake driven through the victim's chest, and one through his belly. The mercy of unconsciousness overtook the victim just moments before a young warrior set fire to the stake embedded in his chest, burning the victim alive.

The settlers in the blockhouse cannot hear the chirping of crickets, scurrying through the tall dry grass outside the blockhouse. Nor can they feel the burrs that had grabbed their clothes as they ran for shelter. Their senses are dulled by the shock of their experience, and by exhaustion and hunger. They sit sweating in the blanket of heat, and nurturing the hope that word of their plight has somehow reached the outside world.

The third morning of their ride, Jenkins and his companions stealthfully approach the blockhouse. They are soaked from fighting the currents of the Hillsboro River. Through a storm of sand flies, they approach on their horses, single file. Dreading the eerie silence, they hope to find at least one survivor.

Newburne yanks at the reins of his horse and jumps down from the saddle. Dashing to the rough-hewn door of the blockhouse, he pounds his gloved fist against its surface. Seconds lapse into minutes – agonizingly long minutes as his riders dismount and circle the structure. Finally he hears the latch lift from the other side. He cries out with a whoop, "Men! Men!" His rider's race to where he is standing as the door creaks open to reveal a bedraggled woman. Her face is stained with dirt and tears, her sleeve torn, and her hair tangled.

"Survivors? Are there any more survivors?"

She burst into tears and nods, leaving way for Newburne's men to dash up the stairs into the dark cavernous pen.

* * *

REMINISCING ON BALTIMORE

Mrs. Colburn gathered her full skirt in one hand and reached out for Mr. Jenkins' arm with the other as the two of them stepped off the wide-plank sidewalk. They strolled away from the water toward Bay Port's central plaza.

She had befriended the local legislator while vacationing with her daughter in the small resort town of Bay Port, Florida. Before she could decide whether or not to pursue her plan, she would need to know more about Mr. Jenkins' past.

"Do go on, Mr. Jenkins. You've never spoken of your family before."

"Hmm, no I haven't, I suppose. Well, let's see. I was sitting on the bottom step of the stairs, which would have been typical. The bottom step offered the best vantage point for seeing what was going on downstairs. As soon as Mother came out of her bedroom, I signaled to my brother, Ambrose, who was hiding behind the dining room door. To this day I can smell the talcum powder she wore. She tucked her ruffled umbrella under her arm, and pulled on her gloves. Nurse was just bringing Enoch out of the nursery. Her timing was impeccable. Nurse didn't want to miss the surprise either. Mother stopped to stroke Enoch's face and cooed at him before she descended the stairs toward Father. I stood up to make way for her and then looked over at Ambrose. He was grinning at me. He and Mother looked so much alike." "It was one of the happiest moments that I can remember. I was ten years old at the time. Life became very difficult after that," C.T. Jenkins was recalling a moment from his Baltimore youth, thirty-seven years later.

Jenkins Confederate Blockade Runner • Emily Hill

"Difficult?" Asked Mrs. Colburn.

He nodded. "We were celebrating Mother's birthday. I remember Father calling up to her, 'Anne Marie, are you coming with me, or not?' Father was waiting in the foyer of our home, Huntington Manor. Mother was undoubtedly primping, and taking much too long at it, I might add, considering we were *all* waiting for her." Jenkins shook his head and looked down as he dug the toe of his boot into the Florida sand, chuckling.

"As he waited, Father pushed the curtains aside and peeked out the window to Jenkins Lane. He looked up the stairs again to see if Mother was coming down, and then glanced over at me and winked. He knew exactly where each of us was hiding. As hard as it surely was to keep eight children quiet, the house was totally silent. We had spent the week leading up to Mother's birthday planning special surprises, all of them orchestrated by Father. Once more he called up to her, 'Anne Marie! The carriage is out on the lane, the furniture designers are waiting! Shall we make it another day?'

Jenkins took out his pocket watch and flipped it open with his thumb nail, then snapped it shut before continuing. "Father was waiting for Mother at the front door with his hand on the latch. She probably thought he was anxious to leave in the carriage; but actually he was eager to show her the surprise he had chosen for her birthday. She descended the stairs, and at the front door she smiled at him. Father smiled back and offered his arm. I can see them as if it were yesterday. They walked out the door and across the porch arm in arm. Ambrose whispered across the dining room to get my attention, 'Cyprian?' That's my given name, actually. I took the moniker 'C.T.' about the time I left Huntington Manor—and Baltimore.

"Anyway, I signaled to him that the coast was clear, and he came to join me on the stair steps. Father left the front door open so those of us hiding downstairs could see what was going on.

Mother stopped short at the sight out on the lane. The umbrella that had been tucked under her arm clattered to the porch. Father was looking down at her, he was so happy, smiling and quite pleased with his, and our, ability to keep the arrival of her birthday gift a secret. It *was* quite wonderful for the whole family, actually."

As C.T. and Mrs. Colburn continued walking toward the city park, he looked around, surveying his Bay Port surroundings, before resuming. "In the lane, waiting outside the wrought-iron gate to Father's manor stood two Tennessee walking horses pulling a high box wagon. The wagon was filled with furniture designed for our foyer. The delivery had come from Brown Imports. Poor Mr. Brown! He grunted as he got down from the driver's seat. I thought of him as very old but he was probably the same age that I am now."

Mrs. Colburn smiled appreciatively.

"Mr. Brown realized immediately that he was an unwitting participant in the delivery of Father's wonderful gift to Mother."

"Not to rush the telling, Mr. Jenkins, but with such devoted parents, it is a curiosity to me why you are not surrounded by your family."

"Hmm." He looked at his companion sidelong. "Well, let me go on. I remember Mother exclaiming, 'William! What have you done?' Once again she had been surprised by Father's ingenious schemes to celebrate her birthday. Old Arthur stepped forward quickly and opened the gate to the drive, as the horses high-stepped forward, pulling the delivery wagon toward the house. Charles and Frederick, my oldest brothers, had hidden in plain sight of Mother. At the time, they were probably twelve and thirteen respectively. They had perched next to each other on the gate that Old Arthur had swung open for Mr. Brown. Mother burst out laughing. We all ran out of our hiding places, conspirators in the surprise. We were jumping and yelling-all eight of us-wanting to tell Mother our own story of where we had been hiding, wanting praise for how quiet we had been."

My Father had arranged a dinner party for Mother that evening. The party was a swirl of chatter and boisterous laughter. It was wonderful. As midnight approached, it seemed the celebration would never wind down. Father stood up to make his toast. Corks popped as the champagne bottles were opened. He shushed all of us—even his own parents—and everyone laughed. Old Arthur poured the champagne ceremoniously and for those few moments everyone *was* quiet.

"Then Father raised his glass and toasted my Mother, 'I love you, Anne Marie, more than anything else on earth. You are my greatest joy.'

Everyone cheered and carried on. Mother stood up to receive diamond-drop earrings from Father. Then she kissed him as we all looked on. We were all so very happy. The tears came later."

* *

OBITUARY
Baltimore Gentlewoman Mourned by Family
Anne Marie Wells, consort and muse of William Valentine Jenkins,
Died the 25th instant February;
Leaving one daughter and ten sons motherless.
Known for her beauty, kindness and gaiety this pious woman has departed, at a most vulnerable moment, immediately following the birth of her eleventh child—a son. Gone from those who will love her eternally; Her disconsolate husband mourns bitterly his fate and seeks solace in his family, the kindness of his community, and the wisdom of the Almighty while attempting to understand the cruelty of this most unjust misfortune.
- Baltimore Gazette and Daily Advertiser
February 28, 1826

**

OBITUARY
Complications from Childbirth

On the 27th Instant of February in her 28th year,
Harriet Wells,
Wife of Mr. Frederick Jenkins
Unexpectedly departed the loving arms of her family, to join her
Sister, Anne Marie, in Heaven.
We forever struggle to understand the mysteries of the Lord,
As Two families face a dark future as a second Wells'
Daughter,
Wife and Mother enter the Kingdom of Heaven in the same week.
These two lovely women leave behind thirteen children, and now
Two devout families must now make the journey through
Life without the calming serenity of a Mothers' gaze.

Baltimore Patriot, March 02, 1826

* *

DIED
Baltimore Lady Succumbs to Old Age
Margaret LeBlanc Wells on the 20th day
of this month.

Into eternity passes the beloved delight of
Cyprian Wells,
Mother to the late Anne Marie Wells.

Baltimore Patriot, October 31, 1826

* * *

Jenkins Confederate Blockade Runner • Emily Hill

3

JENKINS LANE 1831

Cyprian was jolted awake, escaping an unsettled sleep. Glancing around his room apprehensively, he swung his legs out from under the comforting warmth of multiple goose-down quilts and into the cold winter air. As he reached for his heavy brocade robe he thought, *One blessed day closer to leaving these miserable piercing-cold winters and Father's incessant demands.*

He shuddered as his feet hit the ice-cold floor and reflexively he brought them up. The tip of his nose and his fingers were already beginning to chill.

A soft orange glow from the crisp, late autumn sunrise played against the walls of Cyprian's bedroom. The early morning brilliance streamed through beveled glass windows. The windows offered a view overlooking the sloping, dew-prismed landscape of his father's estate. Later that afternoon the sun would warm the room, though only slightly.

As he crept about his room in the pre-dawn light Cyprian stealthily gathering what he would need for the day. He could hear the household stir as Old Arthur started a fire in the fireplace of the main foyer, and then efficiently moved to start a cooking fire in the kitchen for Lettie.

Perennial witnesses to the Jenkins' triumphs and struggles, Old Arthur and Lettie MacDonald continued on with the family after Anne Marie's death. The household also included *Nurse*, a brusque and slightly unfeminine woman who enjoyed no prospects. She fretted daily over the light mustache that decorated her

upper lip. Nurse arrived at the estate in response to an advertisement in the *Baltimore Patriot*, to take over direction of the lives of the younger Jenkins' children after their mother's death.

An hour after Cyprian's departure his father rapped lightly on his son's bedroom door and peeks in.

"Damn it!"

The four-poster bed stood as a cold testament mocking the patriarch. Sheets and comforters, twisted and tangled, spill from the bed onto the polished plank floor. The bed is empty. The room is still.

As William surveyed his son's room, the fragrance of beeswax candles and a light layer of smoke hung in the air; evidence of Cyprian's late night spent studying maps of the eastern seaboard. Drips and blotches from the careless use of a dried quill pen mar the paper and tattled Cyprian's future.

Later that evening William sat at the head of the table surrounded by his sons. Each one was seated in their established places; the oldest son, Charles to the patriarch's left. Cyprian is seated beside Charles, with Frederick to his left. The younger children are seated to the right of their father, with the exception of Constantine, still too young to dine with the family and who takes his meals in the kitchen with Nurse and Lettie. The older brothers sat facing the dining room windows, looking out to the wrought iron gates.

Supper was a glorious celebration featuring roast veal seasoned with bay leaves, simmered through the afternoon in fragrant, fresh rosemary, slow-baked potatoes and late autumn tomatoes. But it was marred by William's brooding. The vibrant fall colors of the meal, arranged on gleaming white plates went unnoticed by Cyprian who kept his eyes downcast in the knowledge that his errant activities of the day were the cause of his father's bad mood.

The silence was broken only by subdued requests from one diner to the next and by the passing of dishes, assisted by Lettie who stood behind the male heirs as the turrets and platters were passed down the table. At last, William spoke.

"Cyprian, did you deliver the portfolio to Judge Sanders today?"

"Father, the sheaf of papers sits on the console in the main foyer. Surely your notice of that fact is what sours your mood."

"That sheath of papers contains business contracts that should see to the financial stability of this family, Cyprian."

Cyprian remained silent as his father continued.

"It is through the efforts of all of us, pulling together as a family, Cyprian, that food is put on this table; and that you are furnished your fine attire; and an education is provided to your younger brothers."

I've got to get away! Even if it means I am cut off from Mother and Grandmother's estate. The constant tugging—doesn't Father realize I cannot leave Huntington soon enough? Cyprian hopes his thoughts will float their way into his Father's subconscious.

"I hoped that you would become an active partner in 'William Jenkins & Sons Tanning and Currier' by now. If I am ultimately going to hand over my position to my sons, it is going to have to be with a little less chasing and cajoling. Cyprian, and you too, Charles, for that matter, are a little too distracted from the family's business and your grandfather's agricultural interests."

"Father, as much as I respect what you do, I do not think I want to work in the same shop, in the same city, doing the same type of work for the rest of my life. I want to be among men who are imagining what lies beyond Baltimore. Conestoga's are heading out every day. Why, Charles Carroll is looking for investors for the railroad that will open routes to the south. Does that interest *you*?"

His face red, William coughed into his napkin before tossing it down. "Cyprian, your namesake grandfather and I invested in that railroad three years ago. If you were the least bit involved in our family interests and investments I would not have to be telling you this."

"Father, your curiosity of my delivery of the estate papers is a moot premise for this conversation. Maybe Frederick or Ambrose can make the delivery tomorrow. They certainly know more about Grandmere Wells' estate than I do."

"Well Cyprian, let's test how well your line of thinking goes. I invite you to ask Frederick, or Ambrose, for that matter, if either one of them is willing to take on *your* family obligations. Go ahead, ask! Who among your brothers should sacrifice their days at the solicitor's office so that you, and that chum of yours, may spend the day at the rail station? And all the while you're sharing the same meals and the same fine clothing. Frederick? Ambrose? Will you do your brother this courtesy?" William's challenge was not met by either Frederick or Ambrose.

William, looking up at the ceiling, shakes his head. He nods to Lettie to remove his plate as the rest of the family members stare straight ahead, waiting to be excused from the table.

"You'll be disappointed with the results if you push me too far, Cyprian."

After his father left the table, it took Cyprian only a moment to return to thoughts of that morning's truancy. Creeping down the stairs and across the foyer, he carefully lifted the latch on the front door. Cyprian made his way down the frost-covered bricks leading out to Jenkins Lane, where he met up with his boyhood friend, John Donohoe. Together they rushed to the platform of the Baltimore and Ohio rail station to catch the five-thirty morning train to Frederick, Maryland.

And, thinking back over the morning, one particular moment made him smirk.

John started in on his chum as they crossed Druid Hill Avenue and West Lafayette, "Morning, Cyprian."

"Do *not* call me that. I've told you, I'm going by 'C.T.' from now on."

John shrugged his shoulders, "Fine, C.T., fine. I just keep forgetting, that's all."

Once they arrived at the Mount Clare Station, C.T. went on ahead to the ticket cage while Donohoe retrieved their bags from the buggy. Tickets in hand, C.T. returned to the platform where he thought John would be waiting, but was confused to find their baggage sitting unattended. Looking around the station, then up and down the tracks, C.T. saw John in the distance loping back toward him with a silly grin on his face.

"*What* are you doing?"

John shrugged his shoulders, grinning sheepishly.

Realization struck and C.T. demanded, "John! You must quit this fooling around! My God, what if you're caught?"

In response Donohoe laughed. He would retrieve the flattened pence from the railroad track the following day. Sauntering across the platform to the passenger car, John climbed the first step leading to the compartment. C.T. reached down for John's duffle bag and tossed it up to his friend.

"Feel better now?" John asked after they had boarded. C.T. and John, and hundreds like them, had watched over the past three years as Charles Carroll and his partners invested in the railway, speculating on the B&O Railroad, they pumped several million dollars into laying tracks from Baltimore to points west with a wary eye on the increasing volume of cargo being shipped through the Erie Canal. Carroll's speculation paid off, handsomely.

The conductor called out, "All aboard," over the expanse of a now empty station platform. Then, as the train pulled out of the station, westerly towards Fredericksburg, a smoke plume puffed skyward from the stacks of the steam-powered engine. The driving rods began their slow circular grind. As a shingled sign printed in block letters, "BaltimoreTown" swung in the light breeze, the last well-wisher turned and walked away from the station in solitude.

C.T. and John slid into their seats and resumed their conversation. John asked, "What are you going to do about your father, and leaving?"

"Well, leave, of course! You and I, just like we've planned! Get out of here. Isn't that what we've intended all along? I'll talk with my Father and my Uncle Frederick. Sometime. Soon. I just don't want to upset things while Father and Grandfather Wells are so involved in settling my Mother's and Grandmother's estate. Father is exhausted and angry by the time he gets home each day. And, it doesn't help that he locks himself in the library until dinner, reading the estate papers and sipping his sherry. He writes his own responses to the court and wants me to present them to the Chancery. I can't bear it much longer. Dinners are composed of vegetables and silence until he decides what to be angry about. Even Charles is afraid to be the first to ask Father about his day. My biggest favor to Father right now is to stay out of his sight."

"I can't imagine. It's been over a year since I've seen your Father, I suppose. It's not like when your..." his voice trailed.

C.T. interjected, "It's not like when Mother was alive; you're right. Father is not the same person as he was then. Not at all."

C.T. saved his ticket stub and the timetable from the maiden run of the Baltimore & Ohio's *Comet*. John shared C.T.'s anticipation to see the world beyond

Baltimore and also C.T.'s love of maps and adventure. But he had his own reasons for having spent the previous two years working with C.T.: to provision the flat-bottom wagon that stood in the Jenkins' carriage house being readied for the trip south.

For their expedition, the two boyhood friends had teamed up with Connor McAllister, a blacksmith on Baltimore's north side. McAllister was moving his family to Georgia hoping to establish a life in Gainesville, following the recent death of his wife.

It was C.T. who had decided that he and John should pair up with McAllister, calculating McAllister could provide the blacksmithing skills, scouting, and veterinarian experience for the journey. Georgia was 'gold country,' and advertisements of the Georgia Land Lottery in Baltimore's newspapers were attracting thousands to 'The Empire State of the South'.

"If we join up, I'll be bringing me kin along," McAllister offered one day to C.T.

"Well, if we join up, I *won't* be bringing me kin along," laughed C.T. The younger man shared his maps and suggested routes from what he had heard about the successes of other expeditions. Beyond that, it was all business between Jenkins and McAllister.

"You *could* get to know Mr. McAllister and his family before we go, you know. I am." Donohoe suggested.

"John, are you getting to know Connor McAllister, or are you getting to know his daughter, Sallie?"

John had met Connor's oldest daughter Sallie one afternoon as he and McAllister chatted and the blacksmith shod John's palomino. Sallie had come bustling into her father's business out of breath. John remembered the day clearly.

Connor nodded a silent 'excuse me' to John and turned, asking his daughter, "My dear, has your Aunt Jessica arrived?"

"Yes, father. Aunt Jessica's coach has arrived. She's settled and refreshed." Her melodious Scottish lilt captured Donohoe's imagination. "When would you want supper served?"

"Right away, of course! Right away, Sallie girl! Let me finish my dealings with Mr. Donohoe here and I'll be on my way home. Tell my dear Jessica I won't be long. And, that we'll spend the evening discussing the plans for the trip that Mr. Donohoe and I have been going over."

John noticed that Sallie nodded her head and blinked, an instant's recognition. *Well...she's heard her father mention my name, then.*

**

C.T. heard the gravel crunch as he worked in the carriage house one evening, and knew it was his father approaching.

"Son, your chair was empty at the dinner table," began William, "This tension between us is as upsetting to your brothers as it is to me."

C.T. barely looked up but his father pressed on. "What are you doing?"

C.T. wiped his hands on a rag and tossed it to the floor. It occurred to him that at five-foot-eight he was quite possibly the taller of the two, finally. He stared intently into the face of his aging father. William's hair was thinning, he had grown thick around the middle; his eyes were bagged and swollen from too much sherry, which he nipped at throughout the day. Five years of estate and filings at the Chancery's office, plus running the household and attending probate hearings had taken a heavy toll on the father of ten sons. In the years following Anne Marie's death he had become an apparition in his own home, able only to maintain a minimum influence in the family's tannery and currier business.

William's question hung in the air as the younger Jenkins tried to think of an appropriate response.

Finally C.T. responded, carefully, as though explaining to a child, "I'm building a spring board wagon, Father."

"You're leaving soon, aren't you, Cyprian?"

"Father, it's been nearly seven years since Mother died. When will you allow us to get over it? I can't live here like this," sweeping his hand toward Huntington Manor, the shadows of the brooding home was cast in darkness as dusk began to fall.

Seeing his father wince, he amended, "Father, I am truly and deeply sorry."

"Cyprian, I thought that at some point you would realize that we need you to help carry on what your grandfather built, at least for the benefit of your younger brothers. Your Uncle Frederick and I are ready for you, Charles and Ambrose to claim your legacy."

"My legacy? My legacy, Father? Is my legacy to live in a cold house that reminds me daily of the Mother this family has lost? Is my legacy to watch Constantine and how he cowers in self blame, hugging the shadows of Huntington Manor? You mean *that* legacy? Father, Uncle Frederick remarried after Aunt Harriet's death. Look out at *his* house as you return to your glass of sherry," inviting the conversation to come to an end.

But his father didn't leave, and so Cyprian continued. "The chandeliers in Uncle Frederick's home are lit brightly. There are candles in the windows, the drapes and sheers are open. He and Aunt Mary Louise entertain constantly. It's a house that any one of us would want to live in, or visit. Are you implying that my legacy is *this* house? Huntington Manor? Because, if the house and the currier business are my legacy, then I am happy enough to pass my share to Frederick and Ambrose."

"My God, Cyprian. What is happening between us? I don't have the strength to make things different, as Frederick has. And, more to the point, unlike Frederick there is no other woman I can see myself loving, other than your mother. I have *only* my business interests now, and as you can see I'm not managing even that all that well."

C.T. placed his hand on his father's shoulder, "I'm sorry, Father. I cannot continue in your footsteps. Truly, I don't even want to."

William stared at his son, stunned at these words. It took only one moment for the shouting to begin. "Damn it, Cyprian! Do you think that *this* is the life that I planned for? I thought if I came out here to speak with you this evening, you would be reasonable! I've built a fine business, mind you! You try it, if you think it's so easy! Yes, damn it! The tanning operation *was* to be your legacy! Is that so bad, Cyprian?" William waited for a response, but got none. "My God! Your mother and I had such dreams for all of you!" C.T. reached out to comfort his Father.

Angered by his failure to make his son understand his perspective William brushed C.T.'s hand away. He shoved his hands into his coat pockets and stormed away from the carriage house and up the driveway toward his manor; but not before a furtive glance toward his brother's brightly lit estate.

**

That's odd, thought C.T. as he roused from sleep. *Didn't I just go to bed? Could it be morning already?* Exasperated, he threw his covers back. *It is so damnably cold!* He stumbled around the bedroom locating his slippers and robe in the flashes of unusual light.

Morning was coming much sooner than he would have thought possible. Cocking his head he listened for the perennial sounds of Old Arthur. The house was silent. The servant should have been moving about the house tending to the fireplaces, which would have offered some warmth and signaled that the kitchen staff was preparing to feed the household.

Something didn't feel right about the growing light from outside. It came not steady like the dawn, but in bright flashes. Giving the sash to his robe a sharp tug, C.T. shuffled across his bedroom to the door and quietly raised the latch. He took a step into the hallway and ducked his head so that he could peer downstairs. He realized that the light *was* coming in increasingly brighter streaks. Hearing a noise from Ambrose's bedroom door, he watched as the door began to slowly creak open. "Shh," he quieted Ambrose as their eyes met.

In a loud whisper Ambrose asked, "What *is* it? Is something on fire?"

Together C.T. and Ambrose padded softly to Charles bedroom to wake him. "What time is it, Cyprian?"

"I think it's an hour or so after midnight."

"Really? It's like morning already." He got out of bed and padded to the window. "In the carriage ride home I was thinking, '*what a bright full moon*'. But the moon isn't full at all. It's a yellow crescent. It was so light out I could even see the occupants of the oncoming carriages along North Avenue as they passed. The sky has been lit up for the last few hours. Everyone was coming out of their houses, lining up along the street to see why it's so bright out. And, there were flashes and a bright yellow glow on the horizon."

It was at that point that Frederick opened his bedroom door to peek into the hallway and joined his brothers in their discussion. "Why is it so light out? Someone should wake Father up!"

"No. Let's see what it is, first." Frederick, now also awake, stepped in to direct the group. "Charles, what time is it, actually?" Frederick asked.

"I'll go get my watch," and Charles went back to his room.

Waiting silently in the hall for Charles to return, the four huddled against the cold, "Don't look so worried, Cyprian. The world isn't coming to an end."

As the four brothers chuckled nervously, Charles returned with his pocket watch. Flipping it open Charles observed, "It is two fifteen in the morning. Cyprian, go get *your* pocket watch. It shouldn't be this bright outside at two in the morning." Taking the cue Frederick and Ambrose also rushed back to their bedrooms to retrieve *their* pocket watches.

"Good God! What was *that*?" asked Charles as Cyprian, Frederick and Ambrose returned.

"A flash! That was a flash!" said Frederick. "Is something on fire?"

"Charles, the whole sky is lighting up! You said yourself it's been going on since you got in! What could possibly be on fire?" asked Ambrose.

Frederick broke from the group and hurried down the hall to his Father's suite, tapping lightly on the door, opening it slightly, "Father...Father, are you up? There's something happening." Turning back to his brothers he beckoned them, "He's already up. He's looking out the window." The others piled into their father's suite.

Dutifully each son acknowledged their father as they entered his room and tiptoed toward the bank of bedroom windows on the north side of the house. William nodded to each of his sons as they entered. Frederick stood next to his father as they scrutinized the sky together at one window, William's arm around the shoulders of his oldest son. Frederick joined Charles and Ambrose at another window. C.T. paced the room, biting at the quick of his nails.

"What do you think?" asked C.T. "Falling stars?" No one answered. "*I* think it's falling stars!" A white flash lit up the brick facade of the manor. C.T. ran over to an unoccupied window. "You can see the hedge along Jenkins Lane – in the middle of the night!"

"Well, at least in the earliest morning hours," his father corrected.

Another burst from the sky lit the lane outside the closed wrought iron gate once more; a flash of phosphorous yellow. C.T. watched from the window farthest from where his father was standing as a bright white celestial flash bathed the room. *Dear God, the sky is on fire! The whole neighborhood is visible. How could stars be bright enough to light up everything around us?*

"Father, what do you think?" ventured Frederick.

"I think we should wake the younger boys! And, make sure Old Arthur is awake! Get some heat in this place! Everyone should see this!"

Cyprian stared at his Father. The right side of his face was lit by another white flash, the left side by candle light. William and Frederick dashed out the door, grinning at each other.

"Let's go down and watch from the back porch. From there we'll be able to see if your Uncle Frederick is awake", suggested William.

"My God!" William Jenkins uttered, as his ten sons huddled around him on the porch scanning the sparkling heavens. From Charles, the eldest; to seven-year-old Constantine, the family witnessed the celestial spectacle of the century together. The sleepy-eyed younger boys joined the huddle, bundled in their coats. Mark and Augustus hugged to keep warm, laughing and carrying on. Leoline and Constantine rode in Frederick's arms, and Augustus was left to cry quietly. Looking down at him, his father asked, "Don't you want to watch all of this little fellow?"

C.T. stood back and took in the scene, surveying his uncle's home, and the direction of North Avenue, taking in the skies above Druid Hill. *How could this be happening?* He stared intently at his father, standing amidst his brothers. Their faces reflected the flashes and trailing glow of the meteors.

1000's Fear End of World as Meteors Light Sky

13 Nov 1833 - Thousands of Baltimoreans woke up in the middle of the night to a sky ablaze with the intensity of 240,000 lumens as Leonid meteors fell to earth in equal number.

"As bright as the morning sky," proclaimed Mrs. Mary Bryan of Park Avenue. Mrs. Bryan added, "In spite of the fact it was in the middle of the night, the sky was so bright that my husband and I were awakened!"

Many residents of this fine city scrambled to windows and porches when the brilliant celestial exhibit, which had never been seen in the lives of most Baltimorean residents, prevailed until the light of dawn overtook the historic cosmic occurrence. Residents who were not awakened by the bright sky were finally awakened by the clamor of neighbors gathering in the street as the display continued toward dawn's hour.

Mrs. Mathew Ringwood, a neighbor of Mr. & Mrs. Bryan reported, "We couldn't settle our two sons down. They were actually quite delighted! Although the light flashes were blinding. Once the children were awake we all stayed up the rest of the night." In response to our question, the Northend housewife added, "No, we certainly didn't go back to sleep. When the traces from the meteors faded the next morning my husband left for the brokerage house as usual." The Bryan's and Ringwood's being the exception, very few other residents continued their day as usual. Baltimore residents congregated on the streets throughout the next day discussing the historic phenomenon.

The Leonid meteor storms occur every 33 years and can be expected to return around the year 1899.
Staff Reporters, Baltimore Republic

* * *

4

GAINESVILLE

Georgia Gold!

News of the richest gold vein to be discovered thus far in Georgia's Cherokee Country has reached Baltimore this week. Prospectors from far and wide are making their way to this Promised Land, forfeiting fear of Indians in order to claim their bounty. Visit Conestoga Outfitters, located at Calhoun and Winchester Sts.

Advertisement, Baltimore Republican Star, 1833

The cicadas droned on in the shimmering midday heat. The Conestoga and spring board wagons had been pulled to the side of a well-camouflaged foot path overgrown with bramble bushes and scrub trees.

"We'll stop here!" McAllister had called back to John and C.T. one week into their journey out of Baltimore.

The sun shot blinding pinpoints of light through fluttering leaves of aspen stands. As late afternoon faded to early evening, a light breeze made a feeble attempt to cool the air.

The horses swished their tails to shoo away robber flies and stomped their feet in unsuccessful attempts to loosen burrs clawing into their hooves.

The Conestoga served as the McAllister family's refuge, its contents neatly organized reflecting a woman's touch provided by Connor McAllister's sister, Jessica.

C.T. and John were travelling in the open flat-bottom spring board wagon that C.T. had built. It was lighter in weight and much easier to keep hidden as the two parties inched their way through Indian country. The flat limestone geologic table to the side of the foot path represented a detour the party had taken at the urging, that morning, of John E. Coffee's militia.

It was too hot a day to expend energy on unnecessary talking. The three men had trudged through the morning in silence, signaling silently their agreement where they would stop for the day. The setting, a short distance from Hartwell Lake, was shielded from the foot path by the rustling curtain of tall grasses. After the two wagons were positioned on the limestone slab, the McAllister children scrambled out of the wagon to restore the trampled grass; hoping to hide the wagon tracks.

John tossed the reins to C.T. and hopped down from the wagon. "If we can stay at this hidden site for a day or two we might have enough time to clean our equipment and sort the provisions," John said. "Perhaps even dry our rumpled clothes and buckskins in the sun. Then, we push for Gainesville."

Walking around the Conestoga, taking stock, McAllister called over, "John, later on help me reposition the Conestoga to face the main path. For now, the women can set up dinner while we settle the horses." John ambled over to help McAllister with the reins and gear on the Conestoga, while C.T. concentrated on unhitching the smaller team of horses.

Some days the party accomplished their goal of covering fifteen miles, some days they didn't. But they continued on, day after day.

"Here you go," offered Jessica McAllister. She dished out ample portions of beans salted with bacon onto the heavy white plates. The plates were now chipped, several tossed beside the trail broken as the result of the wagon wheels bumping over rocks, tipping the lumbering Conestoga.

Each member of the party took a helping from Jessica and found a spot around the campsite. They ate in silence, picking up their conversation after satisfying their hunger.

"Mmm," they all agreed as the nine Baltimoreans enjoyed a dessert of peaches that the two older McAllister boys had gathered. Ripe, fragrant peaches, fuzzy and soft, dripped their sweet juices over chins and fingers and were devoured down to the pits, which were then pitched into the brush to continue the harvest cycle.

"Ma'am, if you'll excuse me. Thank you for the meal," C.T. handed his plate to Jessica and wandered to the spring board wagon after nodding to Connor and John.

"A bit of a loner, that one," observed Aunt Jessica to Sallie.

C.T. noted that John was spending an increasing amount of time helping Connor grease the wagon wheels and maintain the draft horses.

After John and McAllister re-positioned the Conestoga the McAllister camp was less than seven yards from C.T. and John's. "What do you think, John?" mulled Connor.

"I think it's fine for the short while that we'll be here. The Conestoga is going to be the most difficult to move out in a pinch, so let's keep it in forward position with enough room to harness the team. I'll help you. I'm sure that C.T. can manage hooking up the springboard. At least the militia knows we're out here, which should help."

"I'll sleep light for three hours or so, and then wake you up before midnight. We'll trade watch on two full cycles. How does that sound?"

"Sure! Thanks." John placed his hand on Connor's shoulder and bid good night. The older man nodded and dragged himself wearily back to his bed roll.

The two camps bid good night to each other after tending to their individual chores. They settled quietly to rest, surrounded by the sound of crickets and the fragrance of honeysuckle and wild roses. Aunt Jessica pointed and whispered the names of the constellations to her nephews as they lay on their backs. It didn't take long for the little boys to fall fast asleep.

The next morning, a dusky peach sky advanced on the cobalt blue of night, and a welcome chill nipped the air. Donohoe, who was awake, tossed a pebble at C.T. to wake him. Rolling over onto his belly and propping up his elbows C.T. ruffled his hair, and briskly rubbed his eyes with the palms of his hands.

John held his finger up to his lips, his eyes imploring C.T.'s silence. C.T. cocked his head and was able to hear the swish of horses moving through underbrush, and a few shouts in Tsalagi. A small band of Cherokee scouts were passing within a quarter of a mile to the west. Bands of Cherokees and the settlers migrating to Georgia were moving in opposing directions that year. Both populations were using the currents of the Savannah River as their guide.

God help us, Donohoe prayed.

C.T. made a couple of pointed jabs toward the horses. They were becoming restless.

Donohoe nodded.

"John, be careful. Go slowly," whispered C.T.

"If I go slowly, it will be too late to calm them down. If one of them whinnies, it will give away our position. Can you slide my rifle out from under the back wheel of the wagon?"

"Here!"

Donohoe crept softly to the horses, corralled adjacent to the camp in an oval enclosure of brush and tree branches not more than a stone's throw from the lake shore.

John surveyed the landscape, remaining

crouched as he hand-fed the horses sweet grass and stroked their snouts. Although they stomped in anticipation, Donohoe was able to keep the animals calm as the band of Cherokees rustled past on the wider, well-traveled trail that the two chums and the McAllister family had been advised to avoid the previous day. After taking care of the horses, he treaded barefoot over to McAllister who was sleeping on the ground at the foot of the Conestoga wagon. Donohoe gently shook the man's shoulder until he woke. C.T. watched as the two men discussed the situation. McAllister sat up and looked over at him apprehensively and then pulled on his boots.

The precipitous warning by John E. Coffee's militia regarding the Cherokees moving north, resisting a move to reservation lands in the west had been well timed for the settlers.

But with Cherokees so close, the dream of a morning camp fire, crackling and snapping as summer wood burst into flame was out of the question. So was a breakfast of coffee and last night's reheated stew. The adults contemplated how close they had come to a confrontation that could have cost them their lives.

For the remainder of the day the adults were edgy, on alert. The children stayed close to the Conestoga, looking about furtively through the remainder of the day. The men spent their nervous energy pulling trunks out of the wagons, making mental notes of the condition of their equipment, ropes, gun powder, bed rolls and pots.

Long, brooding silences had begun to fall between John and C.T. following their departure from Baltimore, and the tension heightened at times such as this.

"How's Sallie holding up?"

"That's an odd question, coming from you, C.T."

"Look, John, I'm just trying to make conversation. If you want to court Sallie McAllister, that's fine. I appreciate that Connor knows the tanning trade as well as my family; and it sure helps us that he is a blacksmith. But I don't have to check with him on every single little issue just to impress him for the sake of his daughter. I can form my own opinions. No reason for us to form a three-headed monster, now is there?"

The second morning after their near encounter, Connor McAllister nudged his team of horses forward for the final push toward Gainesville. His sister sat beside him peering into the distance. The five McAllister children peered out from the perches of trunks and bundles inside the Conestoga wagon. John and C.T.'s horses pulled the springboard out of the weeds as the two fell in behind the McAllister's Conestoga. The silence between them hung between them as the party moved southwesterly.

When it finally occurred to C.T. that John and Sallie had intentions beyond being sweethearts, he withdrew completely. He no longer included John in on his expansive plans for establishing a gold mine in Gainesville or in any of the other plans they had spoken of before Sallie McAllister came into John's life. The practical jokes and silliness that were John's stock and trade were now directed toward the McAllister clan. In the evening he would chase the McAllister children around the campfire while Jessica and Sallie cleaned up and readied the bed rolls and Connor put the equipment in order for the next day.

It was Sallie who began the campaign to bridge the growing divide.

"C.T., join us!" She would cup her hands and call him to join their party for supper. C.T. would respond by waving to her.

"He thinks I'm just calling *hello*," she would tell John.

"No, he gets it."

Sometimes in response to Sallie's invitation, C.T. would hold up a saddle that needed waxing, or pantomime some other task in order to ward off her invitations. In the evening, as the dinner dishes were being cleared, John remained around the McAllister's campfire. Connor would nod in the direction of C.T.'s camp, asking John, "What's he doing?"

"He's sitting in the shadows at the back of the spring board."

The McAllister's continued to summon C.T. to join them. But, C.T.'s response continued to be as crisp as it was clear, which he explained to John. "My point is to get to Gainesville and decide if I want to stay or push on. Visiting and chatting is not what I have in mind, thank you all the same." To his old chum his words were more direct, "John, it was easy enough to slip away from the generosities of my father, and in so doing I now have control of my own destiny. Can you say as much?"

"How is he today?" Sallie would ask John, when they were gathering wood and out of earshot of the camp.

"The same. Pouty, silent."

"Why don't you two approach him together?" suggested Jessica.

"He certainly wouldn't appreciate that. He sees a life that transcends family. That was his whole point in leaving Baltimore. He could have had it all, tried harder at finding his own niche in his family, but that opportunity is gone now. I love Sallie. She loves me. Everyone understands, except C.T. Things have simply changed since he and I started out. I can't help how he feels, and I'm not going to run from my life like he wants to do."

"Oh John, what should we do? Maybe if we all went to talk with him," suggested Sallie.

"Sallie, would you want to go back to the camp with me and force a conversation on C.T. that he's not interested in having, to tell him the obvious?"

"I would do whatever I needed to do so that you two would be friends again. That is, other than giving you up. There isn't any reason for him to not like me personally. So, I have to go forward in my own happiness, which is with you, John. I hope that someday his life will bring him to understand what I understand; that a family is what you build around yourself in order to gain happiness—not what you *run from*. He certainly seems to cling to his anger."

"Do you have to be so sore all the time? There's a girl waiting for you, C.T." John admonished one day as they packed their wagon.

"Right, John. And maybe you and Sallie, and me and 'that girl' will do a little mining for gold. Maybe tame a few horses; just like you and I had planned. All four of us, together."

Fifty-nine days after they rolled out of Baltimore Town, the men pulled the wagons up at a small ridge to take in the promise of Gainesville, Georgia. The frontier town stood in the distance welcoming them.

John sat beside C.T., driving the wagon they had built in what seemed a lifetime earlier. "Be happy for Sallie and me. Please. At least be my best man."

"Sure. I'll be your best man, if that's what you want. You can find me in town. Send for me the morning of the wedding."

And so it was, a short time later that a stoic Jenkins stood at his friend's side as Connor McAllister walked his daughter down the aisle to wed John Donohoe.

A bit player, C.T. disengaged from the scene, a prickly witness at best. Before the fiddlers struck their bows and the music began, C.T. left the post-nuptial party, charging into his life as an independent man.

"I'm James Rawlins. How do you do?" introduced one of the scouts as he and C.T. stood at the bar at Gainesville's most lively saloon.

"C.T. Jenkins. I'm pleased to meet you. You were with Coffee's militia when I passed through coming in from the north, last month, weren't you?"

The man nodded.

"Do you recall a Conestoga wagon and a spring board coming down from Baltimore Town?"

"Yes! Ha! You?"

In response C.T. threw back his head for a long swig of whiskey.

"So, Jenkins, what was your business in Baltimore?"

"My family's in the tanning business. I know some about leather finishing as well as tanning. I came to Georgia a few months ago to prospect, but I'm thinking of giving that up. Where are you coming in from?"

"We're on our way back to the Piedmont from surveying the new boundaries of the Cherokee Nation. I'm so damned tired from riding and happy to be at Indian Springs. My wife's people are from here. Tomorrow after I've cleaned up I'll go over to their house for a home cooked meal."

C.T. nodded and turned back to his drink listening intently as the men bragged to each other about their experiences on the trail and their description of the life of the militia. "Scouting, that sounds more like what I'm looking for," he admitted to Rawlins. "Panning for gold is not what I have in mind to hold to, now that I've tried it."

"Well, if you're looking for something to do and you've really given up on prospecting," Rawlins advised, as the other scouts snickered, "I hear they are looking for someone to help out at the Coffee Plantation's tannery operation in Telfair."

"Good enough."

It was late in the evening and the noise from the saloon had grown to a cacophony of laughter, the relentless pinging of the piano, and drink orders called out to the bartender. Surveying the saloon, C.T. downed one last shot of whiskey and bid the men at the bar good night. The following day, he would be heading to Telfair and a job, if John Coffee would hire him.

The next morning, C.T. gently closed the door to his hotel room, ready to deposit the room key at the front desk. He glanced back at the bed as a curly-haired brunette dozed lightly, her body barely covered by the rumpled sheets. As the latch fell, the woman's smooth, caramel-throated voice floated out to the hallway, "Bye, Hon." And C.T. was on his way.

* * *

5

VERMONT ~ MRS. COLBURN'S STORY

The soft glow from hundreds of flickering white candles produced an amber veil over the Congregational Meeting Hall. Shards of prismed color splashed across the hall's interior emanating from the Venetian-style stained glass windows at the green-flash moment of sunset.

Fair Haven's most prominent families were gathered for the social season's highlight wedding, the Reverend Rufus Cushman officiating.

Guests filed into the meeting hall through the massive carved doors. While still in the small annex, each gentleman removed his black silk top hat while the women straightened their lace shawls before proceeding into a high-ceiling chamber. A somber quiet prevailed, with the exception of the rustling of skirts and murmurs of 'hello' as each arriving guest stepped into their pew.

Looking down from the gallery above the choir mistress, Miss Larsen, turned and offered a reassuring nod to her choir. Raising her upturned hand she signaled the beginning of her first selection chosen from *The Bay Psalm Book.* The choir began sweetly and with confidence, and a low pitched melody filled the rafters of the hall.

Taking a deep breath, and lifting her chin, Lucy Davey nodded to her father that she was ready to proceed into the life of John Peabody Colburn, widower: The one man in Fair Haven who could provide her with all the security and comfort any woman had reason to wish for.

The bride glided past the approving gaze of the guests, making a mental note of the role each of her husband's business partners and Fair Haven's community leaders, would play in her life as she moved from the eligible daughter of one of Fair Haven's most prominent businessmen to the wife of Fair Haven's wealthiest resident.

Jacob Davey was pleased that his daughter had so enthusiastically agreed to the proposal which John Peabody Colburn had presented to him six months earlier.

A business relationship that had developed five years earlier between the groom and the bride's father was the catalyst for the union between the two families. John Colburn's home, Quinton Estate, stood just south of the Davey paper mill, making neighbors of the Davey and Colburn families.

Colburn had built the estate for his late wife, Elizabeth, who had died three years previous leaving Colburn to raise their two small children Moses and Betsy.

As Lucy took her place at the base of the pulpit beside the groom, Miss Larsen's choir softly drew the pastoral processional hymn to a close. John Colburn looked straight into the eyes of Jacob Davey. The two men nodded to one another.

Having escorted his daughter to the altar Jacob took his place next to his wife of twenty-nine years, Phoebe Dey Davey. He looked at his wife and contemplated what had brought him to this moment.

Many years earlier Davey had left Phoebe and the children behind in Bridgeport in order to take a job as superintendent at the Smith Iron Works. He promised he would summon Phoebe and their children to join him in Fair Haven, after his position was well established. That day came fourteen months later.

The Smith Iron Works flourished under Davey's management as did his young family's fortunes. The iron works was a bevy of activity, with orders received, nails and sieves and other metal tools manufactured, and products packed and delivered to local merchants.

In a few years Jacob had advanced from superintendent of the iron works to owner. The success of the works was in direct correlation to the expanding community of Fair Haven, a perfect time for the young Davey couple to have made their investment.

After years of effort by men such as himself, the village of Fair Haven, first surveyed before 1800, reflected the gentility of a lovely, well-planned community not far from the Castleton River.

Phoebe Davey squeezed her husband's hand to bring him back from his daydreaming to the ceremony.

The groom was no more fixed on the scripture being recited by Reverend Cushman than the father of the bride. John Colburn's mind wandered over the youth of his bride and his hopes that the burdens of his children would be eased by having someone in their lives to take the place of their mother.

Colburn enjoyed an income from a number of lucrative Fair Haven business interests, built on the relationships he and his brothers had cultivated over the past twelve years. He had begun his journey toward the ultimate pinnacle of his career in the unlikely trade of blacksmith, in a shop purchased by his father. Early on, the blacksmithing business generated enough profit for young Colburn to set aside money for the purchase of one half of a scythe factory, a transaction John completed as he turned thirty years of age. Ultimately, John Colburn would become a learned attorney, then a judge in the county's court system, elected by the men of Rutland County.

**

The ceremony continued as Reverend Cushman described in hushed tones the mysteries of the cosmos, a sermon which ultimately wound back to something having to do with the day's events. The rustling of taffeta skirts and light coughs interrupted the Reverend's lengthy nuptial sermon and the bride's mind wandered to an early spring luncheon held at the Quinton Estate shortly after her engagement to John was announced. The occasion was held at the invitation of John's parents.

After the cordial luncheon and dessert, Lucy, her sister MaryAnn, and their mother were given a tour of the estate. During the tour Lucy was informed by her soon to be mother-in-law on how the household was to be run.

A visit to the nursery concluded the tour. It was on this occasion that Lucy met John's children for the first time.

"Moses, please meet Miss Lucy Davey who will be wed to your father this summer," coached the grandmother of the melancholy five-year old.

Clearly preferring the possibility that his departed mother would reappear, Moses bowed his head and whispered to his shoes, "Nurse says she will live with us."

"Why, yes, Moses," instructed the grandmother. "Miss Davey will live here with you, and Betsey, and your father."

"Like Nurse?" further pressed Moses.

"No, dear," resigned the grandmother, "not *quite* like Nurse," as she smiled wanly at the bride's mother.

There were tears of regret during the ceremony as Reverend Cushman reminded the attendees of the importance of a mother in the lives of children, skirting biblical references in deference to the progressive congregation.

Lucy had long been fascinated by John Colburn despite their difference in age. He caught her attention during the visits he made to the Davey household following the death of his wife. John's string of successes and his ability to bring his ideas to fruition intrigued her. Already a village selectman who served with her father, John participated in the planning and development of Fair Haven with its fee-paid Central

Park. He encouraged the engineering of Fair Haven's water supply into a progressive water works system, and promoted the manufacturing that took place in factories along the Castleton and Poultney Rivers. The plans and development of Fair Haven's six churches, halls, mercantile and schools all carried his thumb-print. She took note of the similarities between John Colburn and her father, but observed to her older sister, Mary Anne, before the wedding, "He's more refined isn't he?"

"More refined than whom?"

"Well, I mean John is statesman-like. If he promises that he will someday be a county judge, them someday he will be. And, did you notice the staff? I will have the assistance of so many more servants than mother."

"Oh, I see. Really Lucy, sometimes you disappoint me."

**

"This concludes this evening's service. It is God's will that this union provide the two of you a lifetime of peace." And with that Reverend Cushman nodded to John.

The musical chords of Miss Larsen's choir swelled and the guests stood during the recessional of Mr. John Peabody Colburn and his wife, Mrs. Colburn.

One evening two years later, Lucy Colburn surveyed her home as she walked through the upstairs bedrooms carrying her infant son, John, Jr. She had just retrieved him from the arms of Edwina, the Colburn's live-in nurse. It was nearly bedtime for her first-born, who squeaked happily as the exchange was made from domestic to mother.

"Oh, Edwina! Isn't he a dear?"

"Oh yes, Mum. The most beautiful baby I've ever cared for. He'll grow up to be just like his father some day, 'tis my estimation. A man of fine character."

"Come to me, John Jr., you beautiful joy. Let's go show your father how handsome you are today." She carried him through the generous upstairs hall that ushered the occupants into any one of the four expansive bedrooms, each one pointing in a different direction like points on a compass. Her husband enjoyed having an office on the second floor. The arrangement allowed him to confer more easily with Lucy on his endeavors as he wrote in his journal each evening while she pulled the hair pins that held her braid in a proper chignon.

Lucy settled in easily at the Quinton Estate and kept the household, as well as her husband's office, in perfect order with help from the servants. The estate was every bit as grand as the one in which she had grown up in, although it was certainly more modern. The shuttered windows to the west looked out over bountiful apple orchards, and beyond to a line of leafy maple trees that formed a keyhole-shaped boundary for the property. The main house of the estate had been placed in the center. In the distance, logged woods and clearings marked her husband's harvesting endeavors.

Lucy proceeded through her stepson Moses' bedroom to the east, and looked out the window to survey the stocked pond and vegetable gardens near the carriage road. The secluded road, lined by mature oak trees and stenciled by railed fencing, allowed one to approach the estate from the southeast. The oak arbor on the east side of the estate stretched like a long ribbon toward Fair Haven, past the pasture and barn, past the meadows and through deep woods that would eventually be logged, and milled into lumber.

A mud room had been included off the kitchen. Installed at the deep sink, a water pump disgorged and sputtered water from the well for the use of the servants who gathered the spring-to-autumn harvest from the gardens. The brick oven, which either roared to herald the beginning of the day or glowed providing the final warmth before nightfall, had been built next to the delivery door. And, open shelves in the breakfast room hung over the wainscoting and displayed mixing bowls, sifters, platters and china. The Colburn's dining room was situated to the right of the kitchen.

Five years passed in harmony, as the couple observed all the expected protocols. Each evening, after the children were fed by the kitchen staff and readied for bed, Lucy would visit the children in their bedroms.

"I want my mother," was Betsey's bedtime lament for the first two years. Moses receive her attention each evening, and the child with whom she shared her own evening prayer. "Heavenly Father, please bless my Mother," he would begin night after night.

"What a perfectly beautiful way to begin your prayers, Moses," Lucy reassured.

Next Lucy would say good night to her own son, John Jr. before moving on to her daughter Susan's room.

After 'good nights' had been delivered to each child Lucy welcomed the company of her husband.

"I so treasure hearing about how you come to your business decisions, darling," Lucy observed one evening after listening to a long recitation from her husband. She questioned him endlessly over dinner or when the upstairs had settled down for the day. "I wanted to wait up for you," would be her greeting as she took his cape and hat when he returned from meetings at the Old Lyon Tavern.

"It's fascinating what you and Father are planning regarding the development of Fair Haven. It's truly exciting to see everything being settled, to envision what it will be like in the future." She hung on John's every word as he described how the sawmill was turning a profit, what the Selectmen had decided regarding the development of Fair Haven; and, his perceptions of court cases he studied in preparation for the practice of law, which was his next goal.

John taught Lucy the theory of business cycles and how to overcome the supply problems of the iron works related to keeping up with the growing population of mid-state Vermont. She soon understood the challenges of the deep freezes of winter that threatened both live stock and factory operations, and how to determine which forest tracts were ready to mill to keep the kiln going through the spring and summer.

Coming up behind his high back chair one evening after saying her evening prayers with Moses, she placed her hand on his shoulder. He took it softly and drew her palm to his lips. "How are you faring, Lucy?"

"Darling, I'm fine, and the children are fine."

"I'm sure that's true. Lucy, you are so self-sufficient. You are the lovely wonder in my life."

Once he had finished his law studies, John became Fair Haven's Constable. Just a few years later he realized his dream of being elected a judge of Rutland County. By now his two brothers, along with a crew of foremen, managed the extensive mill operations and real estate holdings. At the beginning of each week, Lucy would watch from behind the silk drapes, as John's carriage took him away from Quinton Estate to the County Courthouse in Rutland. He would return after each week's cases had been heard.

"Darling, what are you reading," asked Lucy leaning over her husband's high back upholstered chair to peer at the object of his intense scrutiny one evening after dinner.

"The filings to a court case that is on the docket for tomorrow," John mumbled. "The case has gone on for two miserable years now. These are the two most tenacious, adversarial, wretched jurists I have ever encountered. When they are not attacking each other, they are attacking the bench. I hope to God in Heaven this case closes this week and I never see these two again," he concluded by slapping the folders shut and staring forward.

"Oh dear! My poor darling." Lucy pulled the step stool up to the base of his chair and sat at his feet, gathering her long hair over one shoulder. "John, it is only one court case. You have no vested interest after this case has been decided but to put it behind you, square your shoulders, and show the legal community and Rutland County your mettle."

John stared dismally at the fireplace, the flames reflecting in his glasses.

"Get through this one case, John."

He sighed.

"You've been taking your work load too hard this year. Let's take a holiday to upstate New York. We could go to Malone, or even up to Ottawa. It would do us good to get away after the baby is born."

He responded by looking down at Lucy, stroking her hair. He rested his hand on her shoulder and tilted his head back, closing his eyes. Lucy laid her head on his knee and they spent a quiet moment together while a servant made their bed ready for the evening, sliding bricks warmed at the hearth between their bed covers.

"Sir," the servant signaled. "Madam, if you would like to retire now."

The next morning Lucy trundled down the front steps of their home, heavy with child and supported on the arm of her personal nurse to see John to his waiting carriage. She clung to her husband as the two embraced in a lingering farewell; he more concerned for her welfare and that of the children than for his own. His exhaustion transferred to Lucy as they released their hold on one another.

The Judge's black carriage proceeded slowly away from the Quinton Estate down the long line of mature maple trees; then on through the colonial village that he had helped design. Lucy's concern over her husband's fatigue and malaise lingered throughout the day.

That evening the candles in Lucy's bedroom burned long into the night, casting strange specters across the chilly bedroom as she dozed, fully clothed.

The silhouette of a lone rider loping along the darkened carriage road advanced slowly toward the front steps of the estate. A rider dismounted his pony and lifted his lantern from the hook in the saddle before proceeding up to the porch. Allowed entry by the evening butler, the rider waited for Mrs. Colburn, a message pinched between his fingers.

Lucy swooped down the staircase into the foyer.

"Ma'am. A message from the court house."

She looked at the messenger quizzically as she slipped her finger nail under the flap of the sealed envelope, pulled out the folded sheet and shook it open.

The message began, *"Madam, I am sorry to inform you."* It only took her an instant to intuit its message.

"Oh John, my dear, sweet husband," she broke down crying, looking helplessly around the expansive entry before continuing to read the words of condolence that had been sent. "I held so much hope that we would bring up the children together." Looking up at the messenger she informed him unnecessarily, "He was only forty two years old."

"I'm so sorry Ma'am." The messenger did his best to not glance down at the woman's abundant form, wondering. The butler eased the front door open behind him so and the messenger rushed his retreat down the long, dark road leading away from Quinton Estate.

It was now up to Lucy Colburn to hold on to the mill operations and raise the children who represented the Colburn legacy.

**

OBITUARY
John Peabody Colburn, one of the Judges of the County Court
Died on the 9th instant of this month.
His widow and seven children are residents of Fair Haven, Rutland County, Vermont.
New York Mercury, December 28, 1831

**

BORN
In Fair Haven, Rutland County, Vermont on the 9th instant,

A daughter, Eliza, to the late John Peabody Colburn.
And his widow, Mrs. Lucy Colburn, currently of Fair Haven, Vermont.
Fair Haven Republican - December 30, 1831

Two weeks later Mrs. Colburn sat in the office of her husband's solicitor. Her brother, Israel, sat to her left and her father to her right.

"Please accept my condolences," Robert McCutcheon began.

Her brother had warned, "Lucy, listen to me. You will most likely not have any idea what John's solicitor is saying as he reads the Will. Or, you may remember some details and not others. There is no need to ask a lot of questions. Father and I can help you think things through; we will attend the reading, of course." She looked at McCutcheon's mouth move and thought she heard, "...an untimely and unexpected death ... leaving such a young widow..." Disjointed words from her husband's closest confident and long-time associate.

Lucy shook her head, clearing it as her father placed his paw over her hand.

John's solicitor continued, "Of course your husband's Will was drawn up before the birth of Albert and Eliza—but Moses and Elizabeth" he paused to clarify, peering over his wire rimmed glasses. "Err...Betsey, that is, and Susan and John are specifically provided for." McCutcheon tugged at his stiffly starched collar and shrugged into the sleeves of his coat. He began by picking up a sheath of papers. "Gentlemen, Mrs. Colburn."

"Mr. McCutcheon," Lucy replied, dabbing at the corners of her eyes.

"If I may now read the Last Will and Testament of John Peabody Colburn." He paused, looking up.

Israel nodded.

Arranging his lanky body, Robert McCutcheon began to read John's Will:

I, John Peabody Colburn, of Fair Haven, County of Rutland in the State of Vermont, being of sound body and mind on this 13th day of December 1829 do make and publish this, my Last Will and Testament, in the following manner:

It is my intention that Robert McCutcheon serve as executor of my estate. I charge Mr. McCutcheon to provide to the Chancery's office of Rutland County a full, true and complete inventory of my debts, properties and interests within one year of my death.

I attest hereto that at the time of the writing of this Will I am a married man. My family consists of my wife, Lucy Davey Colburn with whom I share a son, John Peabody Colburn II; and a daughter, Susan Sibley Colburn. I was previously married to Elizabeth (Betsey) Dennis, late of Fair Haven, Vermont, who precedes me in death.

I recognize son Moses McClellan Colburn and daughter Elizabeth (Betsey) Dennis Colburn from that union.

Oh Dear God, Albert and Eliza are not mentioned at all! Lucy realized. Advised by her brother to resist the impulse to ask questions of the man who expressly did not represent her interests, she tried to shut out what she was hearing. She let Israel, a solicitor himself, determine what questions were necessary.

"The appraisement hereunder shall be entered into these proceedings ... thusly shall my debts be settled ... Each of my children named herein will be entitled to the proceeds of said sale of those properties and enterprises deemed necessary by Robert McCutcheon to provide for the appropriate... which will accrue to Lucy Davey Colburn to be distributed in such manner as my Executor deems..."

Lucy gasped. *As my Executor deems?* Lucy did not want to process the fact that her fate and future depended on the charity of Robert McCutcheon, Solicitor, as negotiated by her brother and father.

"...that my wife, Lucy Davey Colburn shall provide for the comfort, education, necessities and wants of my children from the funds made available to her for this purpose..."

'My children'...but, the Will must have been written before Albert and Eliza were born. Is support for them to be provided? Lucy steadied herself, clutching the purse she held in her lap. It held smelling salts, should they become necessary, and her lace handkerchief.

"...and she will carry on management of my investments, listed herein, all rents, proceeds and properties provided so long as she not remarry..."

Lucy thought through the futility of the moment, *"There is no way I can cope with seven children by myself day after day, night after night. This will be the end of John's dream for the children. Are there even enough funds to run the household; support the servants?"* No solution presented itself during the afternoon's proceeding.

"Do you understand the foregoing, Mrs. Colburn? You will *not* continue to receive proceeds from your husbands' current estate should you remarry. Those proceeds would transfer to John's brother, Charles; and your husband's children, Moses and Elizabeth, Susan and John Jr. You would only have what you generate through the management, with my assistance, of those assets. I only point this out to you because you are of such a young age."

"Yes, I'm sure she understands, as do we," was her brother's crisp reply. "If copies of John's Will could be delivered to Mrs. Colburn, as well as to my office?"

McCutcheon nodded. Israel stood up while Lucy remained seated. Her brother offered his hand, and after a moment she was able to ease herself into a standing position to conclude the meeting with the proper pleasantries.

* * *

6

Fort Brooke 1835

C.T. looked across the noisy saloon taking in the ping of the piano, the heavy smoke from cigarettes and cigars which caused his eyes to burn; and the chatter and laughter that rose and fell, like a billow stoking a furnace.

This confusion was in total contrast to the moment *after* Pickett burst through the saloon doors. The quiet started at the doors as Pickett, a scout riding with Newburne's Company, fell on all fours, red-faced, sweaty, and panting to catch his breath. Then it spread over the room like water spilling across the floor of a room that was flooding. Two men recognized Pickett immediately and rushed forward. Another man, an officer, grabbed a chair and the three hoisted the scout off the floor and into a sitting position. No one said a word.

Dead silence, life in pantomime. C.T. remembered thinking that the scene didn't seem at all real. The men in the saloon waited, drinks held in mid-air. C.T. watched intently. Someone signaled the barkeep for a drink, just the swoop of his hand – no words. A canteen was tossed into the air, its strap flailing until it was caught by one of the men standing over Pickett. The proffered shot glass was passed from hand to hand – less than a minute
had lapsed. Pickett took a swig from the canteen, wheezing after the first swallow. He then wiped his mouth with the back of his sleeve. Waving away the shot glass he looked around the saloon for the first time.

C.T. was off to Pickett's left, he stood up and edged forward, along with the crowd of men who had been strangers to one another five minutes beforehand. He was unable to hear the man's words. It didn't matter.

An interpreter of sorts called out each sentence that Pickett spoke, "Injun attack. One survivor made it across the Hillsboro."

And the words were repeated to the crowd at large, "Injun attack. One survivor made it across the Hillsboro," and so it went.

"He's dead. But maybe a dozen or so settlers made it to the blockhouse on the north side of the river."

The men looked wide-eyed at each other. Not a damn thing had gone right since the skirmish at Hickory Sink. Word of the incident had spread west from Gainesville to Fort Brooke and now rumors and facts swirled together in the shot glasses of every saloon in Northern Florida.

A staff officer separated from the tight-knit cluster surrounding Pickett and shouted across the room, "We're heading out first thing. All Cavalry members and we'll need a couple volunteers!"

"I'll join you! I'm ready!" C.T.'s voice shot across the room and the den of the saloon started up again over speculation on whether they would find any survivors.

The next morning C.T. left his hotel room and hurried over to the saloon, the militia's rendezvous. He ordered a plate of breakfast and wolfed it down, knocking back coffee that scorched his throat. Within minutes his plate was empty and he slid it back across the bar to the cook.

The militia member seated one table over from C.T. tilted his head toward his follow officer who had crouched down to talk with him. The soldier nodded in agreement and began gathering up his hat and Cavalry gloves, and pushing his own breakfast plate away.

"We're saddling up?" C.T. asked the soldier as the man stood and adjusted his felt Cavalry hat so that it sat straight across his brow. The acorn band was frayed and the chin strap was sweat stained.

Mid-thirties, was C.T.'s guess.

"Yes, son. If you're coming, gather your gear. It's going to be a tough ride."

Nodding, C.T. reached down and ran his hand over his pack, gear, and rifle, all cleaned and ready. He stood up and walked across the saloon, after sliding a few coins across the bar. He hoisted his gear over his shoulder and winced at the weight.

C.T.'s life as a scout in the Seminole Wars had begun.

**

Dade ~ Christmas 1836

It had taken over two weeks to gather the ninety-five men willing and able to ride out to the palmetto field that had been described as a massacre scene.

"I'm Jenkins," C.T. extended his hand over his saddle to the paunchy rider next to him. After listening to Colonel Leigh Read's account of the latest Seminole attack—this one on Major Francis Dade's men—the two men stomped down the steps of Colonel Leigh Read's field headquarters. Over the grumblings, predictions, and projections of the huge field of humanity that surrounded them, the man leaned over his saddle to accept C.T.'s handshake. He surveyed the chaotic scene of volunteers, each at a different stage of checking their packs and mounting their steeds.

"Well, I hope we get going before this turns into a stampede. The horses are as anxious as the men," the man observed.

It was total disorder as the horses stomped their feet and whinnied, testing both their riders' skill and patience. Some of the men backed their horses away from the confusion to gain control of their animals. The horses of less experienced riders turned in circles, not helping efforts to fall into formation. Sharp whistles and shouts among the men trying to get organized added to the bedlam. C.T. blew on his cold fingers and transferred the reins to his left hand to shake some warmth into his right hand, waiting to see if the stranger was going to introduce himself.

"Stone Barrett. My brother's out there, I'm afraid," Barrett explained. "We *need* to get going."

Colonel Leigh Read came out of the field headquarters to take the reins of his own horse from the private who had been waiting for him in the crisp cold.

Colonel Read expertly mounted his horse, a beautifully groomed Morgan, and raised his gloved hand, signaling for the men to move out. C.T. nodded to Barrett, who maneuvered to untangle his horse from the knot of riders gathered in front of the weather worn buildings. C.T.'s own mount snorted loudly in protest at the crowding before it fell in beside Barrett's horse. The progress of getting all the volunteers organized had been agonizingly slow for those men who had scouting experience.

Forty or so groups of twos and threes and fours moved northwesterly. The bands of men in the front of the formation moved slowly, while the bands of men at the rear trotted to catch up. C.T. and Barrett were at the front, not far behind Colonel Read.

"I've been scouting along the Coffee Road until a week ago. You from around here?" C.T. asked, looking Barrett over and wondering if he would get a response.

"Nah. That is, not originally. My people's from Macon, Georgia. I'm in Withlacoochee working the Harrell Plantation this season. Overseer. I came down to Florida 'bout the time my brother got assigned to Fort Brooke under Colonel Dade. My ma and pa will be goin' crazy when they get word about Terrence. I don't know too much about what we'll find, but if anyone could survive an injun' attack it would be my brother."

"Well, I hope you're right, Mr. Barrett."

"What have *you* heard? All that I know is what Read," Barrett nodded forward toward the Colonel, "said durin' his talk, '*to prepare for th'worst*'. Ya' hear that? Dade's a good man. My brother's proud ta' be serving under him. If there are men holdin' out, my brother will be among them."

C.T. studied Barrett. He wondered how different from his brother Dade's Georgia recruit could be. He also wondered if Stone Barrett could make the heavy ten-day ride in the mid-winter cold. His paunch wasn't helped by his age and ill-fitting leather coat. C.T. noted the shoddy tooling and worn buttons. His mud-covered boots were cracked across the toe. His bulbous nose was already red from the crisp morning air, the capillaries flaring.

"Well, the scouts have only heard what Clarke relayed to the command when he made it back to Fort Brooke. He was half dead, his right arm nearly shot off. Supposedly, Dade had pulled in his flanking scouts and at that point all hell broke loose as they quick-stepped through the palmettos. Micanopy and his men had been lying flat to the ground, God knows for how long, their rifles loaded and pointed. It was nine o'clock in the morning, cold, and Micanopy's men were ready. I guess you can take hope in one thing: Mr. Clarke said some of the men were able to stack logs and build a fortification. If that bought them time, they might have gotten away or something." C.T.'s voice trailed and the two rode next to each other in silence.

During the silence, C.T. watched Colonel Read's back as he looked about, flanked by two of his Cavalry. C.T. was thinking about skirmishes he had been caught in, or had encountered afterward. They were few in number, but coming upon the casualties was always horrific. If Clarke's description hadn't been blown out of proportion in the retelling, things were going to be bad. *Prepare yourself for the worst.* He thought back on Read's words to the volunteers. He stole another look at Stone Barrett, silent in his misery, and wondered. The man had not spoken since their introduction. *Pulling forward and leaving him in his thoughts for the ride out would be cruel.* C.T. reconciled himself to being Barrett's expedition partner.

"Stone, that's an interesting handle," C.T. commented after nearly an hour's worth of silence. He hoped Barrett wasn't going to be mute for the entire ride.

"Quarries. My pa and grand pappy worked the quarries. It's a nickname, my name is actually Samuel, Sam Barrett. C.T. nodded and fished through his pockets for his flask.

"Hmm. I see."

The sun was just beginning to warm his fingers which felt frozen around the reins of his horse. The group was now moving in a uniform, steady formation. No telling when they would stop to eat, so C.T. leaned back in his saddle and fished out his flask for yet another sip. He held the flask out to Barrett, who raised his eyebrows and welcomed the offer. Stone tipped his head back and took a generous swallow.

He handed back the flask. "That's all, don't offer me anymore. But thanks, all the same. Where you from? Where's your folks?"

"I'm from Maryland - Baltimore, actually. I left almost three years ago. Just after the meteor shower. I wouldn't really say that I've got folks." C.T. assessed his situation neatly. "I landed in Gainesville and then headed to Telfair. I signed up with Coffee's men after doing tannery work on Coffee's plantation. We've been scouting the Coffee Road for the past year. I came over to this side from Tallahassee six months ago. This spring I'll do some more scouting, maybe some tannery work—whatever comes up," ventured C.T. wondering if Barrett might have some leads.

The next four days continued in the same pattern. One question asked, one question answered over the distance of fifty miles each day.

"So, you're not married? No family?" ventured Barrett, his turn to speak.

"*Ha!* No, I'm not married and I guess you could say that I've got no family. Yep! That's a fair assessment."

As the party approached the Withlacoochee River, a slight breeze picked up, the air chilled.

"Early in my life I had promised myself I would never be this cold, stuck out in the elements. But here I am, molded into my saddle, my fingers so cold I can't feel them, the calluses on my feet screaming. How are you holding up, Mr. Barrett?"

"Pretty good, I suppose. We're close, I can feel it. It's quieter than I expected. I just know I don't feel so good, that's all."

Barrett fell silent as Read held up his hand and signaled for the march to slow. The volunteers approached the wide swatch of palmettos that edged the river. He gestured to two men to dismount. C.T. recognized one of the men as a scout he had worked with in the past; experienced, older, wiry and strong. His rifle, slung on the outside of his coat, slid down his arm on the dismount but he retrieved it handily. Some of the men in front also dismounted, Barrett among them. He rubbed his knees and scrubbed his face with his hands.

Colonel Read walked into the formation. The men circled around him as he spoke quietly, "I suspect we're getting very close. Get your rifles ready! Six of us will walk forward one hundred yards or so." He pointed to four volunteers, "Forsell! Davies! Maybe you two men," indicating two more, "flank us at four points while we decide who will be tracking to the river with me."

"I'm coming! My brother's somewhere out there." Barrett stepped forward. C.T. could have seen that decision coming from a hundred miles away, and dismounted too. He checked his carbine and pulled his pack from his horse. Barrett would need someone who would stay right beside him and who was experienced in scouting the area. He handed his reins to the man next to him, who had remained mounted and stepped forward with Barrett. Five volunteers and Colonel Read moved to the front of the formation.

"Move very slowly, and don't be caught off guard by anything. Keep your eyes open, and anticipate what might happen as you take each step," instructed Read. "Your rifles should be out and ready every step of the way."

C.T. stepped toward Read, his boot sinking into the sand. His pack slung over his left shoulder, he stayed to Barrett's right. His finger remained on the trigger of his firearm. In the cold air he wondered if he would be able to pull the trigger at the right moment. He studied Barrett's rifle curiously. *Dear God, I've never seen a rifle in worse condition. 'Poor bastard probably can't shoot his rifle any better than he can clean it.*

The six men fanned out into the palmetto field, widening the distance between themselves and the volunteers they had left behind. C.T. knew they were moving beyond the Colonel's original plan by one hundred yards or so, but something was pulling the experienced colonel forward. Barrett was sweating in spite of the biting cold. The hair on the back of C.T.'s neck was standing up. He suspected that Barrett was probably sick with fear and anticipation. Read silently studied the fauna in front of them, the sand, the sparsely spaced pine trees.

The smell of death hit C.T. like a black wave. He looked over to see if Barrett or the other men were affected.

Read stopped, "We're here." Pointing to two of the men included in the advance team, he commanded, "You two go back and select ten men to return with. As you leave, follow the footsteps that brought you here; and retrace those footsteps to come back to this exact point."

Then he ordered C.T., "You're a scout, I hear. Take that direction and walk along this line." He indicated a longitude through the palmettos. Barrett stuck to C.T.'s side with no protest from the colonel.

"Mr. Barrett," C.T. warned, "I fear this is not going to be good. No part of it, until we find your brother, one way or the other." Barrett nodded, his lip quivering. The two men, C.T. in front, advanced slowly. The first body they came to was laying face down, his arms over his head as in surrender. His legs had flailed out from under him when he took the shot. *Puzzling, he has his coat on over his rifle.* The man's bloated body was stuck to the ground in a pool of dried blood. C.T. looked over to Barrett, he was shaking his head. *His brother must not be blond*, because face down, the age and identity of the man was indeterminate.

C.T. swatted at a fly. He could hear the horse flies buzzing. Shallow breathing was going to save his stomach. He stood there watching Barrett move into the massacre scene, looking for his brother. The additional men had now joined the site. They edged slowly into the macabre scene. C.T. shadowed Barrett as he moved through the carnage. He looked desperate, forlorn, as he moved past each casualty, taking in the magnitude of the massacre. The stench was overwhelming. C.T. pulled out his flask, and caught up to Barrett, not really caring if the man, whose family waited for word in Georgia gulped what remained of his second trail flask. *One hundred and ten men. And one of them, almost certainly, is this poor devil's brother.*

"They're tangled in their coats! Every damned one of them, near, is tangled in his coat! Look at this one, his rifle is under his coat! And that one over there has his rifle tangled *in* his coat." They were beginning to realize the extent to which the attack had been a surprise to Dade and his men. Suddenly, Barrett let out a cry across the scene of a one-sided battle.

"Terrence! Terrence! It's me! Samuel!" Barrett screamed at the pine trees that stretched for miles. His words reverberated off of the trees and the men, but did nothing to locate his brother's body.

Trying to silence him as Barrett's words echoed, C.T. leaped toward his stricken companion, knocking him down. They grappled as C.T. attempted to cover Barrett's mouth with his hand. The two men were tangled in each other's limbs, next to a corpse whose leg had been shot off.

"Shh! Please Mr. Barrett. Please be quiet!" Barrett and C.T. struggled against each other. Several men rushed over to separate the two and pull them to their feet. Barrett burst into tears of futility after he was righted and helped to his feet by the sympathetic men.

Some years later, C.T. sat in a saloon knocking back his third whiskey as he described to a stranger what became known as the Dade Massacre.

"Walking through the palmettos, trying to identify men tangled up in their own limbs, *that* was the loneliest feeling I've ever had. Their bodies were nearly frozen to the ground in their own blood. The silence was vivid, except for the buzzing flies. And Barrett, of course," he explained to the stranger. "You know they were on their way from Fort Brooke to Fort King. It was so cold and crisp during that part of the year. It would have been a beautiful sparkle of a day, except for the massacre."

Anytime he told of his Dade experience, his listeners would watch him push through to the conclusion of his reflections with a swig of the last of whatever amount of whiskey was in his shot glass.

"Our own fingers had frozen around the reins and we had only gone half the distance those men had. God knows how we would have gotten off a fast shot if ambushed. Hell! We had *our* coats on! When we found Dade's men, we saw they had their coats on *over* their rifles! Dade and half the officers were killed in the first volley. It took the Seminoles a year to plan, and one hundred eighty braves to execute". He shook his head at his own words.

Jenkins would set his glass down and turn it between his thumb and forefinger, "The attack could not have caught Dade's men more by surprise."

* * *

7

HERNANDO

C.T. threw the latch on the barn door, leaving the cool, dark air behind. He turned toward the fields and squinted, wiping his shirtsleeve across his forehead, his fist clutched around the wide brim of his felt hat.

"Not a bad day," he concluded, late in the afternoon. After he checked that Anwok had put away the scythes and plows, he gave himself permission to concentrate on other things. Limping tiredly toward the bottle of whiskey stored under his bedroll in the bunk house, his mouth watered for the sting of that first nip. The long log cabin bunk house was hidden from the vista of the main house. The slaves' quarters were located behind the bunk house, even farther out of view of the plantation owner, Mrs. Harrell.

He eyed the cotton fields. *We're exactly where we need to be, this time of year*, he thought as he navigated the triangular course between the cotton fields, the barn and the bunk house. The fields of the Harrell's Plantation stretched outward as far as the eye could see, a lush emerald green, promising and decorated with little snowballs of white cotton. Each snowball pointed skyward from its own brittle, scalloped casing.

Please let dinner be ready, C.T. begged as he reached for the post and pulled himself up each step of the bunkhouse porch. Walking through the main room to the dormitory he sunk onto his cot.

Christ, he proclaimed to his sore muscles. He reached for the bottle he kept under his bed roll. Holding it up for inspection C.T. shook his head. *Damn! I will be out of whiskey before payday at this rate.*

He had to pull his boots off. Tugging mightily he was able to complete the last strenuous task of the day. He fell over onto his pillow and closed his eyes.

An hour later he awoke with a start. The cook was standing at the door of the dormitory softly calling his name. He could easily miss dinner if he didn't get up and dust off.

"Dalia, thank you," nodding at the forty-something woman, dressed in calico. "Corn chowder?"

"Hmm," she nodded before adding, "Mr. Stockard rode up a few moments ago, Mr. Jenkins."

"Well then, he should join us for dinner and I'll show him around afterward. Where is he now?"

"With Mrs. Harrell,"

"Fine, I'll go up to the house and join them. Then he can come back with me and sit down to dinner with the rest of the men." C.T. returned to his bunk and slipped on a fresh shirt, agonizing over the fact that he would have to struggle back into his boots if he was going to go up to the main house.

"Cyprian," Mrs. Harrell greeted him as he approached the front porch. He shook hands with Mr. Stockard, twenty-years old and the newest hand on Harrell's plantation. "Mr. Stockard, you've met our overseer, Mr. Jenkins, haven't you?"

"Yes Ma'am, I have. Pleased to see you again, Mr. Jenkins," greeted Mr. Stockard as he extended his hand.

Mrs. Harrell addressed C.T. as the two men shook hands, "Mr. Jenkins, I've gone over the basics with Mr. Stockard; pay, what we expect of our hands in terms of behavior, and such. If you would like to show him to the bunk house and get him settled, that would be nice. I'll leave the rest up to you."

"Well, Mr. Stockard, shall we? Dalia is stirring a fragrant pot of corn chowder in the mess hall. Why don't you bring your gear along and we'll drop it off at your bunk. Then you can sit down with the rest of the men and get acquainted." C.T. allowed Mr. Stockard to precede him from Mrs. Harrell's porch.

"Ma'am," Mr. Stockard tipped his hat to Mrs. Harrell before placing it on the back of his head.

"Mrs. Harrell," C.T. bid adieu to the widow and joined his new charge out in the front yard, pointing in the direction of the bunk house. "You can unpack your bedroll after dinner. We have supper at two o'clock and dinner in the evening, around eight o'clock."

Stockard nodded.

"You'll have an hour or two to look around after we have toured the fields. I came off the land an hour ago. The crops are doing fine and we are on track to bring in a good year."

"Hmm. How long have you worked here?"

"Six years or so. I started when I was about your age, I suppose. Rode in with a man from Macon, Georgia and other than scouting, I've spent the last six years with Mrs. Harrell and her family. Nice people. If you mind your business and you're an honest worker, you'll do fine."

The two men walked the boundary between the main house and the fields as they talked.

"Who's that?" asked Mr. Stockard, nodding to a young woman being helped off an open flat bed wagon that had arrived at the front of the Harrell's home.

The young woman popped open her lace umbrella, shading her light skin from the sun, and waved to Jenkins. C.T. smiled and tipped his hat.

"Hmm, that's Victoria Harrell, Mrs. Harrell's widowed daughter-in-law. Her husband had a riding accident three years ago. Lost his balance on a runaway horse. His boot caught in the stirrup."

Stockard gasped.

"Anyway, helping her down from the wagon is her uncle, Thomas Harrell. Mrs. Harrell's brother."

"She's a sight for sore eyes."

"Like I said, Mr. Stockard, if you mind your business and you're an honest worker, you'll do fine here."

**

"Mr. Jenkins." Smiling, Victoria offered a serving bowl of fragrant Cuban sweet potatoes to C.T. the following Sunday at dinner.

"Thank you," C.T. nodded and looked into the lush green of the cilantro combined with the bright yellow sweet potatoes. He placed a small portion of vegetables on his plate and continued his observations regarding managing the Harrell's tanning operation to Mrs. Harrell.

"If Stockard, here, takes over all post-tanning operations, we can increase production within the month." He passed the serving bowl back to Victoria.

"I'll take some of those sweet potatoes, Ma'am," Stockard cut in. "My, my! Everything looks so delicious Miss Victoria. You must be awfully good in the kitchen to supervise over these good fixins'," Stockard continued.

C.T. noticed Victoria Harrell's knitted eyebrows and nudged Stockard's boot under the table; although Stockard continued to beam at Victoria.

Dear God, was all that C.T. could think. He put his napkin down for the moment to draw Stockard's attention back to the discussion. "Mr. Stockard, as I was saying, if you are able to manage post-tanning operations we should be able to increase production. What are your suggestions now that you've had a few days?"

"Well, I'd like to take another week and then lay out my suggestions to you, Mr. Jenkins."

"Well, I guess that's fair."

"Mr. Jenkins, how do *you* like your dinner this evening?" Victoria asked, leaning forward toward C.T.

"Very nice meal, Ma'am. Your management of the kitchen staff is evident in every meal. It's clear that you and your cook get along well together. My compliments."

"It's a great meal! I've never eaten so much in my life! Why the roasted chicken is the best I've ever had, if I could have more?" interjected Stockard.

This time C.T. chose not to provide a cautionary signal to his new employee but he was bemused by the fleeting look of horror on Victoria Harrell's face. He then turned his attention to Mrs. Harrell. The report of the week's progress continued. *Please be listening,* was his silent chant to Mr. Stockard who was staring openly at Victoria.

Scooting back her chair, Victoria came around the table and stood over C.T. The fragrance of gardenias was evident as she reached across, "If you're done may I take your plate, Mr. Jenkins?"

He leaned away from her, "Once again you have provided a most generous Sunday meal. How can I ever thank you?" instantly regretting his words.

Handing over C.T.'s plate to a little girl who had just come from the kitchen, Victoria responded, "Well, would you care to escort me through a walk of the orchards?"

"Oh! I didn't mean...what I meant...I meant simply 'thank you' for the nice meal, Mrs. Harrell. It takes a lot of effort to manage the kitchen staff and plan such nice meals each week. Yes! That is what I meant!" Rushing into his words he added, "I was planning to ride into town after dinner actually," thinking about the shot of

Evan Williams and the ample company that awaited him at Jesse Black's Saloon.

He sat helpless as he watched the flush of rejection redden Victoria's face. She blinked back tears of embarrassment. C.T. glanced over at Stockard and caught the tail end of a smirk.

"Why Miss Victoria, I happen to know that Mr. Jenkins has plans that cannot be set aside. But I'd be more than honored if you would show me the upper yard of the plantation from something other than a work hand's perspective. Please accept *my* invitation for a stroll, won't you?"

Looking from Stockard to Jenkins, Victoria lifted her chin and accepted, "How lovely, Mr. Stockard. Yes, just let me run upstairs and get my shawl."

"Well, gentlemen. If you will give me my

leave, I'll excuse myself so you can talk over the work that needs to be done to bring the crops in," said Mrs. Harrell as she stood up.

Hearing the footsteps of their boss trip up the stairs after her daughter-in-law, Stockard laughed, "Mr. Jenkins, you might be a highly capable overseer, but you will never settle down and have a family if you keep that up!"

The two men parted on the front porch. Mrs. Harrell stood with C.T., watching the younger man tip his hat and offer his arm to Victoria, and the two stepped forward together.

Jenkins continued to watch as they carried on pleasantly with one another, feeling as though he had witnessed many such pairings over the past several years.

He had enough experience to know that his first sip of whiskey at Jesse Black's Saloon would make him feel fine again.

AOA ~ Armed Occupation Act, 1843

C.T.'s horse loped leisurely, leading the way through the thick underbrush of tangled morning glory vines and dwarf palmettos that fanned out across the Annutteliga Hammock. It was early morning and the damp sand clumped under horse's hoofs. C.T. rode his favorite horse from Mrs. Harrell's stable. "You know the way, don't you, Buddy? There, there. What do you think old boy?"

The response was a toss of his mane and a high step, as horse and rider proceeded deeper into the thick brush that formed a botanical carpet under towering hickory and juniper trees. The salt air rolled in with the gulf breeze the night before and was burning off, leaving a clean fragrance of fresh cut bamboo. Wafting over gentle hill crests. A mottled blue haze hung in the distance, promising a tropical downpour later that afternoon.

C.T. was on a personal mission that morning, going over in his mind his choices of possible tracts of northwestern Florida land he might stake claim to under the Armed Occupation Act. Committing to the Act was an easy decision for Jenkins. He ran the provision through his mind. *Claim one hundred sixty acres of land, and within the first year after the permit was approved, then cultivate five acre.* Twelve years after leaving Baltimore he had made up his mind about Florida, *I'm staying. It's a new frontier. Yes, full of risks, but the men who are settling Florida have a vision of the possibilities of commerce and community. They see what I see in Florida's beauty and bounty. Yes, I'm staying.*

And with that personal commitment, the only decision in completing the permit process of the land grant was the final difficult choice between two tracts of land: the rise north of Bay Port, next to Francis Ederington's plantation, or a tract along the shores of the Homosassa River which would make a neighbor of visionary and statesman, David Yulee.

C.T. imagined what his life in Baltimore would have been like had he followed his father's wish that he join with his brothers, Frederick and William, continuing the legacy of *William V. Jenkins & Son's Tanning and Currier*. He would have dealt daily with the same Baltimore businessmen, their sons, and their families. His days would pass in repetitious, mind-numbing decisions about their respective enterprises, designed by past generations controlling the future from the grave, as was the case with the Wells' enterprises. *To Hell with the clawing and the plotting*, he had decided years earlier.

His only discomfort was any thought that brought him to the bundled letters collecting in his bureau bearing the return address, 'Huntington Estate, Baltimore, Maryland'. *Oh Father! I've made my decision. I have no choice but to go forward with my life here, and no idea of how your days are spent.* And, that last question would not be answered as long as the letters from his father remained unopened, as they had.

**

"And, I'll carry your permit, along with all the others, to the Lands Office in Newnansville," Garrason reassured, once again outlining the Armed Occupation Act to C.T. as they continued their conversation over breakfast. C.T. was in town on business, and had stopped in at the Garrason's Bay Port House before going over to the Ederington's store for supplies to take back to Mrs. Harrell's plantation.

"Well, that interests me, Isaac. One hundred sixty acres, you say? I guess I've decided that my
interest is in the tract across the spine of the Annutteliga hammock. I could build a cottage there. Do some farming. Probably hire out to survey the cedar stands."

"Surveying? Really, who is hiring?"

"Eberhard Faber, I hear. Faber bought land out at Cedar Key, and I hear he needs it surveyed and logged."

"Never heard of him. What's his business?"

"Pencils," C.T. laughed. "Pencils and stationery stores; it seems his family owns a pencil manufacturing plant in Germany, supplied by high tariff lumber from the U.S. He has been buying cedar in the states, shipping it to Germany for manufacture after paying the tariffs, and then paying to have the manufactured pencils shipped back across the Atlantic to his New York stationery store. Figures he can manufacture pencils right here in the states using Florida cedar and save money on the tariffs and cross-Atlantic shipping. Ederington is going to pay Faber for use of Faber's southbound schooners in order to bring furniture and supplies from New York to Ederington's Tampa and Bay Port general stores. If all parties are in agreement, I will survey and supervise the Cedar Key logging operation"

"Pencils," Garrason mused.

Placed on the table in front of C.T. was the application that needed to be completed if the Baltimorean was to become a land holder.

Garrason handed him the quill and together they concentrated on filling out the application.

"To the Register of the land Office at Newnansville, Florida. *Under the provisions of the Act of Congress approved on the 4th day of August, A.D. 1842, entitled, "An Act to provide for the armed occupation and settlement of the unsettled part of the Peninsula of East Florida."*

C.T. relished the idea of being among the first to stake a claim on Florida's future, he read each word of the permit carefully, rubbed his hands together as if to warm them and then picked up the quill to fill his name in the space provided,

"I, Cyprian T. Jenkins*, do hereby apply to the Register of the proper Land Office for a Permit to settle upon One hundred and sixty acres of unappropriated public land, lying south of the line dividing townships numbered nine and ten, south of the base line, and situated as herein described..."*

C.T. unfolded the piece of paper providing the legal description of the property he had staked out and began to write. After thirty minutes he re-read the permit and stopped for a moment to look around the dining room of the Bay Port House. It was empty and elegantly quiet, the breakfast diners having left to go about their day. The gravity of making application for the land grant permit left him light headed. *If only Ambrose or Charles were here to share this moment with me!*

But that was not the case. He looked across the table to Mr. Garrason, who waited patiently for the young man to date and sign for his 'intended settlement'. Mr. Garrason's proffered the inkwell to C.T. who signed his given name, 'Cyprian T. Jenkins' underlining it for good measure; adding the date, 04 April 1843.

* * *

8

Fair Haven

It was incredulous to Mrs. Colburn that so many years had passed since the death of her husband.

Day after day during all the years of her widowhood she would wake to the same routine of breakfast on a tray upstairs in the space that had been her husband's library; the space that adjoined her bedroom. After breakfast she would write in her journal or answer her correspondence, which was posted each week by Abby.

"I do love writing letters, Abby. I can almost hear my sister's voice responding to my thoughts."

"Yes, Ma'am. Just pull the cord and I'll come up when they are ready to be posted. I can pick up your subscriptions while I'm in the village."

If the *New York Mercury* had been brought in, she might read it after lunch. Later, she would look at the accounts and jot notes in the margins of the reports that her son Rufus or her brother-in-law Charles would leave for her.

And so it had gone, attending church, working on social committees with the wives of the newest generation of Fair Haven businessmen, and talking over topics of art and culture with the women's luncheon group, and fundraising.

She had recently pulled down from her library shelves the journal containing the words she had written immediately after John's death. His library had been redecorated into a more feminine sitting area, with a generous roll top desk and a much smaller library collection. A fireplace kept the room warm through the long bluster of winter and its frequent ice storms. Mrs.

Colburn welcomed visits to this private space from Eliza and her sister-in-law, Olivia.

When she pulled down that first journal, Mrs. Colburn passed her hand over the journal's pages which had yellowed to a soft sepia. The ink was faded, tattling how many years had worn on. Her more recent journals contained notations of the accomplishments of her four sons.

My life has simply gotten away from me; it's passing while I watch the children achieve their dreams, she read. Mrs. Colburn had to remind herself how many years it had been since she was the twenty-two year old bride arriving at Quinton Estate to take over the care of Betsey and Moses.

If John were alive we would have so much to discuss, to plan for. If only Susan and MaryAnn weren't so far away.

She felt isolated, as first Moses and then John Jr. left the estate to begin their lives. She was lonely in spite of Eliza's company, in spite of correspondence from MaryAnn and visits from Olivia, and in spite of the fatiguing demands of the operations of the Colburn properties.

Someday this sorrow and focus on John's death has got to end, she thought.

After twenty-five years, even Robert McCutcheon's interest in the Colburn properties had waned. The day-to-day management of the foundry had been turned over to Rufus rather unceremoniously.

At the end of each week, Mrs. Colburn and Rufus poured over the ledgers. When he left, Mrs. Colburn would climb the stairs to her gabled library, remove her glasses and dim the gas lamps. Seeing her shadow she thought ruefully, *Aha! There you are. My only companion.*

Her mother also seemed overly fatigued.

"Mother, darling . . .?

But her queries were always brushed away, though it had become increasingly difficult for Phoebe Davey to climb the stairs to the sanctuary library. Her heart condition caused such trepidation that her mid-morning visits were usually capped off by a nap before the carriage took Mrs. Davey back her own estate.

It had also been years since the tear-stained letters from Lucy caused her sister, MaryAnn, to pace her own home worrying about Lucy's ability to get through the worst burden possible, the death of a child. It was Lucy's darkest moment, and the greatest blow to her confidence since John Sr. had died.

John Jr. had just graduated from law school in Burlington, Vermont. He had taken a position with the Office of Commissioner of Lands, State of Iowa. Mrs. Colburn and Eliza had travelled by rail to Iowa City after John's graduation to celebrate the promise of his new career.

"You'll do beautifully. I will look forward to hearing the most wonderful news in the letters you send us," Lucy praised her son. "I have the greatest pride and boundless confidence that things will turn out fine for you, now that you are done with your schooling," she promised.

Lighthearted, she and her daughter boarded the eastbound train and rode back to Quinton Estate. Lucy felt rich, empowered. "It's not becoming," she admitted to Eliza, "but I think I even feel a bit smug at John Jr.'s success." She felt that she had successfully handed her most handsome son over to the brightest of futures.

Four months later the telegram arrived, heralding an inferno of devastation. Abby had answered the door that day, and summoned Mrs. Colburn to receive the telegram.

Mrs. Colburn wrote in her letter to MaryAnn, describing the moment, *"Actually, the moment I saw the messenger standing in the foyer I was filled with a sense of dread. He was serene, even formal as he held an envelope in both hands, arms extended in front of him. The setting, the season, the circumstances were so different from the last time a telegram had arrived that it didn't occur to me that I was about to receive news that would leave my life in shambles."*

She took the envelope from the middle aged man quizzically. Nodding, she pulled the door open so that he could take his leave. Listening to the hoof beats of the messenger's horse as he retreated, Lucy felt protected by the privacy of the estate. She slipped a fingernail under the flap and opened the envelope marked, "The New York and Mississippi Valley Printing Telegraph Company".

> *L. W. Babbitt Law Offices*
> *Sioux City, Iowa*
> *We. Regret. To. Inform. You:*
> *Accidental. Death. John. Colburn. Jr., Esq.*
> *Please. Make. Arrangements.*
> *Arrive. Immediately.*

Lucy stared at the words on the page. She simply could not comprehend the words pasted into the message. She held the telegram tight in her fist, and then crumpled it, listening to her heart pound wildly. The words didn't make sense to her. Not yet. She was confused by the message and then not at all able to comprehend it. A white storm raged in her mind. Her heart raced. A loud, bright ringing in her ears prevented her from hearing anything.

Afterwards – when the deadening calm came – she would recall dragging herself toward the drawing room to sit down; the weight of her skirts, the length of the hallway.

Abby found her on the sofa, leaning heavily into the armrest and staring straight ahead in unresponsive, dazed.

"Oh dear, oh dear! What is it Mrs. Colburn? Please, what is it?" Abby dropped to her knees in front of Lucy as she continued to stare straight ahead. It sounded like Abby was speaking to her from the bottom of a well. She could hear her name being called, but because of the high pitched ringing in her eardrums Lucy could not hear clearly.

"Please, Mrs. Colburn, what is it?"

Finally Lucy held the telegram at arms' length and dropped the crumpled message into Abby's outstretched palm.

Abby struggled with the message, sounding out the words as best she could until she too understood. She was stricken by the loss of John Jr. Abby had enjoyed happy friendships with each of the children, a secret life full of joyful experiences.

In a bustling kitchen smelling of vanilla and cookie-dough Abby had spent years listening to and comforting all of the Colburn children as they grew to adulthood. She fed them cookies and sweet dumplings as their ideas buzzed around the kitchen like little honeybees.

Abby wasn't thinking, in the foul moments of the telegram's news of John Jr. as a grown man fresh from law school; but as the studious little child who wandered into the kitchen. She remembered him curiously poking at sifters and cooking pots until she was able to ply him out of his bashfulness. He would grab at warm cookies just out of the oven, or lean against the entry just to see what was happening in the kitchen. How could Mrs. Colburn know that this brilliant young man had created special, endearing memories for the woman she saw merely as a house servant?

Abby had always looked at Mrs. Colburn's children and thought, *Look at these beautiful children for whom I am responsible. They'll achieve so much more than I ever would have*, realizing how limited she was by her own circumstances.

"Abby, have Gerald saddle a horse and instruct him bring Charles to me," the words, even in their crisp delivery, were welcome. "We'll settle things after he arrives."

Mrs. Colburn and her brother-in-law spent the following day discussing matters at the Quinton Estate, setting things in order before Charles left to board a train for Iowa City. His and Mrs. Colburn's parting was as tender as thirty-two years of knowing one another from a distance would allow.

In spite of her age, Lucy's mother became the stronger of the two in the weeks that followed John's death. "What is happening to our family, Mother? One by one we're dying."

"I suppose we are," admitted the matriarch. "But, I didn't expect to outlive my children, let alone my grandchildren. *I* should be next." Phoebe foretold her own death with those words. She began to grow frailer. Her lacy white collars, now loose, sat unbalanced on her neck and shoulders. She became easily tangled in her long skirts and ruffled sleeves. Her silver hair, once worn in a thick braided bun, now fell out in clumps. Her nurse's solution was to place crocheted bonnets on top of her little skull, which did little to capture the carriage and elegance of her earlier years.

Pneumonia killed Phoebe the winter of 1856.

**

DIED
Buggy Accident Fells Vermont Lawyer
In Iowa City, Iowa on the 10th instant, December
John P. Colburn, Jr., Esq., late of
Fair Haven, Vermont.
Iowa City Press-Citizen - December 13, 1853

**

OBITUARY
Rutland County Loses Pre-Eminent Hostess
In Fair Haven, Rutland County, Vermont

On the 19th instant, January
Phoebe Dey Davey, widow of Jacob Davey
At Eighty Years of Age.
Rutland Advertiser - 1856

***

9

West Point

Lucy caught her son, Albert, eyeing himself in the mirror, his left side and then his right, brushing a tuft of hair over the thin spot that was developing early in spite of his youthful age of twenty-two.

"Oh, you handsome devil," were the words she was sure she heard as she entered from the kitchen with a basket of sandwiches and sweets prepared by the cook.

"Here darling, you do look perfectly handsome." Lucy brushed her hand over the shoulder of her son's suit, looking at his face but seeing the face of his paternal grandfather, Moses Colburn.

"You'll do well, Albert. And New York is such an exciting place for you to be; with so much to look forward to. Your Uncle Israel will introduce you to Lieutenant Colonel McDowell at the Convocation next week. Eliza and I will visit New York during the holidays, and we'll make the trip up to see you. We'll all be waiting to hear great things from you."

Mrs. Colburn thought back to Albert's youth and the scattered wood carved army pieces that had been lined up in proper formation on the rug in front of the fireplace or scattered under his Uncle Israel's feet ever since Albert was a small child. For hours he would command and cajole his soldiers, catapulting them into the air, scolding and celebrating their imaginary victories. Now Albert had a commission to the Class of 1856 at West Point. His pride could not be more evident.

"Here's your portfolio, and your letters of introduction. The telegram confirming that your trunk arrived in New York is right here." Lucy pointed out to

Albert how she had organized his paperwork. She had choreographed her son's entire life to that moment, and the last seconds of her tutelage were arriving.

"Thank you, Mother. Do I have everything?"

"Albert, just let me say this. You will be as successful in military sciences as your father and brother were in law school, and your life will be as happy as Susan's. Your career at West Point will be as successful as Rufus' business career. You are entitled to this success."

Her words of send-off delivered, she turned her attention to Eliza, "Where is your sister?"

"I . . ."

Not waiting for Albert's response, she added, "Uncle Israel will be here very shortly. I know she's not reluctant to see you off; but it's unbecoming that I should have call for her."

Lucy Colburn fussed and tugged at Albert's bow tie.

He shrugged her off as best he could and said, "Eliza is finishing an embroidered handkerchief that I'm to keep in my lapel."

Mrs. Colburn looked up at her son quizzically.

"She left her embroidery hoop in the parlor last week." Then, glancing up, he interrupted his explanation as his sister quietly shut the door to her room and turned to start down the stairs.

Looking over the banister Eliza smiled at her mother and brother, holding something behind her back as she joined them to wait for her uncle.

"Out with it, then. What do you have for me?" laughed Albert, stealing the moment from her.

Mrs. Colburn stepped aside as Eliza thrust a tissue-wrapped package, bound with gold ribbon at Albert. Grinning, he tugged at the ribbon and folded back the wrapping, revealing four delicate white handkerchiefs bearing his initials, AVC. Mrs. Colburn peered down at her daughter's embroidery work. "Nicely done, Eliza. You should be proud of yourself."

Then, with the flourish of a magician, Albert draped three of the handkerchiefs over his extended forearm, each next to the other. Taking the fourth handkerchief, he stuffed the middle of the handkerchief into a ring made by his joined thumb and forefinger. Once the linen square was stuffed into his closed fist, he bowed his head and peeked at his mother through sandy blonde eyelashes. As she feigned impatience he blew into his hand which sprung open less one linen handkerchief. In mock surprise at the trick taught him by his grandfather, he turned his hand, fingers spread, in the air and winked at his mother.

Impeccably timed, his Uncle Israel entered the parlor. He removed his hat, and handed his black walking stick and cape to Abby.

Israel went straight to his sister. "Hello dear," he kissed her cheek, then her forehead, "Are you well?"

"No, actually, I'm not. I feel quite out of sorts, actually."

"I'll take good care getting him there, Lucy."

"It's his dream, I suppose. As much as I wish he weren't leaving, at least he's going off to be with fine officers, men of high caliber."

"It will be fine."

"That's what you always say, Israel, even when it's obvious that it won't be." Her voice was tight and controlled as Mrs. Colburn followed them all to the foyer. She realized she was speaking to herself as she trailed through the house.

Eliza folded her arm into the crook of Albert's and walked her brother beyond the front porch to where his horse was hitched. "Write us often, Albert!"

"Certainly, Eliza, every day. No formation, no classes, no military school training. I'll just sit in my room and whine into letters about how much I miss you."

"Stop making fun of me, you silly!"

"Mother?" John called to Mrs. Colburn.

She plucked at her ruffled skirts and made her way to the son she had always referred to as *My Little Comedian.* "I know you will take care and be a credit to your father. Write when you can, we understand you'll have demands made on your time," and she backed away leaving him next to his black saddle horse.

Israel and John mounted up with the practiced skill of expert equestrians and tipped their hats.

"I hate this, John."

"I know, Mother," he said as he coaxed his horse.

Mrs. Colburn and her daughter waved, and Israel and Albert turned in their saddles to wave back before sauntering down the lane. Soon they had made their way through the orchards of Fair Haven, Vermont riding toward the station where they would board the horses and catch the train for New York.

"Eliza, are you coming?"

"Yes."

Mrs. Colburn turned and made her way back up the steps to the manor, calling over her shoulder, "We'll have to try to fill the void of Albert's departure together," not waiting for Eliza's reply.

**

Lucy Colburn was frantically packing, scurrying back and forth across her bedroom. She retraced her footsteps, traversing the polished plank floor of the generous alcove she had been the sole occupant of since the death of her husband. Tiny sparkles of perspiration collected above her finely arched eyebrows as she packed clothes into two open-jawed trunks placed side by side at the foot of her bed. After turning her options over for the past year, she was now convinced that she was setting the most practical course for herself.

And her course was to leave Fair Haven as immediately as possible.

She clawed at clothes that had hung symmetrically in the cabinet, leaving most of the hangers askew and tangled. She plucked through clothes that had been neatly folded in the regal old sleigh-front bureau, leaving the contents in an unusual state of disarray.

Concerned over Mrs. Colburn's frenetic pace, Abby offered to help. "Really, Mum, it's not good that you won't accept my help!"

"I know what I'm doing and by the time I explain to you what to pack, I'm doing the job twice now, aren't I?"

Letting the skirt she was holding fall to the floor in soft folds, she stopped for a moment. "We've been through so much together, haven't we Abby?"

"Yes'um, I suppose we have."

"If you could please check on Eliza for me, dear, that would be most generous."

"Of course," Abby's voice trailed as she curtsied and gently pulled the door to Mrs. Colburn's suite shut.

Lucy Colburn's plans to leave Fair Haven were prompted by her mother's death, which left her as the last Dey-Davey woman in Rutland County. Her sister MaryAnn Moore's funereal visit, all the way from Florida, had prompted her to action. MaryAnn and her husband, Reverend Harrison Moore, had moved from Fair Haven twenty-two years earlier when Harrison had been called to minister a congregational church in St. Petersburg. Their son was involved in the timber business in nearby Bay Port and seemed to be doing quite well.

Since MaryAnn's departure from Fair Haven, Lucy had only seen her older sister twice—the year their father died and this past year after their mother's death.

Two visits in twenty-two years. Of course there had been telegrams, but the sisters had depended primarily on the postal service, sending letters via steamer routes along the eastern seaboard.

Dear MaryAnn,

I hope this letter finds you and Harrison well.

Life is exceptionally quiet here, to the point of being unsettling. The children continue to expect so much from me, not realizing that with Mother gone I no longer have my source of strength. Eliza's future is clouded as she does not seem able to make a decision without me. My daughter, I admit, seems impossibly stuck and rudderless. Will I be her sole support for the rest of her life? With Albert's

departure to West Point, and mother and John Jr.'s passing, little compels me to keep Quinton Estate open year-round.

Would you care for a visit from us? I believe that Eliza would benefit from coming to Florida and experiencing a livelier social scene this season. Maybe her favorite cousin could escort her?

I'll begin to make plans and write again soon,

Love in God's Name,

Lucy

**

A light knock on Mrs. Colburn's door interrupted her packing. It was Eliza bringing her back to the moment.

"Taking only two trunks is impossible! It can't be done; even Abby agrees."

My goodness, this just may be the extent of Eliza's problems, Lucy thought as her daughter swept through the door of her mother's room and flounced onto her bed. Lucy looked at her youngest child, now a twenty-five year old woman.

"Look at you Eliza; you're three years older than I was when I married your father. I was so very young when John and I married."

She chided herself as she watched her daughter's face fall, and amended, "Do the best you can, Eliza, and we'll consider a side trunk for our millinery and extras."

Eliza nodded, "Alright, Mother."

Before the words, "Now, go finish packing," left her lips, Mrs. Colburn took a long moment staring at her daughter. *We look so much alike, how could we possibly be so different?*

She realized that the challenges of raising seven children alone had set her strong jaw line and mouth, making her look unyielding.

"Eliza, you have the most beautiful smile. That is, when you smile. Now go do the best you can while I think about business matters and finish packing my things."

After signing what seemed like an endless number of documents, all prepared by Robert McCutcheon, Lucy Colburn had relinquished to her son Rufus, and her brother-in-law Charles, total control of the Colburn business interests.

"Well, Mr. McCutcheon, after all these many years, there is little reason for you to involve me in the management of Colburn Enterprises any longer," she stated as she handed the quill to her husband's protagonist.

"You've provided well for your family, Mrs. Colburn. I'm sure Rufus and your brother-in-law will be able to provide well for you and Eliza."

Mrs. Colburn had established an annual allowance from royalties and income amounting to fifteen hundred dollars. That sum already awaited her in Florida, wired ahead in anticipation of her needs. The possibilities for Mrs. Colburn and her daughter were enormous. With Florida land selling at one dollar an acre, she could only imagine that her own life and her daughter's would be much richer than they enjoyed in Fair Haven.

While planning, Mrs. Colburn's mind had wandered through every possibility she could imagine once she and Eliza left the confines of their roles as the widow and daughter of John Peabody Colburn. She had considered the responsibility of guiding her daughter through the selection of an appropriate husband from the suitors whose east coast families vacationed in Florida each year.

Although several plucky Fair Haven young men had tipped their hats to Eliza and Mrs. Colburn after Sunday services, none of their mothers or older sisters had been extended an invitation to Quinton Estate for the purpose of pursuing 'possibilities.' Mrs. Colburn simply hadn't found any of the young men suitable, advising Eliza after each gentleman's inquiry, "He is not exactly what I have in mind for your happiness, and I don't sense any great interest on your part, darling. We can afford to wait for the right situation."

The family's travel plans were that she and Eliza, along with Gerald and Abby, would take a carriage to the Rutland rail line. Gerald, of course, would assist with baggage and other tasks. The two other servants who had quarters at the estate would be let go to neighboring households. The party of four would then board the train to New York where they would board the steamship *Brother Jonathan* for their first stop—Savannah, Georgia.

Gerald, originally indentured to the Davey's for his passage from Ireland, had transferred to the Colburn household and had lived a more comfortable life once the expense of his passage had been paid. Tall, well-dressed, with a fair complexion, the older gentleman easily navigated the party through the rail stations and eventually onto the docks, as they embarked on their unusually long journey.

Seven lazy sun-drenched days passed while the Colburn party steamed from New York, down the Atlantic seaboard to Savannah. Most of their time was spent lazing on deck chairs, wrapped in light blankets, chatting with other travellers, and pointing out sights to one another. Each day grew warmer as the steamboat made its way into the waters of the Carolinas en route to the Garden City.

"Won't you excuse me, Eliza?" Mrs. Colburn would ask each day before excusing herself from the dining room to make notes in her journal.

They awoke at dawn on the day the *Brother Jonathan* was to arrive in Savannah. Mrs. Colburn was eager to disembark at their first port of call, and had her luggage and papers in order well before the ship docked.

"Eliza, are you awake?" She asked as tapped on her daughter's stateroom door.

"Oh! Mother isn't this exciting, I'm so thrilled; I've been up for hours. Look, Abby has everything ready. Bags packed, hat and gloves set aside."

Mrs. Colburn nodded, "I'm pleased that you are

so enthusiastic, Eliza. I hope this vacation will turn out to be all that you hope for." They hooked arms and strolled out to the promenade deck to watch the stevedore activity.

By eight o'clock in the morning the air was humid to the point of being suffocating. The commotion on the debarkation deck worked into frenzy as the vessel made its wide pass up the Savannah River. Fort Tybee slid by on the starboard shore. Against a treacherous current, the vessel began its trudge toward Savannah Harbor, escorted by tugs. The steamer continued its hard pull past Bird Island, the salt works, and the city's industrial sites. Exuberant friends and relatives lined up along East Bay Street, jumping up and down, screaming, waving hats and handkerchiefs, calling and beckoning to the steamboat's passengers.

Wheeled vehicles—bicycles and carriages; carts and wagons both laden and empty—formed a backdrop to the carnival atmosphere. Young boys in short pants and newsboy caps ran alongside hoops that they kept upright with sticks until the hoops would catch in a plank and topple, or until a constable grabbed at the hoop wagging a finger at the errant youth.

"Abby, Gerald, do come along," instructed Mrs. Colburn as she and Eliza led the way down the gangplank. While the steamer took on coal and provisions and then began the process of reversing its course for the return to New York, Mrs. Colburn and Eliza planned their route out of the crowded port.

Abby and Gerald had been booked into a boarding house adjacent to the port district before the trip commenced.

As they parted company, Gerald negotiated the fare with a waiting coachman for Mrs. Colburn and Eliza who left the waterfront to tour the city.

Wearing top hat and tails, their guide selected a wonderful route meant to show off the most beautiful homes and park-like boulevards of Savannah. Their first stop was at the sidewalk café at 307 West Bryan Street. "This is a very agreeable gathering spot for our city's ladies, if you would care to stop for tea and sandwiches?" The coachman asked.

"Yes," agreed Mrs. Colburn, "that is a nice idea, actually. Thank you."

"Mother, don't forget to gather your parasol."

Pulling the carriage to the side of the boulevard the driver climbed down from his perch and opened the carriage door, lifting each lady down to the plank sidewalk. He then escorted them to the French inspired café.

After lunch, as Mrs. Colburn thanked the café's proprietor, the coachman pulled the carriage up from its shaded post across the street. However, instead of returning to the confines of the carriage, Mrs. Colburn instructed the driver to follow as she and Eliza took an early afternoon stroll along the tree lined streets adjacent to the City Market.

It would be a full week before they made their way back to the bawdy, intrigue-filled port to meet up with Abby and Gerald. Jacksonville, Florida, where they would meet Mrs. Colburn's brother-in-law, Reverend Moore was their next destination.

"Where will we meet him, Mother?" Eliza asked.

"I'm hoping Harrison will be at the dock waiting for us," she laughed, and added, "I also hope to be able to recognize him—it's been so long!"

The arrangement was that Harrison Moore would meet them in Jacksonville; they would all vacation for a few days before continuing through the Keys and on to the Gulf Coast destination of Bay Port, where MaryAnn Moore was waiting.

Leaving Savannah on a day that the weather threatened an early afternoon thunder storm, the steamer *Seminole* blew its whistle and started its coal-fired engines. The ship strained against its moorings as the ships' mates untangled the lines and tossed them down to the dock. The steamship, loaded with cotton, coal and passengers, left the harbor and turned through Wassaw Sound to begin its stately sail southward along the coast.

"Are you excited, darling?" Mrs. Colburn asked Eliza.

"Yes! Of Course! That's when our vacation will really begin. Just imagine the dinner parties and tours of the gardens."

Arriving Jacksonville, the steamship docked at the mouth of the St. Johns River. Boat-weary but delighted passengers surged to the ship's rail, calling out to family and friends waiting for the ship to be properly berthed. It was chaotic fanfare as a band at the entrance to the dock below filled the sky with a flotilla of summertime sounds. Vendors screeched, selling cookies, sandwiches, and selections of cheese to those waiting to be reunited with a member of the throng that pressed itself against the rails of the steamer.

From the upper deck of the steam ship, with Eliza standing beside her, Lucy looked down into the faces of the crowd. She peered anxiously into the confusion of the screaming, manic mass of people. Parties to the mêlée called out to friends and relatives. Children ran up the docks to the waiting arms of aunts and uncles with parents and grandparents rushing behind them.

On the edge of the pulsing crowd stood a tall bean-pole of a man, standing on a crate. It was Harrison. He took off his black silk top hat and waved it in a wide arc above his head until he caught his sister-in-law's attention. In spite of the distance between them, Harrison and Lucy burst out laughing in relief at finding each other amid the wild pandemonium. From that moment until the gangway was lifted, they kept careful sight of each other.

Their plan was that Gerald would collect the trunks and find porters to carry the baggage and parcels up the dock to where Harrison stood ready to greet them. Abby stood to the side, observing the mayhem as other families and friends connected, collected, and departed from the long wharf. A young sailor came up alongside Abby, offering his arm and a wink to the 40-year old woman.

"Abby! Stay close! Don't frighten us so!" Mrs. Colburn admonished.

Lucy turned her thoughts to Harrison, whom she felt was well suited to the Colburn family. He had completed his theological studies at Middlebury College. In Vermont, his family had enjoyed a lifestyle similar to the Colburn's. And, after his marriage to her sister, Harrison enjoyed a lifestyle that was unattainable to most in the ministry.

She watched Harrison survey the bedlam and extended his arm, snapping his fingers at a coachman. The rumpled, portly man gathered the bundles that Gerald had collected, as Harrison engaged the man's services for the remainder of the day.

After the jostling and commotion of loading the carriage settled down, Reverend Moore assisted Eliza, Mrs. Colburn and Abby into the passenger compartment. The quarter-lights remained open so that the four passengers could enjoy the fresh air once they were underway. Gerald climbed up to sit in the open with the carriage driver. As a precaution, a scout accompanied the driver. Harrison explained that a party of Seminole braves had, allegedly, recently taken shots at a party riding in an open wagon on the outskirts of Jacksonville.

"My dear!" exclaimed Mrs. Colburn.

The coachman turned to Gerald, "There's a shotgun; do you know how to use it?"

Mrs. Colburn smiled to herself upon hearing Gerald's response, "Yes, but of course."

The old fibber! She knew that he was dearly depending on the expertise of the wizened scout who nudged his horse to follow the slow rolling coach as the members of the Colburn party settled in for a ride through Jacksonville. They made a stop along the way at the Bank of Commerce, where Harrison accompanied Lucy into the bank for her first Florida transaction.

At Harrison's urging, Mrs. Colburn and Eliza were planning to spend the upcoming days in Jacksonville's Arlington District at the home of the O'Neale family, investment partners of Harrison.

"Harrison, how long have you known this family?"

"Lucy, don't start your worrying. They are so lively. Really, my dear. I know that you and Eliza will find the O'Neales intriguing and generous. Margaret and her husband are such close friends of mine, and this is the perfect time to meet them."

"Hmm."

"Then, after you've had a chance to consider the opportunities Jacksonville has to offer, we will all continue on to Bay Port."

As Harrison chattered on Lucy thought through her itinerary. After their Jacksonville visit, their

party would board the schooner, *W. H Hazard Tucker,* to Bay Port. Taking the much shorter overland route from Jacksonville to Bay Port would have been folly, considering the unrest among the Seminoles that was receiving great attention and much press.

It would take a week for the schooner to dock at the wharf on the St. John's River. In the meantime, they would see Jacksonville, socialize and relax before boarding another vessel and continuing on their journey.

After the stop at the bank and an afternoon of touring—with Harrison pointing out the development of Jacksonville—the carriage pulled up to the Arlington District home of Margaret O'Neale.

"I guarantee, compared to Vermont, this will be lively!" exclaimed Harrison as they peered out the quarter lights to the O'Neale's home.

"I'm not entirely sure that what I'm look for, Harrison, is 'lively.' "

"Nonsense. Margaret's sister, Maria Rose, is visiting from Washington, D.C. Rumors swirl and intrigue blossoms whenever Maria Rose is in town," he added with a wink.

"In these times, that sounds dangerous. Harrison, let's wait inside the coach until our bags are unloaded. It will be cooler here than beside the lane. What else do you know about them?"

"Well, the O'Neale's political influence is expansive. Margaret leads a dazzling life, entertaining visitors as well as the elite of Jacksonville. She holds the most interesting social events and dinner parties." He leaned across the bench toward his sister-in-law and added, "You'll understand why I've recommended you stay here. The O'Neale's home is *the center* of Jacksonville society's buzz."

The Arlington District sat on a slight knoll overlooking the Jacksonville business district. Stately oaks, planted many years before, lined the cobbled lanes providing shade as the carriage pulled up to Margaret O'Neale's stately home. Generous shaded porches encircled of the house on both the first and second levels, encouraging a breeze to fan through the upstairs sleeping porches and the downstairs parlors. On the upper floor, French doors provided access from Mr. and Mrs. O'Neale's bedroom to a widow's walk and veranda. Breakfasts and cocktails were set out each day on the white wrought iron settee placed at the center of the veranda.

From the widow's walk, a panorama of Jacksonville stretched out for the O'Neales to enjoy during their private breakfasts and evening gossip sessions where the O'Neales plotted their lucrative pastimes.

Rather tidy home, actually, Mrs. Colburn thought, as she examined the O'Neale's residence. It was so unlike her stately brick estate that spread over generous green lawns extending beyond many acres. In Vermont, the O'Neale home would not have been considered an estate. Oh *well, it's already arranged.* She acquiesced to the accommodations while dabbing her throat and wrists.

A servant came from the carriage house to supervise bringing the luggage up to the house. A maid waited behind the etched glass door of the home, poised to respond to the anticipated knock.

* * *

10

JACKSONVILLE

Margaret O'Neale's blonde curls bounced as she descended the stairs toward the Colburn's, make her exuberance all the more dramatic.

She led with a beautiful, dimpled smile, paired with chimes of *"Hello's"* and *"Welcome,"* and added a string of questions concerning Mrs. Colburn's travels, the eastern seaboard, and the quality of accommodations onboard the steamship.

My goodness, I hope she doesn't remain this flighty through our entire stay, Mrs. Colburn shot a look skepticism at her brother-in-law.

Reaching the bottom step Margaret rushed first to Harrison, "How nice of you to recommend our home for your sister-in-law's stay, Reverend Moore! It is such a pleasure to see you again." Margaret clasped Harrison's hand and then parlayed through a series of flirts that had earned her the reputation as Jacksonville's leading hostess.

Mrs. Colburn watched with fascination as she moved next to Eliza, "You *must* be Miss Eliza. I hope you don't mind my calling you 'Miss Eliza'. It's a southern custom, you know. No wonder word of your beauty has reached Jacksonville with such speed! I understand that you were treated to a dinner party in Charleston at William Miles's home." She lowered her voice as though what she had to say must be kept in confidence, "I do hope you will find our young gentlemen of Jacksonville as charming as those of Charleston."

Eliza looked at her mother with a helpless expression.

Finally Margaret took a breath and then continued, "My sister, Maria Rose, and I have a wonderful dinner party arranged as a welcome to you and your mother. I've taken the liberty of inviting, as your escort, Taylor Babcock. He's from a fine Jacksonville family. My husband admires Taylor greatly as he seems to be one young man who reads the winds of business better than most. And, he's as handsome as he is intelligent. I'm sure you'll enjoy his company." She stopped there for a moment, once again breathless.

Oh, my gracious, Mrs. Colburn thought. *She's going to hold Eliza's hand all afternoon.*

Her words tumbled out once Eliza was finally given a chance to respond, "A dinner party, how thoughtful! Mother and I are thoroughly delighted to be here in Jacksonville. Uncle Harrison has been telling us how exciting it is to be here in Florida right now. We're so looking forward to a party. I love it here already! Don't you mother?"

Not waiting for her mother's response, Eliza continued, "Uncle Harrison had the coachman give us a tour of Jacksonville. There is so much to see, so many people out! We just hadn't known what to expect!"

"Well, we want you, and your mother," Margaret nodded her bouncy curls toward Mrs. Colburn, "to feel completely at home while you are in Jacksonville."

"Oh."

"Tomorrow morning you must come with me and my sister. We have an appointment with our seamstress. If you would like to join us and pick out a dinner gown for tomorrow evening. Maybe something light weight, in pastel, with ribbons? I'm not sure what style would make you most comfortable; but Jacksonville evenings can be rather humid this time of year."

A younger version of Margaret, dressed in deep rouge scarlett, appeared in the doorway of the drawing room and with a smoky voice interjected, "I agree with my sister. You will be much too warm in your Vermont wardrobe for tomorrow evening's dinner party."

Margaret burst into a peal of laughter, "Oh! Maria Rose, there you are. Everyone, please meet my sister. She's staying with Mr. O'Neale and me through the month.

"Greetings, everyone." And Maria Rose raised her Olorosos (which was her noon custom) in a toast.

Mrs. Colburn lifted her chin, narrowing her eyes at the overly-rouged woman.

Maria Rose continued, "We would hate to lose you to a swoon during your first dinner party in Jacksonville, wouldn't we, Margaret?'"

She nodded. "Well! Shall we make an outing of it tomorrow morning, Miss Eliza?"

The two sisters laced through each other's conversation for several more minutes, describing to each other, mostly, how the younger Colburn might be made more comfortable.

"I see beaded pearl netting for her beautifully waved hair, don't you, Maria Rose?"

"Oh, yes! And Eliza, you *must* order at least two low crowned hats to protect yourself from the sun. Plus a parasol, of course, a month in Jacksonville without a parasol would be impossible. Unless you brought one with you, of course."

Eliza's eyes sparkled with excitement and possibility.

Margaret then changed her cadence and with a soft, rich voice turned to Mrs. Colburn who had remained silent, except for her thoughts, *Harrison, what were you thinking?*

"Oh my," began Margaret. "I got so carried away with your stunning daughter, Mrs. Colburn. I want to welcome you, most of all, to Jacksonville."

Lucy extended her lace-gloved hand.

With a dimpled smile Margaret continued, "It is our deepest pleasure to have you as our guest. There are so many business opportunities in our beautiful city right now. I'll warn you in advance; you might hear our gentlemen speak of the 'Indian Issue' or of the economic sanctions of the Buchanan administration, but never you mind. Southern men do love their overblown conversations of wars and politics!"

"They certainly do!" agreed her sister.

"Why, Maria Rose was in Tallahassee just last month and tells me she attended dinner parties where she overheard the men speaking of nothing but '*War, War, War,*' in their hosts' smoking parlors." Margaret stuttered, but only for a moment before taking off again, "I mean, not that Maria Rose was listening in, or lingers in smoking parlors!" she laughed.

The sisters stole conspiratorial glances at each other, revealing who they might have been as eight-year olds, and giving Mrs. Colburn her first opening.

"Well, my daughter and I have a lot of discover on our own to do, as you might imagine. Although it will

be a welcome respite to enjoy your hospitality before we board the schooner to Bay Port, where my sister waits for us. She—and Harrison, of course—have resided in St. Petersburg for many years and I'm sure can ably continue your tutelage of the subtleties of southern culture.

"Hmm," the sisters agreed in unison.

"But all the same, thank you. We feel so warmly greeted. No wonder Harrison recommended your hospitality. And, of course, we accept your invitation to look over fabrics and meet with your seamstress tomorrow. And, who, by the way, *is* Taylor Babcock, this young man you have in mind as Eliza's dinner companion?"

"Taylor is Jacksonville's most promising young attorney! He is two years out of law school and has a very strong practice overseeing my husband's banking interests. I just *know* that you are going to be delighted when you meet him."

Mrs. Colburn smiled wanly as Margaret went on about 'the fine family' and young Taylor's promising career. She wasn't thinking about 'promising young Taylor' or her own hopes that her daughter be introduced to the right 'match'. Her thoughts were, painfully, on the fact that her own young attorney, first child, John Jr. was no longer in her life. *How unfair that life's losses specter at the least opportune moments.* She was in a transitory fog, cast back to the day she received the telegram notifying her of John's death.

Eliza brushed her mother's sleeve, prompting her to conclude her comments and announce, "It's been a long day, and we appreciate your enthusiastic welcome. It would probably best for me and Eliza to settle into our rooms."

"Of course, how I do go on. You must stop me if I am wearing upon you. You and your daughter will take the three overlooking the garden and shaded grounds. And, Abby? Is it Abby?"

Mrs. Colburn nodded.

"Well, Abby has been shown to an alcove off the sleeping porch at the back of the house."

**

Abby's cool interior room included a narrow bed and a vanity, both painted in the same cool shade of mint green as the wainscot and banisters leading upstairs from the entry foyer. A breezeway and screened porch off the back of the house provided relief from the sultry heat, as the sun beat relentlessly across the face of the estate.

At that moment, Abby was resting on a cot clothed only in her camisole and pantaloons, her blouse and heavy skirt draped over the alcove's straight-backed wooden chair.

**

Margaret continued, "Eliza's sitting room and sleeping alcove is next to Maria Rose's."

She couldn't help by observe the worried look that Eliza gave her mother.

"It is a troublesome floor plan. Now, Mrs. Colburn, your room overlooks the north garden, with French doors leading to the rear balcony."

Harrison cleared his throat as he entered from the coach house.

"Oh, Reverend! We were just speaking of guest rooms. Your room is the first one on the right looking out over the front lane."

Poor Harrison, probably the hottest room in the house, Mrs. Colburn noted.

Their baggage had already been placed in the appropriate rooms by a slave who was called back to show the Colburn's to their rooms.

Eliza ascended the narrow staircase that clung to the right side of the foyer, followed by her mother.

Brass lamps had been installed along the staircase, on walls papered in alternating green and black stripes piped with gold pin-striping. The banisters featured beautifully turned wood, painted a fresh pastel mint, which cooled the entry in consideration of the southern heat and humidity.

At the top of the landing Mrs. Colburn turned to her brother-in-law, "Harrison, when you have a moment?"

"Of course. I'll meet you in your sitting room in just a few moments."

Mrs. Colburn nodded her leave to the two hostesses, gathered her skirt, and made her way down the hall to her suite. The door was held open by a young servant standing at attention, staring blankly into her own future.

The Reverend lingered at the top of the stairs, turning the narrow brim of his hat in his hands. After watching his niece and sister-in-law take their rooms, he turned to the O'Neale sisters.

"Reverend? Was there something else?" began Margaret.

"Uh, Margaret, I was wondering if you had an opportunity since my last visit to approach your husband regarding our last conversation."

"Oh dear. Are you in a rush for funds, Reverend?"

"A rush? No, it's just that I, uhm, thought that with your husband's assistance, and your interest, a new church . . . I mean we spoke about how nice it would be to have a new church in Jacksonville. Uh, that I would be the officiate, of course."

Margaret smiled at her sister playfully.

Harrison took note of the exchange.

"Perhaps this is not the time?" He asked, backing away.

"No, not *quite* the right time, actually, Reverend. Let's see how much our guests take to having Taylor's attention. My guess is that he will be an ardent escort to Mrs. Colburn and her daughter this week."

"Taylor?"

"Why, yes. Appropriate matches are so important to everyone's interests in these times, and Maria Rose and I would love for there to be a place for Taylor in any plans the Colburn's develop should they decide to settle in Florida. Maybe you could be of assistance in persuading Mrs. Colburn what a lovely city Jacksonville is, and how much assistance my husband could offer were she to engage the Bank of Jacksonville in her business dealings?"

"I don't advise my sister-in-law in business matters."

"Ah, how civilized," retorted Maria Rose. "But, didn't Mrs. Colburn ask to speak with you? She must seek your counsel in some matters."

He looked from one woman to the other, and then bowed before going to his assigned guest suite.

"That ought to slow him down," Margaret whispered to her sister. The two of them stood, leaning toward each other. "We need to find investors for Prescott's bank as much as Harrison needs to find backers for his church. I do believe even he is able to make the connection, don't you Maria Rose?"

"Of course, sweet. Do you still think Taylor is the right choice?"

"Darling, my dear Prescott would not have suggested him as Eliza's companion this week if he didn't believe that Taylor would win her interest. I'm sure that the Colburn's will consider Prescott's bank for their investments, and possibly extend their stay in Jacksonville, that is, once they meet Taylor."

"Well, considering the administration's sanctions, let's not speak too strongly against Washington, lest Mrs. Colburn grows wary of investing in Jacksonville. I suspect she controls all the money in that family!"

"So, go slowly? Do you think we may have underestimated Mrs. Colburn? Maybe we could re-think things just a little."

"Margaret! They are leaving within the next two weeks! Unless they change their passage, we don't have time to re-think anything."

The weather the next morning was beautifully clear, with a light breeze ruffling the lilacs. The four women started out just after seven o'clock in the morning to gain on the approaching heat. It didn't take long to arrive at their destination. Their carriage pulled up at the sign on University Boulevard.

Mme. Biscay • Tailor
'Specializing in Parisian Styling'

The sisters dedicated the morning to Eliza's introduction to Jacksonville. Mme. Biscay prompted the women toward soft pastels of cream yellows, light pinks, and peach tones in yards of fabric meant to show off willowy waistlines, and sweetheart necklines.

Margaret selected Mlle. Zoe—a young French understudy whose fashion instincts were used to show off her own creamy soft skin, long doe-like eyelashes and the sparkle of freckles across her nose—to guide Eliza and to coax Mrs. Colburn into southern fashion. Mlle. Zoe instantly endeared herself to Eliza. The soft, frothy summer styles of Jacksonville that she suggested contrasted keenly with Eliza's heavier, dark-colored colonial fashion.

Two hours after arriving at the tailoring shop, the O'Neale carriage pulled away.

"Well I, for one, am looking forward to tea and powdered rum-drop cookies on the breezeway when we get home," Margaret invited.

At four o'clock that afternoon, a package from Mme. Biscay's salon arrived for Eliza and Mrs. Colburn. A peach voile, featuring a deep neckline and two-tiered peach colored lace sleeves; delivered in time for the much anticipated dinner party.

Abby accepted the packages for Eliza, which also included multi-colored sets of lace lingerie; pantaloons and whisper-soft, brushed cotton camisettes all intended to make the humidity of a Florida summer a little more bearable.

Mrs. Colburn had chosen a high-throated navy blue blouse of lace sheer, featuring a ribbon striped pattern and two-tiered hoop skirt, for that evening.

The rest of their ensembles included soft lace with light frames, offering cool alternatives to the heavy cotton dresses that filled the trunks the two women had brought down the seaboard.

Meanwhile, the ladies carried on their discussion on the back porch as Margaret steered delicately toward political and economic issues. "Mrs. Colburn, what news do *you* hear from Washington concerning the free-states issue or economic sanctions? We're never quite sure how much economic power Buchanan's administration is going to wield against the territories and new-states."

"We mostly hear that land in Florida is as cheap as the weather is pleasant. I suppose though, the secession issue makes land less expensive, and investments more risky."

Maria Rose added, "Well, our gentlemen suggest that if Washington sanctions the territories along with the southern states, the talk of secession will grow."

Margaret scowled at her sister as she chattered on. "People who have travelled for years to the South for respite and health will be forced to declare their loyalties."

"That may be true. With my sister and the Reverend residing in St. Petersburg, and Eliza's young cousin

Jacob in Bay Port, we sometimes imagine the unlikely possibility that our future is in Florida. But, I'm not one to make rash decisions. Particularly since, for Eliza's sake, I must make the very best decisions that will benefit both of us as well as the Colburn legacy. That is why I've left my son Rufus, a businessman in Fair Haven, in charge of our investments which will remain, for now, in Vermont."

"You must ask Taylor *his* opinion of the current financial outlook for investments in Florida," Maria Rose added. "It seems like so many prominent families from the North have chosen Jacksonville, and are turning their investment decisions over to Taylor. If you express an interest, I'm sure he will be able to offer admirable references."

That evening Mrs. Colburn and her daughter descended the staircase of the O'Neale home into the foyer leading to the generous ballroom. Margaret, on the arm of her husband, glided toward the two Vermont guests. "May I introduce my husband, Prescott, and once again take the opportunity of telling you how pleased that you have chosen our home for your Jacksonville stay. We want to do everything possible to make your stay pleasant enough for you to consider this your *second* home. My husband and Mr. Babcock can advise you in any aspect of Florida living that might interest you, Mrs. Colburn."

"Thank you, even if short, I'm sure our stay in your home will be pleasant."

"Mrs. Colburn. It's a pleasure to make your acquaintance."

"Mr. Prescott . . ."

Their introductions were cut short, "Hmmm, yes. Oh! Taylor! Taylor, darling," Margaret called over Mrs. Colburn's shoulder. "Excuse me, Mrs. Colburn, for interrupting, but Taylor has just arrived. This is such an anticipated moment! Let me introduce the two of you."

Taylor, a tall, heavy jawed young man, strode over to Margaret's side.

"Good evening, Mrs. O'Neale! Don't you know how to entertain the good people of Jacksonville! Your husband assured me that the evening would be as delightful as it was intriguing—both your specialties."

"Taylor, stop it! Be serious. I want to introduce you to Mrs. John Peabody Colburn of Vermont, and her daughter, Miss Eliza Colburn. I know that you will be a wonderful host to these wonderful guests of mine. Mrs. Colburn will be staying the week here in Jacksonville. Perhaps longer, depending entirely on just how charming you are."

Margaret turned to Mrs. Colburn and Eliza. "Mrs. Colburn, I would like to present Mr. Taylor Babcock to you. Mr. Babcock is three years out of Emory College and now one of my husband's associates."

"Ah, Emory. A wise heart seeks knowledge," said Lucy.

Taylor stepped back. "Oh my! Mrs. Colburn! Not to be underestimated, I'm sure. Very few individuals make my acquaintance by quoting Emory's motto, and certainly no members of the fairer sex. What a pleasure to meet you. I'm sure it will be a lively week, now that you are here in Jacksonville with your lovely daughter." Taylor reassured himself that he also held Eliza's attention, and then turned his rapt attention back to Mrs. Colburn.

"Well, that remains to be seen. Let me present my daughter, Eliza."

"Eliza, what a lovely name for such a lovely young woman. I hope you don't mind," and with that Taylor accepted Eliza's extended hand and caressed her bare fingertips, turning her palm over he leaned down to place a delicate kiss on the back of her hand.

"I would be very interested in hearing your impressions of our fair city, Miss Colburn. How do you find Jacksonville thus far?"

"I . . ."

A short while later, having welcomed all of her guests, Mrs. O'Neale signaled that dinner was about to be served.

Taylor Babcock offered his right arm to Eliza and his left arm to her mother.

Once seated, he regaled them with vignettes of his recent trip to Barbados. Turning toward Mrs. Colburn, he asked, "Do your sons travel, Mrs. Colburn?"

"Yes, when they were your age, they did travel. They are each quite involved in business ventures and service to their country at this point in their lives, however."

Taylor cleared his throat and turned his attention to Eliza, "Is there any chance that you will extend your stay in Jacksonville, Miss Colburn?"

"Mother?" Not receiving her mother's attention, she was left to making conversation without any assistance. "I'm not sure. That is something for Mother to decide."

"The O'Neales say that this is your first visit to the South, Miss Colburn; is that true?"

"It is. And you may call me Eliza. I'm sure that would be fine."

"And, of course, you may call me Taylor

Mrs. Colburn led a conversation with Prescott O'Neale regarding markets and trade, and whether or not the administration would act punitively toward Cuba as the previous administration had done.

Taylor carefully monitored Prescott's conversation with Mrs. Colburn, pleased to have an opportunity to monopolize Eliza's attention. His hand brushed the gardenia wrist corsage which he had delivered to Eliza that afternoon. The dainty corsage was decorated with small tight loops of narrow white ribbon. Cultivated pink seed pearls strung on silver thread were knotted to keep each pearl in place.

Looking down at her wrist, Eliza asked her suitor, "How could you have known that pink pearls are my favorite?" Taylor thought back on the exchange between the downstairs maid and Abby as to Miss Eliza's preferences, smiled and shrugged.

The two reached for the miniature salt shaker that had been placed at their setting at the same moment and out laughing.

"Possibly you and your mother would like to accompany me on a carriage ride to my father's sugar plantation while you are here in Jacksonville. It's not far."

Eliza looked down at the napkin folded in her lap, but did not respond.

"Oh, I do hope I haven't suggested something untoward. Of course, my sister could join us! You'll meet her this week, and I know you'll love her!"

"Perhaps we could. I'll need to ask mother."

"I seem to keep asking, how many days will you be in Jacksonville?"

"Perhaps as many as nine. We'll be leaving for Bay Port where my aunt is waiting for us."

"Bay Port? That's not much more than a day-and-a-half day sail around the Keys. I've been there a number of times. It's rustic, but the coastline of the Gulf is so still, so different from Florida's crashing, blustery Atlantic Coast. I hope you don't become bored there after being introduced to Jacksonville."

"Well, my cousin Jacob lives there, and my aunt and uncle are visiting him this season as well. So, I don't suppose I will become bored."

The dinner party progressed pleasantly. The dessert plates were abandoned after the key lime mousse had been served. The heavy white linen napkins were tossed aside, crumpled, folded properly, or left where they had dropped to the floor of the dining room, after bearing witness to whispered secrets, promised business transactions and delicious gossip.

Taylor scrutinized Mrs. Colburn as Prescott O'Neale stood and offered his arm to her. As she left the dining room, Mrs. Colburn looked over her shoulder to Eliza.

Instead of catching her daughter's eye, she caught the eye of Taylor Babcock who nodded. The two couples moved forward in a promenade to the drawing room where the piano would be put to good use.

**

Two evenings later, the fragrance of orange trees and jasmine welcomed guests to the O'Neale's expansive backyard. The hostess was holding her second party of the week in the couple's tropical garden.

Sipping from a tall glass of tea, the rim of the glass ringed with powdered sugar, Eliza turned just in time to catch Taylor making his way toward her through the guests crowded at the base of the veranda. He waved and quickened his pace.

"There you are! I lost sight of you after your uncle and I arrived. I just said a quick 'hello' to your mother. How are you?" He took her wrist to inspect the corsage that had been delivered that afternoon along with a message she wait for him on the veranda.

"I'm having a wonderful time."

"Perfect. I wouldn't have it any other way. It was so good of the Reverend to hire a carriage so that he and I could arrive together. He has such inspiring ideas for establishing a church here in Jacksonville."

Eliza laughed, "I know. That is all he talks about, to everyone. I'm surprised mother is still engaged in conversation with him and Mr. O'Neale," she stated, motioning over to the threesome.

"Yes, to be honest, your mother seems somewhat annoyed by his plan. Or maybe it's me she doesn't find to her liking."

"Oh dear! Hardly, I'm sure. It's complicated. Mother is trying to make all the right decisions for us now that my grandmother has passed away. My uncle's church may, or may not be part of her plans."

"I'm still not convinced it isn't me she doesn't want as part of her plans. I have quite a promising future, you know. I was hoping she would agree to come out to my family's plantation during your stay. My parents would have been delighted to meet you and your mother. A slice of sweet potato pie and a good chat with my mother about my attributes would have been just the thing to make her want to choose Jacksonville as her home."

Taylor took Eliza's left hand and curled it around his extended arm. Smiling at her, he nodded toward the other guests. "Shall we?"

Eliza tilted her head and smiled her assent.

She was steered in the opposite direction from her mother, who was cornered by her brother-in-law and Prescott. The couple strolled past the copper lanterns hanging in the oak trees that formed a circumference for the landscaped lawn, then around the galleries of needle palms which separated the guests into conversation pockets.

They approached a group of young couples engaged in an animated conversation at the far edge of the garden. Two couples who had married the previous season moved to make room for Taylor and Eliza. The brides looked over the rim of their glassware at each other, sipped their drinks. One of them turned to Eliza to exclaim over her gown.

"You are such a lovely creature!"

Eliza was quick to mention that she had spent her time in Jacksonville at the tailoring salon of Mme. Biscay. The mention of Jacksonville's

fashion authority mollified the sleek-haired sophisticates and the conversation was overtaken by the topic of politics.

Taylor used the excuse that it was time to refresh his and Eliza's drinks in order to make their way to a more secluded corner of the garden, where they turned their backs to the evening's festivities.

As twilight descended, hanging lanterns containing beeswax candles were lit and pillar candles were placed in white muslin sand-filled sacks were set out along the pathways leading toward the house illuminating the grounds with soft light and light shadows.

Jasmine wafted through the air as Taylor continued, "Your uncle told me that he is coming back to Jacksonville at the end of next month, after he escorts you to Bay Port. He said your mother has discussed financing his new church, and they will come back to select a site from the choices that Mr. O'Neale proposes. I hope you are not being evasive at my expense."

"What? I'm quite sure you're mistaken. Mother is fond of Uncle Harrison, true. But she has never shown an interest in helping develop any of his business plans, including this one."

Taylor gently removed Eliza's hand from his arm and stepped back.

"She may have listened to him as he discusses his church, but that would be different from agreeing to finance it."

"Eliza, your uncle spoke of his and your mother's plans at great length to Mr. O'Neale and I, earlier today at the bank. Hmm…maybe I've said too much."

"He did? Oh! I'm not sure. I just can't imagine Mother investing in . . . *Well!* Let's not try to solve this big mystery now," she laughed.

"Somehow, I am still short of one answer to my questions that I need. Will you receive my letters if I write to you, Eliza?"

"Oh! Taylor. Yes, that would be dear to me."

"Good! Then, until we do see each other again, we'll write to one another."

As the sun set, Taylor and Eliza made their way slowly back to the house for a mid-evening Jacksonville fare. Once again the O'Neale sisters had seated Taylor between Eliza and her mother, with Prescott as Mrs. Colburn's dinner companion.

**

Back in their adjoining rooms at the end of a very late evening, Mrs. Colburn asked her daughter, "Eliza, what were you and Taylor discussing at the edge of the garden before we sat down to dine?"

The two women were helped out of their corsets by the O'Neale sister's chambermaids.

"He's invited us to visit his parents' plantation. He seems quite anxious for you to make his mother's acquaintance."

"Eliza, social etiquette has not strayed so far that a gentleman extends his invitations to a young lady instead of to her mother. Besides, getting involved with the Babcock family, the siblings, and the relatives—as I am sure would be expected—is not something we have time for. It all seems so crowding. Do keep your options open, Eliza. Do you give any thought—" She stopped, eyeing the two young girls who all too quietly fussed over the dresses that now lay on Mrs. Colburn's bed.

"Girls, you are *so* generous with your attention! Thank you for helping us with our wardrobe. If you would like to leave us now? Good night, dears."

The two girls hurried out of Eliza's suite. When they were gone, Mrs. Colburn continued.

"Have you given any thought to the interesting pairing of you with Mr. Babcock, or his ardent attention to you? Or, that since we've been here, my constant companion is the investment banker, Mr. O'Neale? Really, Eliza, we haven't travelled as far from Fair Haven as you might think."

"Mother, I know what you are inferring and it's not like that with Taylor. What you *seem to be* afraid of, Mother, is not being the central authority if I were to show interest in a *whole* family, such as the Babcock's."

"Eliza, think carefully before you speak to me. Actually, I've decided that we are leaving Jacksonville very soon. Besides the fact that I am anxious to see MaryAnn, there is a wide world of choices to consider before we accept the inquiry of a suitor whose past has yet to establish his future."

"Mother, I do not know for what reason it pleases you that I remain unmarried."

Nine days after arriving Jacksonville, Mrs. Colburn bid an effusive farewell to the O'Neale sisters on her way to board a steamer and continued on to Bay Port.

* * *

Bay Port

Lucy and MaryAnn walked past the dry goods store, baked goods shop and candy store—all featured attractions in the port town that served as the winter destination of prominent northern families.

"Mrs. Moore." The finely dressed bearded gentleman tipped his hat politely as Mrs. Colburn and her sister strolled past him on the wide plank sidewalk along the store fronts of Bay Port, Florida.

"Who was *that*?" asked Lucy.

"C.T. Jenkins. He owns a cottage and farm on Rose Hill, north of Bay Port. Jacob introduced him to Harrison and me once last year, when we came up from St. Petersburg. He came to Bay Port when he was Jacob's age. For many years he worked as an overseer at the Harrell's tannery operation. Jacob used him as a reference when *he* first went to work for the Harrell family. His family is from Baltimore. Catholics."

"Oh."

After their promenade through the quaint and beautifully landscaped park at the center of the small community, the two returned, arm in arm, to The Bay Port House. Knowing that the evening would be a reunion dinner for the sisters, the innkeeper's wife, Mrs. Garrason, had promised a specially-prepared meal.

As the two walked past Parson's General Store, Lucy peeked in. A group of men stood in the center of the store arguing – or at least debating. Lucy slowed, fascinated at seeing Mr. Jenkins for the second time that afternoon. He was making a statement about timber pricing and crop value and that, "Buchanan needs to actually *do* something."

"Is he involved in politics?" she asked her sister.

MaryAnn laughed, "Is he, indeed! The simple answer is 'yes'; he is a state legislator, recently re-elected to a second term. If the topic is the development of Hernando County, he seems to be involved in some way."

"Hmmm. Like my John," mused Mrs. Colburn. Her sister looked sidelong at Mrs. Colburn and hugged her shoulders sympathetically.

**

MaryAnn and Harrison continued their conversation from earlier that day as Reverend Moore leaned over to his wife, giving thought to what Lucy confided in her about their Jacksonville visit. The couple was waiting in the dining room of The Bay Port House for their son, Jacob, to arrive for their reunion dinner with Lucy and Eliza.

In a low voice Harrison asked his wife, "Did you know the O'Neales were involved in financing the secession movement? They spent quite a bit of time trying to entice your sister with investment opportunities."

"Dear goodness, no! Is that true? It must have been so embarrassing for you to sit there, Harrison. You are steering clear of all of that aren't you, dear?"

"Hmm, yes, as much as I can without being impolite. The O'Neale's may have been hoping that Lucy had come down from Vermont with states' rights sentiments, looking for investments…"

"Honestly, Harrison, they must be desperate for money. Certainly they are ignorant of father's tutelage and John's influence over Lucy where business and investment matters are concerned."

"It seems."

"Well, she seems to have put the episode behind her. The only thing she mentioned was that she had made inquiries regarding a certain Mr. Babcock, and wasn't impressed with his background. It seems he was quite eager to woo Eliza."

Ah, Harrison thought. "Well, it *was* embarrassing to be seated two table settings down and have to listen to 'the sell'! How bold! Mr. O'Neale talked endlessly about the economics of 'The Confederate Nation'. I don't believe for a moment that the Republicans will win the next election, or that secession will be a real issue."

"Well, as I've said, politics is not your forte, so please do not involve yourself. There is simply too much panic and speculation right now. It would be unseemly for you to get involved in all that talk."

The two continued their tea in silence. They nodded greetings as other Bay Port vacationers arrived to the dining room.

A charge of activity at the innkeeper's desk signaled Jacob's arrival. At thirty-five he was fit and tan - and exuberant to see his parents.

"Mother!" Embracing MaryAnn, he kissed her forehead then her upturned cheek.

"My Darling."

"Father," Jacob grabbed his father's forearm and the two broke into a warm hug. "Are they here?"

"Of course! Your father and Aunt Lucy located each other as their steamer docked in Jacksonville. She and your cousin will be down for dinner shortly. And, fair warning, Eliza has revealed that she is still smitten where you are concerned," laughed MaryAnn.

"Well, do tell me all about their visit so far while we're waiting for them. And what have you and Father been doing since your last visit to Bay Port."

MaryAnn's had shook as she reached for her tea cup, looking for Harrison to pick up the conversation."

"Mother? How are you feeling?"

"I . . ."

Jacob's question was interrupted by a cry of delight followed by dazzling laughter, as Eliza danced down the stairs into Jacob's arms. Jacob whirled her around, lifting her off her feet in their spin. They then alternated between hugs and arms-length inspection.

Eliza's outcry caught the attention of everyone in the dining room, particularly that of one diner who watched as the young woman was escorted to her table. The diner, C. T. Jenkins, continued to glance over at the unfolding reunion from his vantage across the dining room while taking appreciative sips of whiskey.

"The waiter, noting Jenkins' seeming interest noted, "pretty glorious reunion scenes here at The Bay Port House."

"Yes, it would seem so." Jenkins turned his shot glass between his thumb and forefinger as he watched from afar.

A short while later Mrs. Colburn stood at the entrance of the dining room. She stopped for a moment and surveyed her surroundings before entering. She found herself looking straight into the eyes of C.T. Jenkins, the only person sitting alone in the crowded, boisterous dining room.

Harrison stood up to greet his sister-in-law, blocking her view of Mr. Jenkins. Jacob strode toward Lucy.

"Look at you! Jacob, look at you!" C.T. heard the woman exclaim. Then he watched as Jacob offered his arm. Jacob, and the woman who had been strolling that afternoon with Mrs. Moore, made a show of walking to their dinner table. As he seated the woman Jacob winked at the young lady who was already seated. He walked around the table backwards to return to his chair. Having attained everyone's attention, he pulled out a pence and rolled it over his knuckles. *Not bad,* thought Jenkins'.

"He's just like father!" He heard Jacob's mother declare. *Jacob's mother – what is her name,* he tried to remember.

Nothing came to mind from their introduction last year.

'Ahh, just like father'. They're sisters. The woman is Mrs. Moore's sister. Then, who is the young woman sitting next to Jacob Moore? C.T. continued his fascination with the party, listening for snippets of conversation that floated across the dining room.

"Yes, he probably is the grandchild most like father," he heard the woman he presumed was Mrs. Moore's sister state.

The other travelers dining at The Bay Port House returned to their own conversations and meals, with C.T. being the exception.

The Davey sisters' reunion continued well into the evening, with stories meant to shore up family history as well as advance family lore.

**

C.T. signaled the dining room host with a nod, and then raised his index finger from the rim of his shot glass. He was fascinated by how the energy rose and fell among the five dinner companions. C.T. realized then that not one person in the dining room seemed interested in *him*, other than the wait staff, who reacted immediately to his every signal. *I have the privacy of a confessional but the visual access of a bell jar,* he mused.

He observed Mrs. Moore's sister lean forward and ask Reverend Moore something. *Ah! The bread.*

Jacob, his back to C.T., handed the basket of bread to his father, who then passed it to Mrs. Moore's sister.

At that moment the woman looked in his direction, but made no indication that she recognized him. *Am I that invisible?* Now she was surveying the room for the wait staff. A waiter brought a tall glass, served on a small silver platter, and placed it in front of her.

The frivolity at Mrs. Moore's table continued. C.T. had not had such a perch for taking in a family gathering such as this for many years.

He fingered his glass, looking into the bottom of his third shot of whiskey. *A portal into the past.* He thought back on his mother and father at their dining room table in Baltimore, thirty-three years before. They were smiling at one another. He remember his father reaching forward and placing his large hand over his mother's delicate fingers. It was obvious to him that they were deeply in love. At that moment, *they* had been the ones in the bell jar—in their own world, in spite of the fact that their many children sat at the same dining room table, kicking, sticking their tongues out at each other, or discussing their studies.

C.T. turned his attention to the young woman sitting across from Jacob, and facing him, albeit from a distance. *Jacob's fiancée, perhaps?* But there was a playful distance between them that C.T. could not put his finger on.

Now Reverend Moore was speaking. C.T. watched the back of the Reverend's head as it bobbed and swiveled in the telling of his vignette.

Mrs. Moore's sister dabbed at her lips with her napkin and took a quick moment to examine her fingernails. *Ha! Not listening! Now there is someone with whom I can identify. That pompous ass has never held my attention for more than one minute.*

Mrs. Moore gazed at her husband, invested in the point he was making. The young lady was also rapt, smiling—*maybe she is a future daughter-in-law,* he mused.

"Sir, we're closing. Do you require anything else," asked the bell captain. The Moore's, and their guests, were also preparing to leave.

"No nothing. That will be all. Thank you very much." C.T. looked at his empty shot glass before standing up and striding through the near-empty dining room.

**

Eliza's Room

Eliza's first weeks in Bay Port were idyllic. Florida mornings burst into radiant warmth as the sun broke over the horizon. Gentle breezes off the Gulf of Mexico brought in the brine of seaweed and salt air that mixed with the cooking aromas from the Bay Port House dining room. Eliza would pad across her room and, throw open the shutters admitting the breezes that were rustling through the marsh grasses of the Weekiwachee River.

From her second story window she watched the seagulls swoop and dive in lacy patterns against a clear blue morning sky. Their cawing and arguing punctuated the day. Shelled sea life would plummet to the shore from the beaks of sea birds, breaking open to spill Gulf delicacies. Looking down on the marsh below, Eliza spied an egret—a lone ghost bird, statuesque and tall on it spindly legs.

Influenced by the sun, the fragrances of the Gulf, and the noisy chatter of the aviary outside her window

Eliza realized that even thinking the name, *Fair Haven,* seemed foreign.

How nice it is to have time to myself, realizing she had spent much of the past month alone. Her mother spent her mornings walking Bay Port with

her sister, after breakfast. Eliza *was* expected to share lunch with her mother, but after that Mrs. Colburn retired to her room to write in her journal, leaving Eliza again to her own devices. Mrs. Colburn monitored the packets of letters that came in weekly on the mail boat. She would respond immediately to those letters received from Rufus. Eliza had not yet received any letters from Taylor.

Mother and her tangled plots, Eliza thought to herself, avoiding her mother's door until dinner. Their distance was caused by an exchange after breakfast a few days earlier:

"I haven't heard from Taylor. Mother, have you been to the post office to pick up our mail?"

"There's no reason to pine after a circumstance you could easily regret, Eliza. That is, one that will deprive you of the comforts you receive from your father's investments."

It's no use. She'll never accept the man I, myself, choose. Aloud she said, "Mother, the Babcock's aren't expecting a 'circumstance'. They merely would like to have the opportunity to meet you. Taylor says that their plantation is breathtaking. What if it turned out that you enjoyed them?"

"My darling, let me frame things in this manner. Why would I want any less for you than what my family wanted for me? The Babcock's fortunes are tied to extraordinary economic hopes. When I married your father, he was not dependent on the fortunes of his family, as is Mr. Babcock. John was independently established. Older."

Eliza watched her mother's mouth open and close not hearing her words.

"And, by carefully thinking through my choices, I attained lifelong happiness, security, standing, and the most beautiful home that any young woman of Fair Haven could have wanted. Why should you have any less?"

One afternoon Harrison sought out Eliza's company. "I've checked with your mother. Would you like to accompany me to Brooksville tomorrow?"

"Yes! Yes! Of course!" Laughing, she queried, "But, what's there?"

"A vacation day? Would you like that?"

"Yes, my goodness! Of course."

Very early the next day they engaged a coach and crossed the corduroy road for the outpost located ten miles inland.

"Why go there?" She asked.

"Brooksville is establishing itself as a commerce hub for citrus crops. There is a lot of activity and interest being generated in building a rail line. Let's go see about it all, shall we?"

"Uncle Harrison, may I have your confidence? Do you think that I will ever marry? I haven't heard from Taylor. And my mother is not at all supportive of my writing to him."

"Eliza, your mother has generous intentions for you, I'm sure; but I'll admit she's almost getting in God's way by not letting you make some of your own decisions. There *is* a fine line."

"So you agree with me?"

Nodding, he added, "Your mother was still quite young when your father died. Think of it. The day you were born, she was one day into widowhood. Thinking that he would have a much longer life and many more years of showing your mother how to manage their investments, he left his business and properties to her, with Robert McCutcheon as executor, instead of to his brothers."

"Oh?"

"It took everyone's efforts to keep the real estate investments and manufacturing operations going, whether your mother knows it or not. And, although the Davey family helped her manage the business interests, particularly her father, she raised you children with very little assistance. She *chose* to be as independent as possible. It is very understandable why she is as controlling as she is."

"So she wasn't always like she is, but became this way?"

"I met her when she was fifteen and, even then, she knew what she wanted and was able to get her own way. By the time I married your aunt, your mother was sixteen and two women could not have been more different. And, although your grandfather loved your Aunt MaryAnn, he cherished your mother. Their business instincts were identical. Your mother was adventurous. She is *still* adventurous. If she decides to remain in this

new environment, in Florida, she will use every skill she has to thrive. She will find a way to make it all work out—for the two of you."

**

"Really, Harrison, you simply must tell me what you said to Eliza to make her so deferential to me?"

"On our trip to Brooksville? I can't imagine anything I told her would make her treat you any differently than she always has, Lucy."

The day after their trip to Brooksville, Harrison noticed Lucy and Eliza leave the hotel together strolling toward the Bay Port post office.

Well isn't that a sight for sore eyes, he thought as he watched them walk, arms-linked as Eliza tilted back her head, closing her eyes to let the sunshine warm her face.

**

One day sitting on the sun porch adjoining the dining room with Eliza, MaryAnn and Harrison, Mrs. Colburn noticed that C.T. had entered. They had seen each other on other occasions and acknowledged each other. Catching his eye she waved and called out to him, "Would you like to join us?"

C.T. acknowledged the invitation and made his way over. He bowed and took her extended hand, "Thank you, what a kind invitation. We haven't been formally introduced. My name is Cyprian Jenkins."

Lucy nodded to MaryAnn and Harrison, "Yes that is what I have come to understand from my sister and brother-in-law, whom I believe you know."

Harrison received Cyprian's handshake, "We met, of course, last year. Our family is obliged to you, I believe. Your letter of reference assisted our son in getting the position as overseer at Nancy Harrell's property."

"Well, possibly my letter was of some consequence. It's a pleasure to see you again." Cyprian remained standing and bowed to MaryAnn, "Mrs. Moore. I've had the pleasure of seeing you enjoy your strolls of Bay Port over the past two months. I hope your health is improving in Florida's fine climate."

"Yes, thank you, Mr. Jenkins. We just mentioned as you walked in that you have not been formally introduced to my sister, Mrs. Colburn, of Vermont, who is visiting Harrison and me for the season."

"Of course. I have seen you with your sister over the past several weeks, Mrs. Moore.

He then turned to Lucy, "I hope that you are enjoying vacationing in Florida as much as I enjoy living here, in spite of longing for my beautiful home state of Maryland. It is my utmost pleasure to make your acquaintance, Madam."

Lucy extended a white-lace gloved hand, which C.T. bowed over, adding a light kiss.

"And likewise, it is my utmost pleasure to make your acquaintance, Mr. Jenkins." She then reiterated her invitation, "I'm sure that we will find that we have much in common. May I introduce my daughter, Eliza."

C.T. bowed slightly and Eliza smiled and nodded, acknowledging the introduction.

"Well do sit down," Lucy invited.

"Thank you." C.T. took the chair pulled out for him by the hotel's bell captain and joined them.

Eliza remained silent through lunch listening to the banter between her mother, Mr. Jenkins, and her aunt and uncle. She took stock of his sandy blond hair which contrasted with his wiry, graying beard. *"Mother, do be wary. Quite a storyteller, that's for sure."*

Mrs. Colburn commented, "Mr. Jenkins, you were saying your *family* is from Maryland?"

"Why, yes, Mrs. Colburn." He laughed, "I must say I'm enjoying your curiosity about my family."

"Well I hope you don't think I'm being too forward."

"Not at all. I don't often use the term family. But, I have ten brothers, six still in Baltimore, one in Texas. Three are deceased. My father, William, passed away three years ago, but my uncles reside in the Cathedral District; if you're familiar with Baltimore. I was born at my parents' home in the Belvederes. I'm not really sure any more what constitutes a family, but I *do* have relatives there."

Mrs. Colburn asked, "Eliza, would you like to join the conversation?"

"I'm enjoying myself, Mother."

C.T. continued on revealing to Lucy and her party the highlights of his life and what had brought him to Bay Port. During their visit diners came in and sat through their meals, some leaving quickly, some languishing over dessert or iced tea. The only constant that afternoon was the party of five northeasterners enjoying an afternoon of animated storytelling, laughing often over how much they had in common.

"When did you leave Baltimore, Mr. Jenkins?" prompted Mrs. Colburn.

"Well, not soon enough for my liking, but it was 1833, the year of the great Leonid shower."

"Oh! The meteor shower! I remember it vividly. I brought the children to the upstairs window as the early morning skies lit. It was as though there were a thousand candles streaking across the sky. Oh my! Eliza must have been only two at the time."

"Oh dear," Eliza murmured.

Twenty Six? Is that it? Not younger? C.T. smoothed Mrs. Colburn's gaffe of revealing her daughter's age by talking over her with his own story.

"By the time I was twenty-two I already felt as

though I was missing out on life. I was suffocating from the expectations of my family—uhhh—relatives."

"I see."

"Anyway, I was twenty-two and headed out for the Georgia gold rush, much to my father's displeasure. I left with a good friend, John Donohoe, who ended up forsaking our adventure to marry the daughter of the man who led our party into Georgia. Telfair County, to be exact. It occurs to me at this moment that I've lost track of John over the years."

Harrison interrupted Jenkins' adventure by calling out to the server, "More bread?"

MaryAnn leaned over to her husband and patted his arm.

As Mrs. Colburn listened she drew parallels between Jenkins and John Colburn as C.T.'s story meandered. "I met up with John Coffee's militia and scouted the boundary of the Coffee family plantation. I was involved in a number of skirmishes between Georgia settlers and members of the Creek tribe. I suppose I developed a reputation for being a reliable sharp shooter," he admitted. "Besides scouting, I tried my hand at the tannery business, having observed the trade of my uncles and being taught some artful nuances of the trade by McAllister. But by 1836, one good friend was married and had settled, and my next best friend, John Coffee, had died. I found myself unemployed, and as seems my preference—alone."

"It's your *preference* to be alone?"

"Well, after being raised in a household of eleven children, yes, it appears it is my preference to be alone. Anyway, to continue, Francis Dade's militia was looking for monitoring the Seminoles, migration, and the like. So, I expanded my scouting experience," C.T. laughed, "and, my language skills."

"You can speak native languages?" asked MaryAnn.

"Yes, Mrs. Moore, as much time as I spend on the land, I find knowing the language of the Creeks and Seminoles as necessary as it is useful. I was assigned to the post of assistant quartermaster under General Leigh Reed and continued as a mounted scout through a number of skirmishes with the Seminoles. It wasn't long before I left Georgia with a group of settlers heading for Florida. We followed an established supply route,

'Coffee Road', which needed shoring up after a number of encounters with the Creeks. My adopted Georgia refugees settled in Tallahassee, in January…let's see … 1839."

There was very little interruption as Jenkins recounted a brief history of how he came to be in Bay Port. He took up his account after lunch was cleared, and was only interrupted when Harrison snapped his fingers to get the attention of the dining room captain. "We'll take our tea now."

"Hmmm…Well! The Armed Occupation Act of 1842 gave me the impetus to explore these parts. Have you heard of the Act, Mrs. Colburn?"

"No."

C.T. explained how the Act had allowed him to establish holdings and settle the Bay Port area. "Anyway, bringing us up to the present, I come into town to take care of the business of managing my stands of cedar, and my pineapple crops. My farm is located on land several miles north of here. Actually, Jacob has been out to my property on a number of occasions. It's quite a comfortable piece of land, which I have named Rose Hill."

Eliza was smoothing her skirt and replacing her napkin to her plate as C.T. picked up his narrow brimmed hat to excuse himself, "Well, it seems we've all finished our meals. I've immensely enjoyed telling you about myself," he laughed, "but I must take care of some business, if you'll excuse me."

He stood up and took Mrs. Colburn's hand and bowed. "It was a pleasure having your company, Mrs. Colburn."

"Likewise."

Then he continued, "And, Miss Colburn.

Eliza responded, "Hmm."

"Reverend, I'm going to stroll down to the Port. I hear the schooner *General Worth* has put in this morning, and I need to see after some supplies I'm expecting and collect any mail I might have from Baltimore. Would you care to walk with me?"

C.T. noted the slightest hesitation before Harrison nodded to the ladies and responded, "I'd be please to join you."

Donning their brimmed hats, they walked in the direction of the Port.

Harrison broke their initial silence, "I hear from Jacob that you influenced the legislation establishing Bay Port as a Port of Entry."

"Well, a lot of good men worked hard for that. Most notably, David Yulee, seeing the benefit of establishing mercantile routes to Cuba, and beyond. It didn't hurt, I'll admit, that I was serving in the Florida legislature at the time. We vigorously promoted, and then backed the joint resolution that was sent to the U.S. House of Representatives for consideration. It worked."

C.T. laid out what was on his mind, "Reverend, what I want to talk to you about, away from the ladies, is the Indian problem. There is no indication that the Seminoles are going to relocate peaceably to Oklahoma, or to Arkansas for that matter. In fact, there has been an increase in attacks between Tampa and Hernando County since Captain Casey passed away. As many as thirty-seven of Capt. Cone's volunteers were surrounded and murdered outside Fort Brooks very recently. Did you happen upon the news accounts while in Jacksonville?"

The Reverend shook his head, but declined to add anything that would indicate that the topic interested him.

C.T. continued, "The account is that the volunteers were in camp and had turned their horses out to graze. The Indians laid in ambush for Capt. Cone, and fired upon him and his volunteers. When they were about a mile and a half from camp, the Indians surrounded them and killed all thirty seven men. The area of the attack is a stronghold of 'Billy Bowlegs' but more than a hundred volunteers, scouts and troops are now in pursuit."

"Really!"

Jenkins continued head long into his recitation of current events, "If Col. Harney were in command, the Indians would be slain in arms, but he's not. Now, however, with a change in command imminent we can only hope for vigorous and consistent policies. Their murdering and burning is shutting out a large portion of Florida from colonization, and improvement. The Shive family being a horrific example of that fact with their little ones killed and their home burned to the ground last year."

"Pardon me, Mr. Jenkins, I have given you ample audience. But, really. I am a man of God. I don't want to say that these issues don't touch my life, but..." He trailed off.

"Well, I understand and respect your reluctance to take a direct stand. But consider, the number of volunteers is particularly low right now, and as the heat of summer approaches and the waterways dry up, it will be more difficult to scout Indian movement around the settlements, and more importantly, to move quickly to protect families. Florida settlers are having a particular problem right now with the troop's levels being so low. You realize, don't you, that just last week a war party attacked the Spencer homestead in Spring Hill and dragged John Spencer away from his wife and children? We found his body tied to a tree and burnt, after pine fat splinters had been stabbed into his chest. Do you know what pine fat resin does when ignited? The resins explode causing the hottest fire to burn under the skin of its victims."

"Finally, Mr. Jenkins! You do go too far!"

"Reverend Moore, in your travels between here and St. Petersburg, you have the privilege of the pulpit. If you were to encounter men so inclined as to assist, you could suggest that they present to the Garrason at Key West.   I understand that Captain Baker, and his commander Col. Loomis, have arrived for a stay over at Key West to collect troops who will operate from Fort Dallas against the Indians there.   If we could raise a corps of volunteer troops by September to take the place of the companies of artillery that are being withdrawn by the United States, we may be able to protect our settled land though the winter.   Particularly the women and children."

"Well, I'm not arguing against the protection of families. But, it simply isn't my calling to encourage anything other than the most peaceable solution, and the patience of a longer time table to encourage the Indian population that the reservation in Arkansas territory, or the Oklahoma Indian Territory, would be the most comfortable place for their people."

How naïve. C.T. finally let the topic drop as the two approached a schooner undergoing extensive repairs after losing its spars, sails and rigging.

As the two men arrived at the port, Harrison observed, "Beautiful isn't it? The late afternoon sun with the birds swooping and the light waves sweeping the smell of seaweed into the air."

"How poetic, Reverend."

"Is there any place on God's earth as wonderful?"

"Yes, I would probably say my Maryland.   Well, Reverend, let me bid you adieu for the afternoon. Think on what I've said." C.T. tipped his hat and walked briskly in the direction of Garrason's storefront.

* * *

12

ROSE HILL

One afternoon as C.T. left the Bay Port post office with a small bundle of letters, he nearly bumped into Mrs. Colburn coming out of the millinery shop. Mrs. Colburn was carrying a hat box tied with navy blue cording. The hat box was overlaid in bright blue lace, with a label, advertising,

Mme. Spurrier Millinery

Charleston Bay Port

"Mrs. Colburn! I am so pleased at this unexpected encounter. Shouldn't you be strolling with your sister?"

"Well, that has become my custom over the months, hasn't it? It's a pleasure to see you as well, Mr. Jenkins. MaryAnn is not feeling well so I am obliged to retrieve, on my own, a new hat from Mme. Spurrier. Mme. Spurrier designed it as a surprise for my daughter. I don't wear hats myself, as you see. I prefer a parasol, but Eliza enjoys fashion and Mme. Spurrier's new shop has become a haven for her. She enjoys the opportunity to speak French with someone her own age and who can gossip and speculate about Paris fashion in French."

"Hmm . . . I see. There was a point in my life that I spoke French. Fluently, actually. My maternal grandmother arrived in Baltimore from Montreal and only spoke French when she arrived."

Jenkins stopped for a moment and inspected the toe of his boot before continuing, "That was so many years ago. But I remember that my mother and her sister would have long conversations in French."

"Really?"

He pressed his fingers to his eyes, "There were so many children hanging on their skirts and hanging on their every word that speaking French became their only sanctuary. They would stroll through the grounds of their adjoining estates, arm in arm, and we older boys would hide behind trees and try to translate their conversations. 'Alors, les enfants,' was pretty easy to figure out," C.T. finally found something in his story that made him laugh.

"Well, Montreal is a lovely city, particularly if one is visiting in the spring or autumn. I have been there a number of times," Lucy remarked.

"Yes, it would be relatively easy to get there from Vermont, I would imagine."

"It is. I made the trip just before we left for this retreat. Well, actually, Eliza and I made the trip together. We go to New York City for a few days and then take the train to Malone in upstate New York where my older daughter, Susan and her husband live. He has a ministry in Malone. They've been there for years. From there we cross into Quebec. I speak only enough French to be able to exchange pleasantries, so I depend heavily on Eliza."

Changing the subject, she noted, "I see you've retrieved quite a stack of mail."

"Yes," he replied, turning the clutter of mail he held. "I get so busy managing my property and then suddenly I realize that I haven't seen any of my neighbors in weeks. Such was the case this morning, so I decided it was time to come into Bay Port to pick up my mail and newspapers."

"I was going to stop by the post office and pick up mine and Eliza's mail before going back to the hotel. Are you going back to your home? Rose Hill is it? That is, now that you have picked up your mail?"

"Not quite yet, actually. I thought I might stroll and say a few 'Hello's' and maybe start back after supper."

"Well, I'm hoping for a letter from my son, Albert, who is stationed at West Point. He is leaving on the Cheyenne and Utah Expeditions very soon. I'm hoping to hear from him before his regiment leaves. Would you care to walk with me to retrieve *my* letters, Mr. Jenkins?"

"Certainly." C.T. offered his arm and the two continued on. It was a few moments before either one of them picked up the conversation.

"It sounds as though your son has an exciting assignment waiting for him. West Point, you say? How do you feel about his choosing a military career, Mrs. Colburn?"

"Well, I worry. Constantly. I've lost my first-born son; and my husband, of course. Both John Jr. and his father were lawyers. My husband served as a judge in Rutland County, Vermont. I assumed that my oldest son would continue his father's career after he finished law school. But, John Jr. died shortly after taking his first position. To have Albert on any perilous mission is devastating my calm. I haven't seen him since his commission. So, yes, I worry about him constantly. What in life is as unbearable as being separated from, or losing, one's children?"

C.T. winced.

"Albert wrote me once after his grandmother's death, but I haven't heard from him since. It was my brother, Israel, who told me of Albert's commission. I seem to hear more about his accomplishments from others."

"Well, it seems your family has suffered an inordinate share of loss, Mrs. Colburn. We have that much in common, I'm afraid." He patted Mrs. Colburn's hand and continued on to the front door of the post office, pulling it open for her. "I'll wait for you here," offered C.T.

"You don't look happy. No West Point letter, Mrs. Colburn?"

Looking up at C.T. from the packet of letters, she responded, "No." He noticed that she shuffled to the bottom of the stack one letter addressed in a masculine hand.

"Not from Albert?"

"No, Jacksonville, I'm afraid."

"Oh, I'm sorry."

"Well, I'm sure that Albert is very busy. I believe he's in St. Louis, which seems so very close..." her voice trailed before she picked up again. "Mr. Jenkins! I'm wondering, as long as you will be in Bay Port this evening for supper, would you like to join us at the Garrason's dining room?"

"I, uh.." *It's all so complicated, how do I decline?*

"It would be wonderful to have your company, Mr. Jenkins."

"Yes, I'd like to think that's true. Well, let's see how you feel about my company once the evening has concluded," he laughed. "You may be taking a lot for granted presuming it would be wonderful. Family gatherings have not been my forte over the past twenty-some years. I mostly dine alone, whether I'm at home or in Bay Port on business."

"Really? How could that be? I'm barely ever alone. I can't imagine not having my children or some members of my family with me at all times."

"Well, I admit I've always had a tendency to bolt when faced with familial obligations. I'll ask Mrs. Garrason to leave a message for you by mid-afternoon if I feel sociable enough to join your merry table this evening. In the meantime, would you care to stroll to the park with me, after which I can escort you back to the Garrason's?"

"Yes, that would indeed take some of the sting out of my afternoon mail."

"So tell me, how are you enjoying Bay Port, Mrs. Colburn?"

"I'm enjoying it immensely. Before this visit it had been thirteen years since I had seen my sister. Her travels no longer bring her to Vermont. MaryAnn's health and Jacob's life here influenced her to make her home in Florida. Harrison has a fledgling ministry in St. Petersburg, and would like to help start a church in Jacksonville, for some reason. It seems like an inopportune time to make such a decision."

Their chat was interrupted by a gentleman overtaking them on the sidewalk. "Your Honor," the man tipped his hat at C.T.

"Your Honor?" Mrs. Colburn tilted her head.

"I'll explain, but later. There's no need for you to interrupt your story."

"Ah, yes. Well, after my mother's death this past year, it seemed only natural that my daughter and I retreat here, to be with my sister for the winter. It means everything to have my family around me. Being here with MaryAnn, with our lively dinners, reminds me of the parties that my father used to have when we were growing up in Vermont. You really don't see much of your family Mr. Jenkins?"

"No, I do not. I haven't been back to Baltimore in years. I correspond sporadically with my cousins, who keep me up on news of what is happening in the family. My mother died before I left Baltimore, and my father died three years ago. There's little reason to go back, I suppose. Unlike you, I'm not much when it comes to family, as I've said. And, after all these years I suspect I would hardly recognize my own home state, although its beauty as I recall from my boyhood remains in my heart."

"Hmm, I've spent very little time in Maryland, actually."

"Well, I do subscribe to *The Baltimore Sun* so I can keep up on the news of Baltimore Town and Washington. All that said about my not having ties to family, it occurs to me that I *do* have a letter here from my cousin Mary, among the letters I just retrieved. I'll read it later this evening. I've always felt a pull in the opposite direction where family is concerned. There's been such a burden of heavy, dreary obligations—all predicated by the ever present specter of death."

I wonder if Albert feels that way, Lucy mused silently, but stated, "We seem to have so much in common."

"I don't know if you mentioned whether you would be staying in Bay Port beyond the season, Mrs. Colburn?
"

"Well, first of all, I want to see to my daughter's happiness. So, if it makes sense to remain in Bay Port, I suppose I will. As much as anything this trip is intended to give Eliza an opportunity to make some decisions concerning her future. After that, I will concentrate on what comes next. But, yes, under certain circumstances I would be willing to stay in Bay Port beyond the season."

"Well, Mrs. Colburn, let me predict that you will remain for a very long while."

"Predictions indeed! We'll see. What about you, Mr. Jenkins? Do you have everything that you need here in Bay Port? Enough to ensure a lifetime of happiness?"

"Ha! Isn't that a complicated question? By establishing my life in Bay Port I have certainly managed to escape the familial obligations that suffocated me as a young man. But, I've exhausted that topic, now, haven't I? My investments here in Florida interest me, as do my crops. So as it has turned out, I manage quite nicely not having relatives, as you say, "with me at all times". Isn't that what you said, Mrs. Colburn? Maybe that's good, in spite of some long periods of loneliness. I've been independent since I was fifteen. I made a decision in 1833 which turned out to be pivotal. I wanted to see for myself what was possible beyond the bounds of Huntington, our family estate, and the life my father had mapped out for me. Father had made it clear that it I should continue *his* dream rather than dream my own. *Ha!*"

Mrs. Colburn, who had been watching the plank sidewalk in front of her, faltered at his single burst of laughter.

"I remember having a very happy life before my mother and her sister died – within days of each other. After they passed on, and later that year my grandmother, our family was comprised solely of men. Business men. My father, Uncle Frederick and my brothers. Can you imagine? I made the choice of living in the outdoors and settling land. Everything that I have is a product of my own choices. So if happiness is guiding one's own destiny, then I guess I am happy; but 'a lifetime of happiness', Mrs. Colburn? Is that what you asked? Hardly. Most days I feel like one little pebble rattling around the bottom of an otherwise empty tin bucket."

"Oh dear."

"Now, getting back to Mr. Parson's greeting, let me explain." C.T. stopped for a moment, "Have you met him? Mr. Parsons?"

"No, I have not, actually."

"Well, his greeting…sometimes I guess I am greeted as 'Colonel,' sometimes as 'Your Honor'. It's flattering. I try to stay busy, settling the community. But, I'm hardly alone in that avocation. We'll have to see what the future brings."

"A legislator *and* a colonel. You're an interesting man, Mr. Jenkins."

"Well, it's obvious that you are flattering me, and here we are at the Bay Port House. Let me think about your dinner invitation. In the meantime, good day."

As their conversation concluded, C.T. tipped his hat, leaving Mrs. Colburn in the lobby of the hotel. Before she sought out Eliza to present the gift of the Parisian-styled hat, Mrs. Colburn tapped on the door of her sister's suite, "MaryAnn?"

"Lucy? There you are!"

"MaryAnn, did you and Harrison know that Mr. Jenkins is a legislator?"

MaryAnn sat propped up against pillows on the "Uhmm, well, let me think. Yes, I suppose we did know."

"Well! I encountered him on my walk this morning. I wish you would have been with me, MaryAnn. I invited him to join us for dinner. He seems," searching for the right word, Mrs. Colburn selected, "lonely."

"Lucy, I'm sure he's not lonely," MaryAnn laughed. "He's busy constantly. As busy as father was, I'd say. He's well-liked. And if he accepts your dinner invitation, fine. I know that Jacob likes him a lot."

"Does he? Well, I'll leave you to go and check on Eliza. She'll probably be pleased to know that we may have company at tonight's dinner table."

"Lucy, Darling, as you leave, would you pull the shades? I'm going to have one more little rest before I come down to dinner."

"Are you alright, MaryAnn?"

"Yes, today is simply a 'resting day' for me. Now, shoo! Go find Eliza."

That evening's dinner party *did* include Mr. Jenkins. By coincidence, Jacob and C.T. arrived at the hotel the same time. Laughing at the happenstance, they patted each other on the back, scraped off their boots as they entered the lobby. After they settled, they were shown to the dining room where MaryAnn and Harrison were already seated with his wife.

"Mrs. Moore, how nice to see you again."

"Mr. Jenkins, it's good that you could join us. Please sit with Harrison and I."

"Reverend?"

Mrs. Colburn came into the dining room and extended both hands to C.T. "I was so pleased to learn that you would join us!"

He took her hands in greeting before seating her. The Reverend and Jacob remained standing as Mrs. Colburn settled, arranging her skirt and patting her beaded hair net

She then turned to her sister, "Hello dear. Please tell me you are feeling better than this afternoon?"

"Yes, I'm feeling fine, thank you. Won't we have a fun evening?"

Hmm, MaryAnn is still ailing, it seems, C.T. noted.

Eliza joined the gathering a few moments after her mother. *My how beautiful she is!*

Skin glowing, bright eyed and rested, she over-staged her moment of entry, tilting her head and turning her chin to show off the bright blue ribboned disk that sat saucily on her coiffed hair. Jacob laughed at her mugging. The Reverend stood up and, striding across the room, offered his arm to escort the ingénue to the table. He seated his niece between her mother and C.T. "Mr. Jenkins, I hope you don't mind my seating Eliza between you and Lucy, since you've already spent so much time with my sister-in-law."

"I beg your pardon?" C.T. responded.

"The park this afternoon, Mr. Jenkins. I took a break from writing an upcoming sermon in order to stretch my legs. You were strolling the park with Lucy. I would have said 'hello', but it seemed like it would have been an intrusion."

"Harrison, really! What's gotten into you?" MaryAnn exclaimed.

"Well, I have nothing to say to that." Turning to Eliza he said, "You look lovely, your mother's gift agrees with you."

"Darling, you remember Mr. Jenkins? We had a lovely visit this afternoon, he's joining us for dinner, obviously."

"Yes, of course. Thank you for the compliment. How nice to see you again, Mr. Jenkins; I so enjoyed hearing of your adventures the last time you were able to join us."

Once seated Harrison shot across the table, "Colonel, I hope you're not going to frighten the ladies with tales of attacking Indians this evening."

C.T. burst out laughing and the women looked on strained, "No, I'm more akin to believing that private conversations should remain just that. And discussing the 'Indian Problem'—did you call it?—might be an unbecoming topic in front of the ladies, don't you agree?"

"Well, enough of that please." Mrs. Colburn turned to her nephew, "Jacob, it would appear you are the link that brings all of us together."

Greetings between tables, the clatter of dishes and occasional laughter from across the large dining room interrupted their conversation. Finally things settled down and the conversation sung its way through the rest of the evening, rising and falling.

C.T. overheard Lucy inquire of her sister, "Dear, are you tiring?"

Harrison snapped his fingers to catch the attention of the dining room hostess and called out, "Tea!" It was only a few minutes later that a pot of chamomile was set in front of MaryAnn.

Just as she smiled at her husband for his kindness toward her, Harrison reached across and scraped the last morsel of chocolate cake from his wife's dessert plate.

"I'm sure we can order more dessert for you, Reverend," C.T. laughed.

"Of course not; it's hardly necessary."

"Well, I wouldn't want you to go back to your room wanting for more food."

MaryAnn looked at Harrison with benevolence as Lucy pursed her lips to a thin line. Catching C.T.'s eye, Mrs. Colburn smirked. He acknowledged her with a nearly imperceptible shake of his head.

As the group stood to end their evening, the men stretched and the ladies smoothed their skirts and chatted. They were led by the bell captain to the hotel's generous lobby, where farewells were exchanged.

"Well, Mr. Jenkins, thank you for joining us. I'm sure we all enjoyed your company."

"Really, Mrs. Colburn, the pleasure was all mine."

Talking over C.T.'s response the Reverend leaned toward his niece and asked in a not so low voice, "Eliza, dear, have you heard from Mr. Babcock? Before we left Jacksonville I remember him mentioning that he might be coming for a visit to Bay Port?"

C.T. noted the tentative glance that Eliza gave her mother before responding to Harrison, "Why, no. No, I haven't, actually."

Soon after that evening, invitations fanned out across Bay Port inviting the community to a mid-summer barbeque, to be held at Rose Hill. Lucy, MaryAnn, and their family were included in the invitation. The buzz that the upcoming event stirred drowned out the local chatter concerning Buchanan's ineptitude, and the price of cotton on the futures market, instead inciting speculation about Mr. Jenkins' 'intentions'.

On the day of the barbeque, C.T. dispatched a buckboard wagon to bring the Colburn family out to Rose Hill. Mrs. Garrason's cook stood ready with parcels of food from the hotel's kitchen as the buckboard pulled up in front of the Bay Port House.

"Here, hand those up and I'll make sure they get to Mr. Jenkins," offered the Reverend.

The Reverend placed the parcels on the elevated bench between himself and the driver. The fragrance of yeast and butter on the fresh-baked bread was overwhelming. Harrison reached under the gingham wrap and pinched off a piece of the bread. He slipped the morsel into his mouth and left it on his tongue to melt while Jacob assisted Lucy, Eliza, and MaryAnn to their places. Two bare-footed children stacked the small overnight bags into the back of the wagon, and then each one jumped onto the wagon's platform, clinging to the vertical bars as the driver gently prodded the horses forward.

The buckboard wagon passed through a mature stand of hickory trees on its way up a small crest. White primroses were scattered in clusters along an overgrown trail.

Finally the Colburn's arrived at the edge of Jenkins property, "MaryAnn, look at this." The Reverend reacted to dozens of tall poles stretching along the trail. Each pole was tied with brightly colored ribbons that fluttered in the breeze, marking the lane up to the cottage. The wagon passed under the Rose Hill arch, arriving at C.T.'s front door and the host stepped off his front porch to greet them.

"Before the other guests arrive, would you like a quick tour of the property?"

"Yes, I think that would be in order," Harrison responded.

"Very well, then. Let's start with a tour of the garden just here to the left of the cottage. If you'll escort Mrs. Moore, of course. Mrs. Colburn? May I?"

The Reverend narrowed his eyes as he watched his sister-in-law and C.T. take up their conversation where it had left off the last time they had seen each other. *Dear Lord! I hope he realizes Lucy is at least ten years older than he is.*

A few moments later, both parties reached the garden and, in the distance, long rows of lush green, bushy-topped pineapple plants.

"It's lovely, isn't it dear?" MaryAnn asked of her husband.

"Sorry, what was that?"

"The setting, looking out over the rises. It's lovely."

"It reminds me of Ecclesiastes 8:17, MaryAnn, 'then I beheld all the work of God'. Shall we return to the cottage and see how the arrangements are coming for the barbeque?"

Taking the lead, Harrison looked back at Lucy and C.T. who was sweeping an arm across the vista. C.T.'s words to Eliza and Jacob were out of lisening range from the top of the path.

By mid-afternoon the festivities on Rose Hill were in full swing. Looking out from the front porch, the open springboard wagons and buggies formed an arc enclosing the children's adventures. The men organized gunny sack races early in the afternoon, with teams of squealing boys doing more rolling on the ground in laughter than in earnest efforts to cross the finish line. Some of the young ladies embroidered in the shade on the porch.   Others rested in the cool of the house, gossiping and braiding each other's hair.

Everyone stopped when the platters of roast chicken were brought out from the kitchen and placed on the six roughhewn tables set on the shaded side of the house. Bread baskets holding fresh baked loaves with light brown, bubbled crusts made up the centerpiece of each table.   Corn on the cob, stacked high like cordwood, tempted the guests along with an array of relishes, yams and slightly burnt thick gravy.   C.T. took a seat at the head of the Colburn's picnic tables, with Mrs. Colburn on one side and Eliza on the other.   Mrs. Moore faced her son, and the Reverend faced C.T. at the foot of the table.   The Garrason's took up a complete table; as did Mr. and Mrs. Ederington and their children.

"Reverend, if you would be so kind?" C.T. asked.

The Reverend's grace began, and then continued.   It grew into a sermon as stomachs growled and children kicked each other under the tables.   Knuckles were slapped as the fingers of the littlest hands tiptoed toward slices of bread and the cobs of corn grew cold.

Finally, everyone settled down to eat.   The chatter and laughter rose as C.T.'s farm dogs curried favor at the feet of the guests.

In the evening the children ran through the property, collecting fireflies in some jars and crickets into others. Grass blades and pine needles were thrown on top of the critters to make them comfortable in their captivity. Covering the mouths of the jars with their hands, the children ran back to their mothers and the jars were secured with oil soaked paper and tied with twine, thus sealing the fate of the luminaries.

At the end of the long day, the men sat down on the wide veranda.   They took up politics and whiskey in equal measure.   Glowing cigar tips, bobbing in the darkness as each man spoke his mind, could be observed from the tree line.   Two of C.T.'s men were posted at corners of the property fifty yards from the house, standing guard, although no incidents were expected.

Having slipped from their hoops and corsets to their embroidered chemises, the women made themselves comfortable on the second story sleeping porch. They spent the humid evening whispering their hopes and troubles to each other.

Laura Garrason and Ruth Kildall took a liking to Eliza, questioning her about her trip down the eastern seaboard, her impressions of Savannah, and whether or not she had a beau.

"Yes, sort of," answered Eliza.

"Oh! Do tell! Who is he? Is he waiting for you in Fair Haven?" began the string of questions.

"No. Actually, I met him in Jacksonville, when we were guests of the O'Neales. My uncle has investment interests with them, and Taylor is seeing to those investments".

"Taylor? Oh, I like that name. He sounds ambitious."

"And charming!"

"Will he be coming down to pay a visit? It's not far, you know."

"I expect to receive a letter from Taylor shortly that outlines his schedule." Then, Eliza added, "Any day now. I'm sure."

Ruth and Laura exchanged glances and the topic waned. The three young women turned their attention to fashion before the candles were dimmed for the evening.

The fragrance of cedar and pine scented the breeze that swept through the expansive, but sparsely, furnished cottage. The guests quieted in anticipation of a long night. A full summer moon, its sharply-defined craters visible from earth, and bright enough to light the landscape, cast long shadows through the rooms of the cottage. The only noise was a steady symphony from the bullfrogs—and an occasional twig breaking in the distance.

Cyprian remained awake as midnight approached. Through the evening he checked that the older boys were staying in the cottage, and not coaxing each other into any nocturnal scouting adventure. He haunted the cottage, moving silently from room to room: from the rocker on the front porch, through the house; then from the living room into the breakfast room, to the kitchen, and back to the rocker. The minutes ticked by as he lost himself in his thoughts. *It's as troubling as it is interesting, I've never seen these men with their families – everyone...together. Am I the only bachelor of my age in this community? Yes, my life is much better adapted to being independent,* he concluded.

He bitterly second-guessed why he had gone to all the trouble of the day. *Having a family of my own is an impractical possibility.* The conclusion came to him in the abstract as he stood looking out the kitchen window into the darkness.

Suddenly, a prickly feeling washed over him. The hair on the back of his neck stood up. He halted his watch and stood frozen in place. Then, slowly, ever cautious, he moved to the side of the kitchen window.

C.T.'s senses registered a presence just inside the tree line to the west of the cottage. It was a human form, majestically tall, standing with his arms across his chest. C.T. felt that he was being watched. His survival skills were at a fever pitch. C.T. knew that unlike most evenings when he had only himself to defend, this evening he had filled his house with his own community, setting up what *could* become, at one o'clock in the morning, a perfect storm of arson and gunfire.

Using his right hand he reached around to his waistband, fingering the handle of the knife he kept within close reach. He turned the glass knob of the kitchen door and made his way down the back steps of his house. His eyes were riveted on the intruder who stood waiting.

"Whoever he is, he has sought this encounter."

Crossing the open space between the cottage and the tree line one powerful stride at a time, Cyprian's only doubt was whether or not it had been wise to leave his handgun hanging in the holster on the hook behind the kitchen door. But, he realized he must go directly to the aberration and not falter or turn back.

Once he was face to face with the intruder, he peered into the man's deep set eyes. The contrast in their age and height kept C.T. just outside the younger man's reach. From his layered dress, leggings, and the kerchiefs adorning his throat, C.T. surmised the intruder was a member of the Seminole Tiger Clan. The native had a powerful, muscular physique. His head was shaved except for the column of hair, combed forward, that stretched in a bow from ear to ear forming fringe bangs over his broad, high forehead. A ponytail, braided, grew from the top of his crown. His presence was imposing, but calm. He waited for C.T. to speak.

C.T. began his conversation in the Creek dialect, "You have been watching us for a long time."

"You've made spectacles of yourselves for a long time."

"You're on my property."

"No. You are on mine." The glint of fire in the man's eyes consumed the space between their faces.

"You have to go. You have to follow your people."

"Maybe for *this* season I must go. But don't ever forget that my people have been here for over a thousand years. You are the speck on *our* history. I promise you that sometime in the future you will witness our return just as, each season, the swallow returns."

And with that, the man who would have been making his home on this lush landscape as his ancestors had, picked up his rucksack and disappeared into the tall stands of cedar.

* * *

13

AN INVITATION

Several weeks after the festivities at Rose Hill, C.T. sent two messages to Bay Port House: One inviting Mrs. Colburn and Eliza to join him for lunch, and the second requesting of Mrs. Garrason that the hotel's cook prepare a waterfront picnic for himself and two guests. The news of the invitation spread and tongues wagged among Bay Port women as they speculated about the solitary Mr. Jenkins.

**

C.T. entered the lobby of the hotel to find Mrs. Garrason reviewing the hotel registry. "Mr. Jenkins, it's a pleasure to see you today. I believe that you will find the arrangements you requested in order. It's a lovely setting."

"Thank you, Mrs. Garrason. I'm sure it's going to be a very nice luncheon. 'A special occasion that we will all enjoy."

She watched him as he pulled out his pocket watch, which was suspended from a heavy silver chain attached to his waistcoat, something she had watched him do on numerous occasions. He flicked the pocket watch open with his thumbnail and noted the time. At one time C.T. had shown Mrs. Garrason a locket-sized daguerreotype of a young couple secreted inside the watch cover. She recalled that the woman appeared serene, and the man's expression was characteristically stern. "My parents," he had revealed.

Although he didn't look up, C.T. realized that Eliza was walking across the lobby toward him. He snapped the watch shut.   Mrs. Colburn, a step behind her daughter, had slowed to look in the mirror, patting her hair.

C.T. spoke first, "Bon après midi, ca va?"

Eliza let out a note of surprise, a soft mezzo-soprano 'ha'!' "Très bien, merci. Parlez-vous français?"

"Mais oui, qu'en je la chance," C.T. countered.

Slipping back into English, Eliza continued, "Mother must have told you that I speak French, Oui? I must practice more, or it won't be possible for me to speak it at all."

"That would be a shame, since the language agrees with you as it does."

Mrs. Colburn laughed and offered C.T. her arm as she joined in, "Allons-nous profiter de l'après-midi?"

"Mrs. Colburn," he greeted as he folded his friend's hand over his offered right arm while offering Eliza his left arm. "I'm delighted to be the host of two such lovely women." He led the way to the setting of a beach-side picnic in one of his most treasured settings in the world, the Gulf of Mexico off Bay Port, Florida.

As C.T. escorted the two women outside they could see, a short distance away, that a small square table had been placed up from the water line. Its white table cloth fluttered gaily in the breeze. Deep blue linen napkins, held down by silverware that flashed in the sunlight, decorated each setting.

The setting was just far enough away from the hotel to ensure privacy, but close enough to deliver, with impeccable timing, fresh baked, still- warm French bread which the three immediately tore into. A chilled cucumber salad was the first course. Later a succulent bouillabaisse, teeming with shelled crayfish and squid; spiced with bay leaves was served.

At a certain point C.T. threw his head back and laughed at Eliza's admonition, "You are ridiculous!" at the conclusion of one of his expanded tales. Her mother smiled at C.T., shrugging her shoulders.

"What can I say? Every word of that account is true! Although I admit, there were no witnesses."

Finally, trays of French pastries were delivered to the table and the three picked at them as they continued their stories. When there was nothing left but crumbs, and seagulls swooping and squawking along the waterline, C.T. stood up to escort the women back to the guest house.

As summer blossomed, Mrs. Colburn continued her long strolls through Bay Port. Her daughter made frequent visits to Mme. Spurrier's millinery. In contrast, C.T. paid close attention to the murmurings over current events and the rumblings of war. He was growing more concerned over what he was hearing, and spending more time in Bay Port discussing its implications.

* * *

14

KILDALL'S READING ROOM

Kildall's Reading Room
The Patronage of Ladies is Not Sought

One day, while walking toward Kildall's Reading Room, C.T. glanced in the window of Mme. Spurrier's hat shop. *Hmmm...not there.* Mme. Spurrier and a matronly Bay Port client became the recipients of C.T.'s nod and tipped hat as they looked up, wondering whether or not the gentleman on the sidewalk might be peering in. He quickened his pace, embarrassed, and a few steps farther was swept into the lively atmosphere of Kildall's Reading Room.

Kildall's, with its sawdust plank floors, smudged windows, and strategically placed spittoons, had sprung up years earlier. It had quickly become the perfect gathering spot for townsmen waiting for the mail boat to dock, and consequently, the place to discuss the news from Washington, D.C. Quite often C.T. would break the twine that bundled his copies of *The Baltimore Sun*, and pour over news of his hometown.

It took a few moments for the street noise—carriages passing on their way to the harbor, the clomping of horse hoofs— to clear from C.T.'s hearing so that he could determine the topic of the day.

His arrival had gone largely unnoticed by the tight core of men standing at the bar, although a few of his Rose Hill neighbors raised their glasses in a welcoming salute.

"Same?" Joseph Kildall, the proprietor, asked him.

C.T. nodded and a shot of Evan Williams appeared in front of him.

Then he picked up the thread of conversation, "We simply can't continue to pay tariffs at *this* rate, even if our crops do yield as high next year as they have this season."

"The Northern senators must know that this can't continue!" someone else added.

"Thomas, you sentimental fool, of course they know. That's the point!" another unidentified patron shouted.

Ah, C.T. realized, *that's Thomas Phillips.* He was the one speaking when I arrived.

Phillips' antagonist continued, "Do you actually believe that Congress isn't aware of what effect this is having on the cotton states? I always took you for a bright fellow." The others laughed good-naturedly.

C.T. couldn't see who was on the other side of the discussion because of the tight knot standing at the bar. But he knew the topic well, "Gentlemen, why, with us holding less than forty percent of the seats in congress, we are fortunate tariffs aren't even *higher* than they are now," he stated.

"Well then, just go ahead and support this Lincoln fellow, if high tariffs interest you," dared an unidentifiable voice.

"If Abe continues his meteoric ascent we'll have more to worry about than a simple increase in this year's tariffs."

C.T. skirted the edge of the group and rested his boot on the well-worn bar's wrought iron foot rest. Leaning forward, he saw the cause of the discussion. A poster, probably yanked down from the exterior wall of Kildall's Reading Room, lay face up. The banner read,

Tariffs Increase imminent!

Buchanan backs move

to increase tariffs!

"I've read that the tariffs are amounting to ninety-five percent of the federal revenue. If true—and it *feels* true—the President is begging for secession!"

"Hell, never mind the tariffs. They only hit the six-percent who own land. What about the taxes! Taxes have risen to twenty percent!" It was Thomas Phillips, once again.

C.T. added "If Cobb would stand up to Congress, we would be greatly helped. What a fine Secretary of the Treasury he's turned out to be! The South is on the brink of being plundered, ironically, under his watch. If he forsakes us, we will have to do what is necessary."

C.T. glanced around the room and acknowledged his neighbors, "You gentlemen have families to support, so I know that you are even more concerned than I am over how much profit from our crops will be scooped up to support the U.S. Treasury. Revenue grabs are not usually rolled back, regardless of which administration has been swept in. Or in Lincoln's case, limped in."

"The South's wealth is pirated at its own hand, and that's the hand of slavery," the voice of Jacob Moore silenced the growing rabble.

"Oh, and now we are to hear from our resident Yankee! That's perfect! Just what are you talking about, Moore?" challenged Phillips, moving through the crowd toward Jacob as murmurs of agreement followed Phillips.

"I'm saying that the Slave States are out-numbered by the North in manufacturing. The South is struggling with a vulnerable monetary system, so untenable even the plantation owners do their banking in Northern banks. And the South is lacking any leaders of significant military training. If anything plunders the South, it will be the South's own misunderstandings of its situation. The states below the Missouri Compromise just might be on the wrong side of the power balance considering the low tolerance of slavery in the rest of the nation," Jacob explained in a tight, nervous voice.

"Ha! First of all, *what* nation are you speaking of, Moore?" an unidentified challenger called out. There was a smattering of laughter.

In his most controlled voice Kildall stated, "Jacob, son, you've been around here for how many years? Young man, I'd take more care with your mouth than your Senator Sumner did, if I were you. Aspiring to be called a Yankee in these parts might not be your smartest stratagem.".

C.T. added another deflection, "Well, we do have solid assurances from France for arms and Britain for naval support. And, as many of our military men are West Point trained as are Washington's. I say it's a solid even fight, if they don't let us live in peace." At that moment he realized that he spoke of Mrs. Colburn's son, Albert.

C.T. circled back toward the door, so that he could determine who each of the speakers were, should Jacob Moore have difficulties later that evening. *Well, He's gotten his hands full for speaking up, that's for sure,* C.T. thought, deciding that he was the best one to determine the difference between a heated discussion and the beginning of a fight. There simply weren't enough fellows decrying the injustices of slavery that afternoon for the topic to be taken seriously, so Jacob was left to the opinions of his youth, as far as the townsmen were concerned.

"Aren't you from the great abolitionist state of Vermont? I'm not really keen on why you're here in Florida, Jacob." Phillips returned to the challenge.

Jacob picked up his mug from the bar and took a long, slow draw while looking at Phillips from over the brim of his glass. When he set the glass down he continued, "I'm just trying to make a tiny point that seems to be overlooked here, Thomas. It's just my opinion, after all. Who would have thought that it would all come to this?"

Jacob's comment was followed by stony silence, broken by a splat as Phillips spat on the floor at Jacob's feet.

C.T. breathed a sigh of relief as Jacob shrugged his shoulders and turned to the bar, tipping his head back for the last sip of his beer.

* * *

15

Eliza Unrequited

Bay Port House
Eliza's Room

04 September, 1858

Dear Taylor,

Your welcome letter of last week was delivered to me by Uncle Harrison. Taylor, I did not receive the previous letter you mentioned. It grieves me that you have written words that I might never read.

As I sit down at my little writing desk overlooking the melancholy waters of the Gulf, I realize how much I miss Jacksonville.

I expect that Mother and I will only stay in Bay Port a little while longer. Each day the dock fills with families departing for northern seaports. The hotel's dining room is growing empty, save for the perennial locals who come in to town to gather their mail and supplies.

You stated in your letter, "We'll see each other again. You must come back to Jacksonville."

Taylor, I have been so hoping that you might be able to make your way to Bay Port. It would be truly wonderful to see you and if your sister could

accompany you, it would be all the more a proper visit that my Mother could agree to. It would not be possible for me to get Mother to agree to my accompanying Uncle Harrison on his trips to Jacksonville.

I hold on to the hope that the feelings you expressed for me the evening we walked through the O'Neales garden have not waned.

Possibly your attempts at securing funding on behalf of Uncle Harrison's project has kept you from travelling to Bay Port? If this is the case, perhaps you could come to Fair Haven in October when your efforts for Uncle Harrison's church will have concluded. My mother and I would be back in Fair Haven by then. And, if your sister would like to accompany you, I can assure you a hearty welcome.

I hope I haven't become tiresome with my worries, and that your feelings for me have not cooled.

Sincerely,

Eliza

**

Using her blotter, she carefully pressed the words into the page of her stationery and blew lightly to set the ink. She then took the three sheets and folded them in half, the scallop of the soft pink stationery forming the top edge. She slid the letter into a matching envelope and painstakingly wrote out the return address on the back flap.

Eliza Colburn

Quinton Estate

Fair Haven, Vermont

I don't think it sounds too overly dreary. If he would just make one last attempt to win Mother over…we were so happy in Jacksonville. Her eyes stung as tears sprang up and she concluded with the vow, *I've got to do something! I'm not going to end up rattling around a house that is too large for me, as Mother has.*

Summoning her confidence, she decided that she would take the letter to her Uncle's room that very instant. *Uncle Harrison will see that it gets to Taylor.* Pinching her cheeks while inspecting her image in the looking glass, her moist eyes and dewy, smudged eyelashes didn't stop her from donning her fashionable Paris-inspired hat; nor did it stop her from throwing a lace wrap over her shoulders on the way out of her room.

Tapping lightly on the door to her aunt and uncle's suite, she waited a moment and then softly whispered, "Uncle Harrison?" Her aunt answered the door. "Aunt MaryAnn, are you alone? We missed you at breakfast. Are you alright?"

"Fine, darling, of course. Would you like to come in?"

"No, I don't want to interrupt your rest. I thought Uncle Harrison would be working on his sermon. Is he down in the lobby?"

"I'm not sure, dear. He could be taking a stroll before dinner."

"Oh, I see."

"Are you alright, Eliza?"

"Uh, I'm not sure. That is, I think so." Eliza held the letter away from her body. "I was going to ask Uncle Harrison to post this letter for me, along with his mail; or deliver it," her voice trailed.

"Well, I'll give it to him when he gets back. Since the mail boat arrives tomorrow morning, it will give him a good excuse to stretch his legs after dinner. Are you going downstairs, dear?"

"Yes. Would you care to join me, Aunt MaryAnn?"

"No dear. The doctor is recommending that I extend my rests. If you see your mother, please ask her if she would like to come visit me. Later on I'll join everyone for lunch. And, if Harrison is in the lobby, let him know that your letter is stacked up here with a note I want to send to Susan."

"Of course," Eliza concluded her visit by kissing her aunt's offered cheek. Buoyed by the prospect of Taylor receiving her letter within the week, she nearly skipped down the stairs to the hotel's front lobby.

Approaching the hotel's sun porch, Eliza noticed her mother and uncle sitting across from one another. She could see her mother leaning forward, speaking in an animated manner, looking slightly cross. *How well I know how that feels*, she thought, empathizing with Uncle Harrison's position as captive listener.

Eliza could just barely make out her mother's words before she opened the screen door to the porch. Mrs. Colburn's words contrasted with serenity of the Gulf, "I will never again spend John's money on another one of your schemes."

"Am I intruding, Mother? I thought you were out on your stroll."

"I *was* on my way, until Harrison indicated his need to speak to me."

"Mother, Aunt MaryAnn is hoping you will sit with her before lunch."

"Of course." She nodded to her brother-in-law as she departed for the company of her sister. "Harrison."

Patting the arm of the chair Eliza's mother had just vacated, Harrison invited his niece's company, "Oh my dear, nothing pleases me more than to have you share your company with me. You are my one bright ray. Sit down and visit, Eliza."

She sat down and demurely waited for her uncle to start the conversation.

An hour later, Mrs. Colburn was tucking a light cover around her older sister's shoulders. They had spent the time discussing their memories of Fair Haven and their parents.

"I don't remember even thinking about our means or our future, do you?" MaryAnn asked. "The thought that what was happening in Washington could have anything to do with our happiness never entered my mind."

"Mine either. Well, let's just be careful and not make the wrong decisions. I hate discouraging Harrison, but really, MaryAnn; the thought of financing another church with Father's and John's money really chills me."

"Don't worry, dear, I'm sure Harrison understands."

"I think I'll take a walk before we have lunch. You rest, darling, but please come down and enjoy a nice meal with all of us later."

Lucy closed the shutters, softening the light that filtered into her sister's room.

"Lucy, would you take the mail that's stacked on the console and give it to Harrison on your way out? If he's too distracted, he won't remember to take it down to the port this evening, and the mail boat comes in tomorrow morning."

"Of course," Mrs. Colburn responded as she gathered the various envelopes, carefully tucking the bundle into her drawstring purse before wrinkling her nose at her sister. MaryAnn laughed and shooed her sister away before closing her eyes to rest.

Just before noon, Mrs. Colburn returned from her walk. Her intention to drop off the bundle of letters at the post office had been thwarted by a discovery that compelled her to return to the Bay Port House and her daughter's room.

Her door ajar, Eliza was sitting in a rocker by the window, reading. Mrs. Colburn entered the room quietly and stood waiting for her daughter to take notice. "Mother! You surprised me! I hope you had a pleasant walk."

"No Eliza, you surprise me. I didn't realize that you and Mr. Babcock were corresponding. I *am* disappointed."

Eliza placed the Bible she was reading on her lap and folded her hands. She stared at her mother, taking her time to respond, trying to gauge the level of her mother's anger.

"Since little escapes your attention, you probably realize that Uncle Harrison and Taylor have stayed in touch. You did know that they have continued to work together on the funding possibilities for Uncle Harrison's church."

Sweet Eliza! If only you realized what part your interest in Jacksonville and Mr. Taylor plays in your Uncle's plans. Mrs. Colburn was beginning to more fully understand Harrison's prompts, prods and interest in arranging their stop-over in Jacksonville on the Colburn's way back to Fair Haven. From her morning conversation with Harrison, she had been able to determine that he had been nursing hopes that she would accompany him on one last visit to Jacksonville, ostensibly to secure funding, but now she could see an ulterior motive as well.

"Eliza, darling, nothing is going to come of this, believe me."

"You mean because you wish it so, Mother? Taylor's mother would have liked to meet us. When Uncle Harrison was in Jacksonville last month, Mr. and Mrs. Babcock attended the fund raiser Taylor had arranged for Uncle Harrison's church. Taylor said his mother specifically wished us to stop over and spend the day visiting Magnolia the next time we were in Jacksonville. We're invited." Eliza insisted.

"How many letters have you received from Taylor, aided by your Uncle Harrison?"

"Mother, have you heard a word I've said? What difference does it make?"

"Please Eliza, don't interpret this as anything more than a summer folly. There's much on the horizon that you wouldn't understand, and too much at stake."

"Mother, you haven't even given Taylor a chance! I don't understand why we had to leave Jacksonville so suddenly."

"MaryAnn was waiting for us, remember? Besides, there are suitors who are considerably more appropriate than Taylor Babcock, Eliza." Mrs. Colburn crossed the room to close the door so that their words would not be heard by the other guests.

"Mother, I am twenty-six. I cannot go back to Fair Haven and face the prospects of the same droll suitors whom you have already had the inclination to pass over in my behalf."

"That suits me fine, Eliza. It's not my intention to push you toward any former or future Fair Haven suitor. I'm sure your father's resources could be stretched to support you if you choose to remain unmarried. I simply hoped you had the capacity to look beyond one Jacksonville dalliance."

Eliza gasps in dismay.

"Really, Eliza! Do you think that you would be happy with someone who chases the coat tails of well-appointed families, with funding schemes and so-called investment opportunities, as your uncle does? I would have imagined you would find the prospect embarrassing."

"Mother, how unkind!"

"Well Eliza, I'm sorry. I know your Uncle has a generous nature toward you, but his associations are ill-advised but well-intentioned. Surely you realize that before we arrived in Jacksonville our resources and background were being weighed carefully by the O'Neales and the Babcock's. Setting your sights on a Southern family with plantation holdings might seem ideal, but they are not. Not in these times. You're simply passing over the most likely solution, Eliza. I think we best go home so you can think about more appropriate options."

Eliza face grew red, tears sprung to her eyes. "Mother, there are no more appropriate options. I've never said this before, but you have stood in the way of every man who could have loved me. You're afraid that I may end up happily married while you remain a widow."

"My dear that is hardly the case. I have remained a widow out of love for your father and in order to properly raise you and your siblings. Now, why don't you gather yourself and think things through. A solution could be right in front of your eyes. Autumn will be coming to an end and we will be leaving for home in a matter of weeks. Without a stop in Jacksonville. If you'd like to write a letter of farewell to Taylor; we can walk it to the post office tomorrow morning before the mail boat docks. In the meantime, I'm going for a stroll with Mr. Jenkins. If you'd care to straighten yourself up, you're welcome to join us."

"Ha! How nice this all is for you. I see."

"No Eliza, actually you don't." Mrs. Colburn fished through her draw string purse for her black lace gloves which she donned as Eliza glared at her. She took her time straightening the seams that ran to the tip of each finger. She then picked up her black satin parasol.

"You can pout through your solution all afternoon, if that's what you wish to do," and she left.

Eliza looked around the room and decided to visit her Aunt's room.

Knocking on the door of her aunt and uncle's suite she found her aunt much improved over her breakfast infirmity.

"Are you here to escort me to lunch, Eliza?"

"Yes, shall we go down together, later?"

"Of course, where's your mother?"

"She is out for a stroll with Mr. Jenkins. They spend so much time together."

"Oh! You should join them. You'd enjoy yourself. That sounds quite pleasant. Jacob thinks the world of Mr. Jenkins. Although for some reason Harrison feels ill at ease around him."

**

Mme. Spurrier's Millinery

"Oh Mimi, what am I to do?"

"Tell me what she said next, Eliza."

She said, '*I didn't realize that you and Mr. Babcock were corresponding, Eliza,*' as though I were a child who needed permission to post letters. She was so unnecessarily cruel. When we were in Jacksonville she didn't say—or do—anything to discourage my interest in Taylor, or Taylor's interest in me. She has become so unkind. You wouldn't believe how much she's changed since we left Fair Haven. She's more overbearing than ever!"

"Oh dear, Eliza; I'm so sorry. How horrid, mon cher, doux…" comforted Mimi Spurrier holding Eliza's hand in her own. "What shall we do with all of this?"

With her free hand Eliza dabbed at her tear ducts, her eyelids swollen from the emotional storm that had progressed from frustration, to humiliation, and finally depression. "She goads at me 'make a decision'. But then she parrots, '*Not* that decision, not *that* decision, until all of my choices are gone. She *wants* me to be a spinster. My only course is to stay perfectly still and let her make all the decisions. I am going to go mad!"

"Eliza, darling; surely that's not true," reassured Mimi Spurrier in her French accent.

"I have no one! What would I do without you, Mimi? I'm going to end up just like Elizabeth."

"Elizabeth?"

"My step-sister, Elizabeth. Betsey, actually. Betsey has never married. Mother never took an interest in

Betsey's prospects, so with her allowance she quietly arranged to have a coach take her from Fair Haven. She now lives with my half-brother Moses and attends his wife, Joslyn, who has been ailing for years. It's the same thing all over again with me. If only Albert were here to reason with her. Mother will only listen to the men in her life. *She'll* be married before I will," and at that thought Eliza finally laughed.

"Really, Eliza! How amusing! Your Mother is...? How old *is* your Mother?" Mimi Spurrier laughed realizing how disrespectful the question might seem; but curious all the same.

"Fifty seven. She's fifty seven."

"*Oh!* I thought she was more Mr. Jenkins age. She looks younger than she is, then."

"Mr. Jenkins?"

"Of course, Mr. Jenkins. They're together every day walking past my shop on their way to the park. He's such a gentleman, oui? Actually, I think she is smitten; but I didn't realize...the age."

"My Mother and Mr. Jenkins? Does the whole town think that? Oh, dear! Now *I* am laughing. You are such a delight, Mimi! My Mother has no interest in being courted by Mr. Jenkins, or anyone else, for that matter. She is still in love with the memory of Father. And, according to Uncle Harrison, should she remarry she would lose the means that Father left us. No, my Mother and Mr. Jenkins is quite an impossible thought, silly! I *knew* you would cheer me up."

Mimi pressed on, "But still, in love all things are possible. And, Mr. Jenkins is a Senator. He's so distinguished, don't you think? Why wouldn't she fancy him? Obviously, he fancies her."

"I haven't given him much thought, actually. Oh, what does it matter? Certainly my Mother would never marry him. Mimi, do you think I should wire Albert?

Maybe he could intercede and convince Mother to be more favorable toward Taylor. What do you think?"

"No, I think this is not a topic that you would want to contact your brother on. And, I don't think your brother would take your side, considering your mother's influence. But what if you wrote to your half-brother?"

"Moses? Hmm . . . Possibly. Maybe if I wrote to him and brought the letter to you, could you post

it for me? No need taking a second chance now that I know I cannot even write an uncensored letter! Oh dear, Mimi! I'm so at odds with everything! Except having you as my friend, of course. Que'est-ce que je ferais sans vous?"

"You would do fine without me. You have your Aunt MaryAnn, your uncle, your whole family, actually. Not like me. My family remains in Quebec. It's so hard sometimes. To be separated by such a distance! Now look what you've done! You are the sunny one and I am sad."

Eliza straightened her shoulders and began the motions of smoothing her hair and straightening her skirts. She reached over to Mimi's cutting table and placed her empty tea cup on the edge, making ready to depart the company of her friend. They laughed and embraced before Mimi shooed Eliza out onto the sidewalk.

"I must return to work, mon cher!"

They waved to each other though the plate glass of Mme. Spurrier's Millinery and Design. Eliza blew Mimi a kiss and touched the rim of the little blue cap she wore, showcasing Mme. Spurrier's work.

**

The calendar moved forward, each day slightly cooler than the previous as tourists leaving Bay Port began to outnumber those arriving. Lucy Colburn and her family continued the routines they had established over the summer.

As Eliza crossed the lobby of the hotel one afternoon C.T. greeted her, "Miss Colburn! Are you finally joining us?"

Eliza accepted a light buss and informed C.T., "Mother has been with Aunt MaryAnn since this morning. She asked that I come down and let you know she is unable to join you for a stroll this afternoon."

"Oh dear! Is everything alright?"

"I think so. Although Aunt MaryAnn continues to suffer from asthma. She had a bit of an attack this morning. She's perennially frail – unlike Mother."

"I see. Most unfortunate about your Aunt. I've come all the way from Rose Hill in the hopes of spending the afternoon with your mother and vying for an invitation to join all of you for dinner."

He was not quite sure what to do about the look of confusion on Eliza's face. "Perhaps you would care to join me on a stroll? We could take a fresh route; maybe walk along the water to watch the egrets' and herons' ballet. Entendu?" He waited for a response.

"Oh dear! Please don't look so melancholy, Mr. Jenkins, you leave me little choice. Well, d'accord!" She shrugged her shoulders and pulled her shawl tightly around her shoulders.

C.T. reached over to tuck the fold around the nape of her neck, then offered his arm.

They descended the steps of the hotel in silence. "Eliza, you are the one who seems wan, or is it sadness? Are you homesick?"

"Oh! Goodness no, Mr. Jenkins. I'm not homesick; although Mother tells me we will be returning to Vermont within the month. I do have a dear friend who I am missing. I regret that it shows."

"I wonder, if only just for the afternoon, would you like to address me as 'C.T.'?

"*Oh!* I suppose, if you wish."

"Yes, of course it would be my preference. Now, back to you, and the possibility that your sadness is caused by the absence of this friend of yours. We humans do tend to wear matters of the heart on our sleeves, don't we?"

"Are you making fun at my expense, Mr. Jenkins?"

"C.T.," he corrected. "And, no. My goodness, dear, I am not making fun of you. Where would that get me? But your sadness over the summer has been so apparent."

They had come to the end of the plank sidewalk and needed to make the decision of whether to walk north toward the cove, joining the larger group of vacationers being enveloped by the warm gulf breeze, or proceed south to the point away from the Bay Port House. Eliza pointed toward the cove and C.T. took the lead, nodding to end-of-the-season vacationers with whom he had made acquaintance.

He was surprised by her reply to his question, "You are the first person to *ask* me, not tell me, how I might be feeling. I'm not sure how to respond, actually."

"Eliza, may I pry, my dear? Exactly how old *are* you?"

"Oh dear! Are you really asking such an unbecoming question? Do you mean to fluster me?"

"Well, let me proceed thusly. I am forty-seven; you must be close to twenty-six. I would suspect that I am at least twenty years your elder. Let me assure you that I do not require that you tell me how correct I may be." He enjoyed her smile for a moment before continuing, "Sometimes we choose to fall into the roles expected of us by our family. Sometimes we do not. It's a matter of choice. Although as strong willed as your mother is, I expect that the free will of her children comes with considerable challenges."

Eliza stopped and faced C.T., "I thought you enjoyed my mother's company."

"Oh, my goodness, I do! We are nearly contemporaries and have become great friends. We have shared many confidences over this season and offered each other many recommendations. Frankly, I hope that she has listened to my advice. I have certainly benefited from her perspectives. I'll admit to you, I now realize that before she came to Bay Port, I *was* lonely. Maybe I recognize that same emotion in you. The thought of not seeking out your mother, not being invited to dine with her and your Aunt's family, not having your audience for my storytelling, does grieve me somewhat. Life will be very different for me once you and your mother return to Vermont."

They had come to the edge of the boardwalk that led to the beach. Eliza stopped to gaze across the water; a blazing orange sun was hanging heavily at flash point above the horizon. Chalky white egrets flew across the sky in silhouette. She turned to C.T., "When Mother and I leave, I'll miss the mood of the water and the birds swooping and squabbling as they do. Florida is *so* different from Vermont. I doubt if it's changed Mother, but I know that I draw different conclusions about my happiness after having taken this vacation."

"...Different conclusions about your happiness? In what ways, Eliza?"

"I suppose I don't feel the same entitlement for happiness, as I did before," she confessed softly.

"What you expect from life, Eliza, is really up to you. Personal expectations are concepts for which we each take responsibility. It's a matter of recognizing opportunities and being open to what is sometimes the least obvious path to happiness or contentment. You are such a lovely, mature woman. You may possess a path to happiness; or contentment at least, that is less obstructed than you might imagine. I know that your mother has given you very few choices in life, but there is one that I hope that you will act upon."

"I'm not sure I understand what you mean, Mr. Jenkins. Loneliness, choice, and solution are such subjective, and even personal notions, wouldn't you say? They strike each individual so differently. Perhaps, as you say, I am lonely, or sad, but how would my expectations fit into all of that?"

"My dear, if one day you have figured out what I am trying to say to you, I hope you will be compelled to let me know, even if it is from Vermont." After some thought, C.T. asked the question that had to be asked, considering how few opportunities he had to speak to Eliza alone, "I haven't made much of an impression on you have I?"

" Oh! You have. I truly enjoyed our picnic on the beach. It was wonderful, the day was memorable."

He shook his head ruefully, "Then the bouillabaisse wasn't served too cold, or anything else that would have put you off?"

"No," she laughed. "Everything was lovely. Why?"

C.T. smiled, "I feel as though I have the pleasure of your company, but not your attention."

One evening when C.T. wandered into the Bay Port House dining room his arrival was noted by Mrs. Colburn who waved to him as he scanned the dining room.

"You're joining us, aren't you?" she asked as he approached. He nodded, smiling at her.

As he sat down he asked, "Will Eliza be joining us?"

"I believe so. She was not feeling well this morning, but I am hoping her mood will not extend into the evening."

The dining room host served tea, while Lucy and MaryAnn's light conversation created a pleasant enough backdrop. Finally, after most of the other diners had been served, Eliza appeared.

C.T. was the first to notice her arrival. Dabbing his moustache, he tossed his napkin to the side of his plate and slid his chair back in order to escort Eliza to their table.

"How are you today? I missed seeing you this morning at breakfast. I had hoped that you might have wanted to join your mother and me for a stroll this morning. I'm not sure whose company you are avoiding, hers or mine."

She responded with a burst of laughter, "Oh my! How brazenly frank you are, Mr. Jenkins!"

"I'm pleased if I amuse, rather than annoy you, Eliza."

As C.T. seated Eliza, she and her mother exchanged cool glances. It became obvious to C.T. that the company Eliza was avoiding was her mother's – not his. She acknowledged her aunt and uncle and C.T. realized that he had the unenviable task of sitting between two women who were involved in a spat.

MaryAnn leaned toward her sister requesting that the tea be poured while C.T. spoke in low tones with Eliza, "I hope you are not too displeased with your mother. I've come to the conclusion over the past months that she has your best interests at heart."

"So she reminds me daily."

"Really, does she? I find that more intriguing than you might imagine."

"Really, Mr. Jenkins? What a curious thing to say. Pray tell what you mean?"

"I implore you to address me as 'C.T.' I hope that someday we can look back on this exchange and enjoy this moment as a pleasant memory."

With that C.T. turned to his other dinner companions and toasted the evening, taking a sip of his favorite whiskey.

**

C.T. held Mrs. Colburn's hand as they all watched the luggage be loaded by the stevedores. In turn she patted C.T.'s arm and eased her right hand away from him. Eliza and Jacob stood behind MaryAnn, who was weeping.

"I wish you wouldn't go, Lucy, dear. You could easily decide it's too much of a trip to make again next year, even if now you think you'll be back."

"Oh, I think it's best for us to return to Fair Haven. The holiday season will begin soon enough, and I'm sure that Eliza will want to participate in the various social occasions..." Then she added, "...and opportunities."

Mrs. Colburn and Eliza were joining other northbound families for the voyage through the Florida Keys, up the coast to Gainesville, Charleston, and on to New York. The rail would take them on to Rutland, Vermont, the closest station to Quinton Estate.

Mrs. Colburn picked up her small bag from the dock and smiled at C.T., asking, "I'll see you again, won't I?"

The gentleman kissed her cheek, "We'll have to see, won't we? But Lucy, my dear, farewell for now." Then C.T. turned his attention to Eliza.

"Well, Eliza, Good bye. You are faced with many decisions. Difficult choices. Thank you for the serenity and comfort the pleasure of your company provided me over this past spring and summer. I hope that you will hold Bay Port in your heart and that you will wish to return some day."

"Yes, perhaps. But, for now, *au revoir*."

The passengers trudged one heavy step at a time up the gateway, turning often to gaze back at the landscape, the sandpipers and the sea grasses of the Florida coast. Finally the vessel's lines were coiled neatly on deck and the steam engines were started. The steamer slowly reversed away from the dock and turned toward the sun, which hung red and brilliant above the horizon.

Long after Bay Port families had returned to their busy routines, one lone silhouette remained looking southward toward the horizon.

"Eliza," Mrs. Colburn acknowledged as her daughter joined her in the shipboard dining room.

"Mother," retorted Eliza as she sat down to dinner and the two continued in this manner, dabbing their lips after each dainty bite. Their first days on ship continued in this manner.

"This silence of yours can go on for as long as you'd like, Eliza."

"Oh, Mother, I was about to suggest the *very* same thing to you."

"Maybe you'd like to put this issue aside and plan for the social occasions that will take place this season."

"Nothing is going to take place this season in Fair Haven that you don't plan for us. Certainly my help in *your* planning is not necessary."

"Eliza, if you want to be angry with me over the evaporation of your friendship with that young banker who had our finances figured out well before our Jacksonville arrival, be my guest. Although Mr. Babcock did not approach me on topics relevant to you, he certainly exhibited keen interest on topics relative to my investment intentions."

"Mother, you have such a biting tongue."

"Maybe I *am* direct, Eliza; but, let me say this one final thing," she was interrupted by her daughter's guffaw, but continued. "There were ideal opportunities in Florida that would have worked out wonderfully for you, if you had been paying attention. If your intention is to *ever* marry I would recommend that you pay closer attention to what is going on around you. I am *very* disappointed in how you have handled your prospects."

* * *

16

A Suitor Heads to Vermont

C.T. stared at his image in the mirror as he pulled a brush through his tangled hair. Setting the brush down on the cabinet beside the wash basin he examined his reflection more closely. The skin under his eyes was beginning to sag. His hands, and the beds of his nails, were unkempt. He splashed his face with water poured from the pitcher and reaching for a towel. His head throbbed.

Eliza and her mother had left ten days earlier. C.T. adjusted the suspenders holding up his soiled work clothes and stole a furtive look at the open cedar wardrobe where his light wool dinner jacket was carefully hung. His white linen shirts were hanging crisply on their hangers, unworn.

C.T. sighed, deciding that his ride out to the hammocks to survey the fence line could wait. Crossing his bedroom, he strode out of the cottage to the pump just outside the kitchen door. C.T. drew a ladle of water and drank it down, clearing his head.

He then went back into the cottage to his desk and sat down at his desk. After selecting a sheet of stationery he centered it on the blotter and opened the small thin case that held his fountain pen. He

set the pen next to the sheet of paper and unscrewed the cap from the inkwell. He stared out the living room window to the palmetto field and distant tree line. After a few moments he began to write.

"I say! C.T!"

"Reverend Moore! What a surprise. I didn't realize that you were in town." C.T. had been looking down, examining the handwriting on a scallop-edged pink envelope when he nearly bumped into Reverend Moore just outside the post office.

"Yes, I was over at New Hope administering to the congregation and thought I'd come into Bay Port. I'll board here and go on to St. Petersburg on Friday. So, have you heard from Lucy?"

"Yes. Lucy *and* Eliza."

"Really? And Eliza, you say?"

"Yes, it seems Eliza has accepted my proposal," C.T. explained, theatrically tucking the dainty envelope into his breast pocket. "I'll be leaving for Fair Haven within the week."

C.T. watched as the Reverend's eyes hungrily followed the placement of the envelope. "Proposal? My God."

"Reverend? Are you alright?"

"I, I—"

"Yes?"

"Your proposal? Marriage proposal? Oh dear. I thought— Well—"

"Do speak your mind, Reverend Moore. After all, we know that under the circumstances I certainly would," he laughed.

"It's just that I—"

C.T. cocked his head quizzically.

"I'm taken by surprise. Speak my mind, you say? Well I would have imagined that Taylor Babcock, the *young* man from Jacksonville, would be a much better match for Eliza." The Reverend took out his handkerchief, wiping his mouth, then his forehead.

"Well, there it is. Finally, the Reverend speaks his mind. What can I say in response to that tidy morsel, Reverend? Other than 'good day'."

The Reverend moved to the side of the plank walk to give way as C.T. tipped his hat and took his leave.

St. John's River, Palatka, Florida
October 1858

The hired carriage driver pulled to the front of the queue of pushcarts and wagons at the Palatka dock. Any mariner taking in the scene would have appreciated the beautiful, slender white schooner lying in the waters off the Florida coast, its foresail lapping in the gentle, tropical breeze, the boom rocking back and forth as the tide slapped against the vessel's waterline. Moored at the end of the long splinter-beamed dock, its course was to ferry passengers northwardly toward Baltimore, and points beyond.

"Are you going far, sir?" the carriage driver asked as he placed C.T.'s bags on the boardwalk leading to the waiting room of the terminal.

"Yes, actually, I am," he replied pleasantly, adding, "with a few stops along the way."

"Very good, Sir," was the non-committal response as the coachman waited for his payment, dutifully holding out his hand as C.T. counted out his coins. The driver watched silently as Jenkins picked up one small bag and two larger bags soldiering on. The throng waited for the lines to be lifted so the surge could move inevitably forward toward the gangplank.

The coachman finally looked down at the coins in his hand. He blinked, furrowed his brow, and looked again. Maybe he had misquoted the fare; or maybe the gentleman had not heard the fare correctly.

In his palm he held thrice what he had expected. *What a generous man, indeed!* The coachman thought for a moment about the possibility of making it a celebratory day, holding onto his hat as he tipped his face into the sunshine. But with luck like this, he reasoned, maybe it would be better to attend to his livery business. Whistling a lively tune, he climbed back into his carriage to make the return trip to the hotel district for more seaboard passengers.

C.T. proceeded into the cool of the waiting room and sat observing the families in all their various assortments.

He turned his attention to his hometown newspaper, *The Baltimore Sun,* and his thoughts moved to the stopover in the city he hadn't stepped foot in, in over twenty years.

An hour later, a young boy came through the terminal calling out over the frenzied din of humanity, "Jacksonville. Jacksonville, Georgia; Baltimore; New York—all aboard the *Everglade.* First class passengers, please board at this time."

C.T. folded his newspaper, tucking it under his arm as he reached down to retrieve a small leather case. A porter appeared beside him to assist with his larger bags, and the two joined the jostling queue making its way up the gangplank. "Sir, with your permission; I'll see these bags to your stateroom."

C.T. nodded and offered the man a tip.

Looking down at the coins that had been pressed into his palm, the porter smiled to himself. Emboldened, he pushed through the crowd along the outside edge of the gangplank and proceeded through the bustle of travelers.

Exhaling a sign of relief upon entering the quiet of his cabin, C.T. gently closed the shuttered door, adjusting the louvers to soften the light coming into his promenade level stateroom.

Later that evening, with the sails billowing the *Everglade* moved northward. C.T. stepped from his cabin out onto the promenade holding a glass tumbler one-quarter filled with whiskey. He was ready for dinner, dressed in a fitted white shirt with abalone buttons, a four button tan vest, and darker tan trousers. His full silver beard was the most striking feature setting him apart from the other middle-aged gentlemen on board.

Entering the dining area at the rear of the main deck, he noted there were plenty of tables to choose from even if all thirty first class passengers happened to choose the first dining. The open canopy dining area accommodated those who wished to stare into their past as the schooner slid through the waters into the future.

Few schooners would be sailing north on the harsh Atlantic after a few more weeks. The distinctive smell of brine scented the air, and C.T. savored each deep breath. His thoughts turned to the two letters that pressed against his chest from the inside pocket of his dinner jacket. The first was a draft of his correspondence to Eliza, which had been sent nearly a month earlier. He unfolded and re-read his copy, not believing his own words:

Posted: *Rose Hill*
Hernando County, Florida

Miss Eliza Colburn
Quinton Estate
Fair Haven, VT

15 September 1858

My Dear Eliza,

I hope your journey back to Fair Haven was pleasant and has allowed you time to reflect on your time in Florida; particularly the time you spent on the Gulf. Possibly you even think back to our luncheon on the shore, the Rose Hill bar-be-que, and other moments that bring Bay Port into favorable light.

My own reflections of the summer now passed bring me such loneliness that I am compelled to pen this letter to you. I must admit that your and your mother's departures have resulted in much quieter days than I would have imagined possible. No longer do I charge away from Rose Hill with the expectation of greeting your family in the Bay Port House dining room. Mrs. Garrason no longer inquires about what plans I may have made to stroll with your mother. Mme. Spurrier no longer asks me if you might be stopping by her shop for a visit as I stroll past her shop on my way to Kildall's.

I am busy, no mistaking; as speculation swirls in the political winds, mandating certain decisions regarding my crops and land management. But, as a middle-aged man I realize now the delights I may have missed in a misbegotten attempt to shield myself from the memories of a troubled past.

I'm sure that by now you understand the depth and dynamic of the friendship I share with your mother. If not, please inform me so that I can assure you of the honor and respect that is enveloped therein.

You may be quite busy entertaining suitors, now that you have returned to Fair Haven. And possibly, I have missed the opportunity of having the frank conversation with you that would more appropriately have taken place during your stay in Bay Port. That is, a conversation that I waited too long to have, hoping for a clear signal that you wished such a conversation to take place. You must understand what I wish now to convey to you, hopefully in person.

If so, and if you wish, I would like to travel to Fair Haven in order to discuss with you a proposal which I presented to your

mother, to which she responds favorably.
Life's moments are fleeting as I wait for your response,
Sincerely Yours,
C.T.

**

The letter that C.T. read next contained Eliza's response.

Posted: *Miss Eliza Colburn*
The Quinton Estate
Fair Haven, Vermont

Mr. C.T. Jenkins
Rose Hill
Bay Port, Florida

06 October 1858

My Dear Mr. Jenkins,

Your heartfelt letter arrived by messenger this morning. I look forward to all that you might wish to discuss with me.
Your arrival in Fair Haven is welcomed and warmly anticipated. I would welcome any correspondence you may wish to send me during your travels.

Have a safe journey.
Sincerely,
Eliza

Time at sea, highlighted by gourmet dinners, passed pleasantly one day after the next until the Everglade glided into its third port of call, Baltimore.
Disembarking, C.T. began the long trudge away from The Basin and uphill toward Light Street to engage an open carriage for the long ride to the Charles Street Hotel. It had been twenty-five years since he had left his hometown. His father had died four years earlier.

* * *

The Randall's of Baltimore

"Jonathan!"

C.T. called out to Jonathan Randall who was about to enter the Charles Street Dining Room for their pre-arranged dinner party. The wind whipped through downtown Baltimore that evening whistling as it circled the brick buildings, menacing the pedestrians. C.T. had made dinner reservations for himself and the Randall's when he arrived in Baltimore the previous day.

Randall stood in the entryway of the dining room as C.T. caught up with him. "Where's Ruth?" inquired C.T.

"She and James will arrive shortly. They're coming directly from home by carriage. I came up from the docks, straight away."

"How's business?" the perfunctory question followed by the customary response.

"Business couldn't possibly be better! And Frederick is managing excellent prospects." C.T.'s face darkened slightly, prompting his cousin's husband to ask, "Will you go to see them?"

"No Jonathan. I'm sure I won't have time."

Choosing to steer clear of the in-fighting that had gone on since the death of C.T.'s father,

Jonathan attempted to segue to another topic. He felt as though he had already gotten off on the wrong foot and wished Ruth was there to steer him to safer ground with her cousin. *Ruth*, he thought of his wife, *so charming, so sought after, always knowing exactly the right words.* "Hmmm, so! You're getting married? My goodness! What news!"

"Yes, I have every reason to believe that my proposal has been received favorably not only by Miss Colburn and her mother, but by her extended family as well."

"Well, Ruth is dying to know every detail, so be prepared to be peppered with questions."

C.T. responded with a hollow laugh, not able to imagine discussing weddings and feminine topics, and also reminding himself that whatever he told Ruth, he might as well telegraph to his Uncle Frederick's widow and his brother's wives.

"Well, do tell me. What is the news in Baltimore of the administration's intentions?"

"Hmm, I seem to rely entirely on Michael's perspective. He's editing The Catholic University Review now, and you know their stand on secession—a little outnumbered, I'd say. Douglas is making things interesting. Or messy. You tell me, Cyprian. In the meantime, how are your Florida prospects? I hear your pineapple crop has become a fine investment."

"Jonathan, it's hard to even say, considering the times. My pineapple crops *are* doing well. Good returns. Beautiful warm weather in Florida. I truly enjoy it. A melancholy beauty hangs over the Gulf that I can't fully explain, except that it agrees with me."

"I suppose I can imagine," though try as he might Randall had no idea what the life of an Indian scout, farmer, and frontier senator was like, except uncivilized. "Ah!" Jonathan's eyes brightened as his wife and son, James, rushed through the dining room, led by the maître de. "Ruth, darling, I'm so happy you have arrived, I'm afraid I'm already out of small talk."

"Silly, silly," she admonished her husband before turning to her cousin, related through their maternal grandmother's family—the Wells.

"Cyprian! Oh my goodness! Look at you! You're so distinguished looking." Breathless from the rush of trying to be on time, Ruth was effusive in her greeting.

C.T. laughed at the compliment, "And, Ruth you haven't changed one bit, 'ever the most charming of my cousins." *No wonder Jonathan is so settled* he reminded himself, realizing that the couple had been married for over twenty years.

"Well I'm sure Jonathan has warned you that I want every word on this young woman who is awaiting your formal proposal. You must have amazing influence to be able to hold on to the attention of a young woman from as far away as Vermont."

"My, my, Ruth. Your eyes are sparkling with anticipation. Actually, though, it was her mother I was trying to influence. She is very much the one

making the decisions regarding who escorts her daughter. Eliza didn't seem to care, one way or the other about the pleasure of my company for most of the summer. It was infuriating, so I gave up for a time, accounting it to our age difference."

Jonathan caught his wife's eye and her subtle signal that a reaction might not be wise. He escaped the balance of the evening's conversation surveying the other dining room guests.

Ruth ventured on alone, "And this young woman's mother?"

"Oh, actually Eliza is twenty-six, not necessarily a 'young' woman. But if you're asking about her mother, Mrs. Colburn is widowed. She relies on her husband's estate for her well-being. She was widowed at about the same age as her daughter is now. Mrs. Colburn is older than I, but who knows by how much."

"Are you enjoying Florida? That is, enough to take a wife back to the Gulf, instead of home to Baltimore? I mean, Eliza is wishing to make her life in Florida, she enjoys it there? And, you - you want to continue on there?"

"You mean, instead of Maryland? Of course I'm enjoying Florida. Maryland is my cradle, but I expect I'll make Florida my grave. I simply cannot abide the cold weather here in the North." C.T. then added, "Mrs. Colburn feels the same way. About the weather, that is."

"Where will the wedding take place?"

"Either at Lake Champlain, a coach ride north of Fair Haven—Eliza's uncle is on faculty at the University there—or at a location Mrs. Colburn chooses in Fair Haven."

"Where *do* you live, cousin?" finally the Randall's young son, James Ryder, mustered a curiosity that garnered him into the conversation.

Pleased to have the interest of his young cousin, C.T. responded, "Not far from the Gulf of Mexico on a beautiful rise. I have a cottage, which I designed myself that looks out over the ridges and hammocks toward Bay Port, Florida. I've planted orange groves and pineapple crops as far as the eye can see; and fig trees form a boundary around the house. Cherokee roses have climbed to the trusses of the porch. The house cools in the evening when the breeze sets in. I've named the property *Rose Hill*. I miss it just talking about it. Someday you must come to Bay Port, James. It would do you good to make the trip. That is, when you're feeling better and have decided what to do about your studies and travels." C.T. surveyed the roomful of diners before finishing the last swirl of cognac and dropping his napkin softly onto his dessert plate.

Aware of every signal, an attentive light-skinned young man appeared at Jonathan Randall's elbow to whisk the plates away.

"Will there be anything else, gentlemen?"

Jonathan looked quizzically at C.T., who waved the air dismissively.

"Thank you, Damien, that's all," indicated Jonathan as he stood up and took Ruth's cape from the maître de.

"The check?"

Jonathan leaned toward C.T., "I'm sure they've added it to my account. You're *my* guest tonight, old man." Anxious to end his long day, Randall began gathering his wife, his son, and his briefcase.

Ruth leaned toward C.T. indicating that a kiss and a hug was in order.

C.T. took his cue, directing his last comments to the Randall's son, "I'll expect to see you in Bay Port, James. Write me when you are on your way." After shaking hands with the patriarch and his son, C.T. balled his fists into the pockets of his wool flannel coat and trudged face-on into the cold Baltimore evening.

* * *

18

A Fair Haven Wedding

The coachman cocked his head to one side waiting for his passenger to reveal a destination.

"Quinton Estate, Fair Haven," C.T. instructed

It had been a long journey. Too long, considering New York, the luggage transfers from the paddle wheel, the train ride, and finally the carriage that would take him to Eliza.

It was a dark, lusterless evening. C.T. put his head back against the tufted headrest of the coach and closed his eyes. He was jolted awake as the surface of the macadam gave way to gravel, which crunched under the wheels of the heavily loaded carriage. C.T. sat up, straightened his string tie, and reached for his silver flask, taking a brisk swig that would have made any other man flinch. He craned his neck to see out the coach window. *Nothing. How could anyone bear to live in the middle of such deep woods? A man would feel completely closed in. Not like the open Gulf, beckoning one to the edge of the map.* In the dark C. T. could not see the turn of the leaves, split rail fences, or symmetrical orchards of Vermont.

Within a few minutes, the coach stopped on the circular brick drive in front of the estate.

"Sir?"

"Yes, yes. Thank you." C.T. acknowledged the

driver and re-capped his flask. He stepped down from the coach and walked up the grand steps that lead to the expansive porch of the Vermont estate. Gerald opened the door at the first discrete knock.

"Gerald," C.T. began. "How nice to see you again."

"Mr. Jenkins, it's a pleasure as always, Sir. I'll see to your bags. Please come in."

Mrs. Colburn rushed forward, extending both hands in welcome. "C.T.! Hello, hello! Come in. Oh my goodness, I must say I'm so pleased! Eliza received your letters, the most recent posted in Baltimore just a few days ago." C.T. gathered Mrs. Colburn in a warm hug. "How wonderful that you're here, C.T." After a moment Mrs. Colburn turned and looked to the top of the stairs toward Eliza's bedroom. C.T. looked up, following Mrs. Colburn's gaze.

"Oh! Eliza, there you are. I was just about to call to you. I was just mentioning that you had received C.T.'s letters." Eliza, who was standing at the top of the stairs, nodded as Mrs. Colburn looked over her shoulder at C.T. and shrugged.

"Well! You've arrived, safely I see," Eliza began as she descended the stairs. "I'm so delighted that you are finally here, as, of course, is Mother. Come in, come in and sit next to the fire. Let's move away from the chill of the foyer." And, like her mother, she extended both hands toward C.T. as though the two might take up a promenade. C.T. took Eliza's soft, dainty hands into his own and kissed each one gently. His apprehension was

assuaged when she let him turn her right palm up, tracing the lines with his finger. Reflexively, she closed her hand around his fingertips and smiled up at him.

Several weeks after arriving Fair Haven, C.T. married the serenely beautiful Eliza Colburn. The wedding took place on the bride's twenty-seventh birthday, 09 December 1858.

The mid-day ceremony was held at the same church where Lucy and John had been married, in the church built by her Grandfather Davey. Once again hundreds of tapers lit the church, this time creating a soft winter glow. The excitement was as palpable as the curiosity over the gentleman who had won over Miss Colburn – and her mother.

The Congregational Meeting Hall in Fair Haven was filled to capacity, Reverend Edward Hooper presiding.

Eliza made her entrance escorted by Rufus. Her brother looked down at her appreciatively and they smiled at one another upon hearing the audible gasps of the guests. The bride was stunning, dressed in ivory satin. A crinoline hoop supported her gown in a bell shape that swayed with Eliza's graceful movements. A guipure lace overlay with a floral design border created the accents for the skirt and bodice. A fingertip-length ivory mantilla was attached to the crown of her upswept hairdo. The comb was adorned with a row of pink cultured seed pearls. Her dark brunette coloring contrasted with the shades of soft ivory her mother had chosen for her.

Susan had arrived from New York two days

before the wedding to serve as matron of honor. As the ceremony began, Eliza handed her white, leather-bound bible to her sister. Eliza's siblings stepped away to join their mother who was seated in the front pew.

The groom, looking distinguished in a European-cut navy blue suit, stepped forward and took the bride's hand. "Eliza?"

"Yes, C.T." And, the couple approached the altar together.

C.T. Jenkins was about to marry into the Colburn family, without one wedding invitation having been sent to his own.

Quinton Estate
One Month Later

C.T. watched from their bed as Eliza held her ruffled flannel nightgown over her head, letting it billow down over her lithe body. He then held the covers up, creating a tent of feather comforters; making it easier for her to return to his side, which she did in a scamper.

"Are you warm enough?" Eliza asked.

"You're teasing me, aren't you?" he laughed. "This northern cold is precisely the reason I have made my home in Florida." C.T. pulled Eliza toward him once she was back in bed, wrapping his leg possessively around her thighs. She responded by cuddling closer into his chest.

"And," she added, "it is precisely the reason it never occurred to me that you would follow me to Vermont."

"Yes, it does seem unlikely, doesn't it? There was a moment when I realized you were …well …most probably out of my life. But…" He changed the direction of his comments. "Well, Mrs. Jenkins, what do you have in mind for us today?"

"Would you like to bundle and take the sleigh down to the river?"

C.T. laughed heartily. "My dear, I just confessed how much I dislike the cold and you want us to spend our day outside? In January? In Vermont?"

She giggled appreciatively. "Not the whole day, C.T. But don't you want to see the property and the river? We could go past my grandparents former home. We can bundle, I'll wear my boots and fur muff. And, you certainly have good boots and warm clothing. It's such a sparkling day! You'll love seeing the Castleton!"

"If that's what you would like then, yes, my dear, we'll bundle and go out to see the surroundings," C.T. agreed.

"A sleigh ride to the river, how perfect!"

C.T. shivered at the thought.

"We'll go past the quarries, and my Grandfather Davey's former estate. It will be quite wonderful, you'll see. I could never live far from the water, and I haven't seen the Castleton or Poultney in weeks. In the winter the rivers are so turbulent and exciting!"

"Hmmm. Well, when we get home to Rose Hill, let's give some consideration to your preference for living close to water. I want *everyone* to be happy, finally."

"Everyone?" Eliza requested clarification.

"Certainly. You most of all, and your mother has dreams of happiness for herself and her children, I can assure you..."

"My mother?"

"Yes, Eliza. She would never encourage you to marry someone who would not have completed her own family. *She* has had everyone's happiness in mind."

Eliza cast aside the doubts that conjured at that moment, "We *should* get out today, it will be fun!" as she placed her palm tenderly against his temple. "We'll ask Gerald to have the sleigh prepared and then leave after breakfast. We can come back for an afternoon lunch and," snuggling closer to her husband, "a warm nap."

"Shall we get up then? Your mother is quite likely waiting for us in the breakfast room."

"Oh, darling, let's linger for a moment longer. We can join Mother for breakfast in just a bit."

Three months had passed since the wedding. Patches of tufted grass were visible as the winter snow pack slowly melted away. It would be another month before a full spectrum of color would herald the coming Vermont summer.

C.T. had decided that he and Eliza would wait until spring to make the southward voyage back to Florida. 'Mud days' made it nearly impossible for the couple to leave and C.T. contented himself with business trips to Fair Haven and stops at the post office and supply store.

He was delighted one bright, sparkling frost morning to have the post master slide a letter from Gainesville, Georgia across the counter toward him. He knew from the handwriting that the envelope had been addressed by John Donohoe. C.T. didn't open John's letter immediately, choosing to savor its receipt. Rather, he planned to open it at the supper table and read it aloud to his wife and mother-in-law.

Over supper, C.T. entertained the two women with his impressions of Fair Haven. He had placed the letter from John face up next to his plate. While the dishes were cleared C.T. ceremoniously took out his pocket knife and slit the envelope open, shaking out a single sheet of paper. The page was filled with the cramped handwriting of a man who had been as good as a brother so long ago.

Posted: *Gainesville, Georgia*

Cyprian T. Jenkins
Fair Haven, Vermont

February 1859

My Dear Friend,
Married, you say?! Is it true? Well, this is one woman that Sallie and I would love to meet.
We are doing well. The children, and the business Connor started, continue to grow. Except for Connor's death two years ago we have been blessed. Aunt Jessica remarried the year after you left for Florida. She is fine and sends her regards.
Back to you and your wife, Eliza. We are thrilled at your news and look forward to your arriving for a visit on your trip back from Vermont.
Anyone in town can direct you to the forge or, better, to our home. You will want to hire a coach to bring you from the docks.

Thanks, old friend, for writing me, I've missed you. And congratulations, we'll look forward to seeing you soon.
Warm regards,
John

C.T. folded the sheet of paper, taking his time to fumble it back into the envelope. *Twenty-five years; how did they slip by so easily? John and Sallie could be grandparents, for all I know. Will I even recognize John, or will he even recognize me?* He tried to imagine their faces, conjuring what they might look like in their fifties. He could barely recall what they looked like on their wedding day, only remembering his own bitterness and sense of betrayal over John's decision to settle in Georgia.

His moment of reflection was broken by Mrs. Colburn.

"How wonderful! I've always wanted to see more of Georgia than merely Savannah! We'll close up the house, and I'll help Eliza pack!"

Eliza laughed one disbelieving burst before covering her mouth. Her husband glanced at her quizzically before responding.

"Perfect, Mrs. Colburn! You can help Eliza with the details of our trip home to Florida and on the way we'll make a stop in Gainesville. The two of you will thoroughly enjoy the Donohoe's, I'm sure."

"Darling, I'm sure that I can manage the details. There's so much that hasn't been discussed," Eliza trailed the end of her sentence as was her practice.

"Well! We're all packed! I've just finished." Mrs. Colburn capped her announcement with high pitched laugh.

"Mother, I didn't realize before the wedding that you were interested, or planning to make your home in Florida…"

"Really, Eliza. I don't know think it's necessary for us to pick at every detail, or intention. It will be wonderful for all of us to be in Florida, together."

Eliza set down her embroidery and stood up, placing her fists in the small of her back, "Mother, won't you miss Fair Haven and Rufus?"

"Eliza, there is no longer anything for me to look forward to here. Susan's children have grown past needing a doting grandmother. Besides, my being in Florida will induce Susan to visit *us* for a change, which is wholly reasonable now that her children are older. There's absolutely nothing that compels me to be in Vermont any longer."

"But Mother; your home, talking over the expansion of manufacturing with Rufus, Uncle Israel— Won't you miss all of this more than you think you would miss me?"

"My goodness, no! It will be exciting to be back in Florida. And in time, I can help you with your new home, and children. I'll be happy there. MaryAnn and I will be close. C.T. and I are dear friends. What is here for me now? Really, Eliza, I've done so much to see to our security and, as it turns out, our happiness. I've always looked out for what was best for you. Aren't you interested in what is best, now, for me?"

Eliza picked up her embroidery without answering her mother's question. *You've never concerned yourself with my interests before, Mother. Why should you start now?*

**

The Donohoe's

The driver of the buggy mopped his face with the back of his dust-covered sleeve. His effort left a streak that divided his forehead from the lower half of his face. He used his stained hat, the brim rolled into his fist, to shade his eyes.

"Well, here you are!" nodding his head.

C.T., Eliza and Mrs. Colburn stared up at an expansive wood frame house with white shutters. A generous overhang protected the front and east side of the house from the pervasive, relentless Georgia sun. The gabled manse stood on the side of a wide, dusty lane. Beyond the residential area were small farms set on a rise, stretching in either direction along the horizon. The fields of each farm were plowed into neat checkerboard patterns. Red barns of various shapes and sizes dotted the rise, and large farmhouses anchored each property, some fenced and some not. Orchards planted in large squares between properties cut the rise into visuals of fruit cobbler.

John was waiting when the buggy driver pulled up. Having following the buggy from town a husky red-haired youth scampered in front and then past the open buggy. The youth took his place next to his father, who placed one hand on the boy's shoulder and trussed his hair with the other.

The driver jumped down and began tugging and scooting two trunks to the edge of the buggy's back platform, seemingly relieved to be done with the trip and eager to deposit his passengers. The only thing, other than receiving payment for his fare, on his mind was the cold drink waiting for him at the saloon they had passed on their way to John and Sallie's home.

"Eliza, Mrs. Colburn, just a few moments, please." C.T. climbed down from the buggy. A long overdue task lay in front of him. C.T. strode up the walkway toward John and his unresolved past. John and Cyprian took stock of each other, until John gently pushed his son toward the driver.

"Go help with the bags, son." The two men continued to stare at each other, looking for similarities and differences in each other's faces. Twenty-five years melted away as though their last encounter was yesterday. "My God, Cyprian."

"Thank you for answering my letter, John."

The men's handshake turned into a gripping hug as John released his old friend's hand and threw his right hand around C.T.'s shoulder. Examining the crow's feet around his eyes, the small pockets of sag at his jaw line at John's craggy throat, C.T. realized that his friend saw the same age indicators in *his* face. John's glossy black hair was streaked with silver-grey, grown over his ears. A lock of unruly hair still insisted on falling across John's forehead.

John stared at Cyprian's weathered, ruddy face. When he was twenty-two, Cyprian had a teenager's stature and a child's sense that expeditions should be never-ending. At forty-seven his waist had thickened. His sandy-blond hair, now flecked with grey, cascaded in unruly waves long enough to sit on a white starched collar. His driven, serious nature had finally met up with his age, and he was complemented by the process. C.T.'s piercing blue eyes were even more serious than two decades earlier; the result of years of scouting, settling, politicking, and drinking.

"Sallie is waiting in the house. Don't embarrass her by looking, but I'd bet that the curtains to the parlor window are askew. I have no doubt she is pointing out your flaws to the children at this very moment," he teased. Taking over the role of host, he added, "Well, let's meet Mrs. Jenkins and her mother, shall we?"

The two men helped the women down from the buggy. C.T. settled with the driver, then introduced the first women, of any significance, to share his life since his mother had died nearly thirty years earlier.

"John, I'd like you to meet my mother-in-law, Mrs. John Colburn, of Vermont. And, this is my wife, Eliza."

"What a pleasure. A real pleasure. My wife, Sallie, is waiting inside. We're thrilled to have your company over the next few weeks. Please, C.T., ladies," and John led the way up the walkway toward the house which was lined on either side with early spring daisies their faces smiling in welcome. A ribbon of brightly colored flower beds stretched across the front of the house, a bounty of various textures.

"Lovely, isn't it?" Eliza asked.

"Yes, it is beautiful. Sallie is obviously a devoted gardener," her mother replied.

Sitting in the parlor one afternoon, a week into their visit, Eliza sat embroidering while Sallie and Mrs. Colburn listened to John and C.T. reminisce their youth. Sallie stood up, and as she retreated to the kitchen she signaled to Eliza.

"More tea?"

"Yes, that would be lovely, thank you." Eliza laid aside her hoop and followed Sallie through the kitchen out to the back porch. The women arranged the mismatched rockers to face each other. Their tea was brought out to them.

"We were surprised, but thrilled, to hear that Cyprian had married," revealed Sallie.

"You were surprised to hear that C.T. had gotten married?"

"Yes. Although, of course, it's been many years, the last time I saw Cyprian he was a rather angry young man. He was especially angry with John. The two had set out to leave Baltimore in—" She stopped for a moment before continuing, "1833. It was seven years after Cyprian's mother had died. Over all the years that have passed, and the many times John or I would bring C.T. into our conversations, I didn't think he would ever get over his mother's death, or his father's bitterness, enough to marry. I've often wondered what his impression of me was back then."

"C.T. doesn't confide many of his impressions to me. But, I'm sure that he thinks you are wonderful. He has long talks with my mother. They are very good friends, I presume you have gathered."

"Yes, it's clear that they are very close. Look who is sitting next to him in the parlor while he and John talk. You understand why that is, don't you?"

Eliza shook her head and shrugged, exhaling a sigh. She didn't try to hide from Sallie the bitter tears of frustration that beaded in her eyelashes.

"He's stuck. He's stuck in the moment he lost his mother. He was fifteen when his youngest brother was born and his mother died. His mother's sister died the following day and his grandmother died later the same year. Imagine. After C.T.'s sixteenth birthday, the only woman left in the Jenkins family was his sister, Mary Josephine, who lived in Washington, D.C. She died just a few years later.

"By the time Cyprian and John left Baltimore, there hadn't been any women in the Jenkins household for perhaps five years. Not until his younger brothers married and he again had sisters-in-law, aunts, and cousins were there any women in the Jenkins' extended household."

Sallie continued in a soft voice and leaned forward, taking Eliza's hands into her own. "I don't understand it all myself, but it was quite clear when I met him that he wasn't interested in starting a family, as most men are at that age. It seems as though your mother has created the best situation for the three of you, by recognizing a boyhood loss that C.T. seems unable to overcome. Following her lead might just bridge the differences between you and C.T. I don't mean to imply that your husband is flawed; I don't know him that well, frankly. But there appears to be a wall between you and Cyprian that your mother seems to have breached. Maybe understanding that he came from a family comprised almost entirely of men will help you find a role for yourself in his life."

"My role has been and continues to be, it seems, defined by my mother. She is as much married to C.T. as I am."

"I see. Well, then, that's that." The depth of Eliza's bitterness was clear.

John foretold C.T.'s future as the two left the house to walk to the blacksmith operation that Connor McAllister had established, "Eliza is really a lovely woman. You will have a family to be proud of in good time, C.T.," John foretold as he and C.T. left

"Well, it was time, John. I'm middle aged, tired of fighting, and Mrs. Colburn is such an enlightened lively woman."

"Mrs. Colburn? Uhmm, I was referring to Eliza."

"Yes, yes. That is, I knew Eliza and I would benefit from her mother's presence. It just seemed right to me. If you're talking of having a family to be proud of, or pride in general, I've done a lot of things I'm proud of frankly. But having Mrs. Colburn and Eliza back in Florida is a necessity in my life, not something on which to build pride."

John looked at him quizzically, "It's interesting to hear you proclaim the necessity of a family, if you don't mind my saying so. But, what are you proud of, more than having a beautiful family?"

"I'm a legislator, John. I'm in my fourth two-year term. I've accomplished as much for myself by settling in Florida as my grandfather accomplished when the Jenkins' were settling Maryland."

"Well, then, Cyprian. You have accomplished all that you set out to do, it appears. "

"Time will tell, won't it?"

* * *

WAR

C.T. called up to the house from the dock of his Homosassa River farm, "Eliza, I'll return tomorrow afternoon! I'll bring back whatever provisions I can find." They had purchased land along the river upon returning to Florida following their wedding.

The cottage featured a wide plank porch, and a generous overhang that ran across the front of the house. The setting of their home was modest and the farm's yield had become meager. Dinner consisted of figs and yams in small portions. The chickens had all been turned over to pay taxes to the Confederacy. And, the cattle had been driven inland toward Gainesville the previous year to feed the Confederate troops.

Eliza nodded and waved, acknowledging C.T. while cuddling their infant son, John-Colburn. Tossing the lines onto the dock that connected their property to the commerce opportunities of the Homosassa, C.T. sailed west to where the river spills into the gulf. He circumnavigated the marsh at Mason Creek, gliding past Porpoise Bay and crisscrossing the mud that was gorging from Gator Creek. He enjoyed every minute of the sail, remembering back to sailing on his grandfather's schooner as the old man brought tobacco to market. Pulling in the sheets and setting the main as the wind rustled across the gulf was calming. C.T. nearly forgot the troubling circumstances of this particular trip.

There wasn't anything noteworthy along the shore between the outlet of the Homosassa River and Bay Port; that is unless you were a Confederate who counted on the salt mines, the hidden inlets of the shallow gulf, the swamps, and the miles of sea grass along the coast where supplies could be tucked away by squads of soldiers operating silently and secretly in the tranquil environment.

C.T. had come to know every landmark, tiny cove and hidden lagoon between the Withlacoochee and Homosassa rivers. So much so that he could draw his own maps of the area. Maps that would be distributed that night, outlining every estuary, inlet and cypress grove along the gulf coast between Bay Port and Pensacola. Maps that had been carefully drawn and tucked into the hold of his twenty-six foot sloop.

He was resigned to the decisions that would have to be made that evening. C.T. tacked out past Pine Island, in at Coogler's Beach, and through the maze of islands toward the welcoming outline of Bay Port's dock facilities.

It was early evening by the time he moored his sloop at the dock adjacent to Kildall's Reading Room, tying a cleat hitch at the fore and aft of his sloop. The water lapped softly, licking the faded hull.

Walking into Kildall's, C.T. found the reading room quiet, the mood somber.

"Anaconda Plan! Ha! That's real good," Richard Hale scoffed and then looked around Kildall's to see if anyone was listening. They were listening, but despondent, they weren't responding.

"Colonel!" Kildall greeted his friend as C.T. strode in, recognized as one of the reading room's most regular customers. That is, a regular customer up until his marriage two and a-half years earlier. It was seven o'clock in the evening when Joseph Kildall slid a shot of Evan Williams and a piping hot plate of cumin-flavored rice across the counter toward C.T.

"Thanks Joseph," C.T. nodded to his friend. No money was exchanged. Kildall had stopped taking money for meals months ago and only collected for drinks on occasion, when a bill featuring Lady Liberty and an unfurled First National Confederate flag was pressed into his palm. The design on the currency reflected the confidence and swagger prevalent throughout the budding Confederacy at the time of its mint. C.T. fingered the Confederate bill. *Our own currency. How affirming to have our own currency. Even if backing it to a funded Treasury has been impossible, C.T.* thought.

One meager lantern lit the expansive space, compelling the men at Kildall's to sit in dimmed lighting that cast deep shadows. Although C.T. could determine the identities of the men sitting beyond the pale circle of light, it would have been hard for a passerby looking in the window to determine who was at Kildall's that evening. Eighteen men sat around in sets of twos and threes, talking quietly among themselves.

"Joseph," recommended C.T., "let's move to the back room. We can spread out the maps out better there." Chairs and tables scraped and creaked as the men moved toward the back of Kildall's business. Kildall picked up the lantern to bring up the rear, leaving the Reading Room dark and eerily empty.

Two more lanterns were lit and the men finally started working together, unrolling maps and setting paper weights at their corners. The charts which depicted the harbors, coves, and lagoons that encompassed Florida's gulf coast.

"What do you think?" C.T. asked Johnny Johns. The swarthy young man was C.T.'s sounding board, and C.T. placed complete trust in the younger man.

"I think we're going to be in desperate straits real soon," Johns admitted. "The Union's East Gulf blockading operation has been in place long enough to encumber any attempts of making it to Bermuda, or the Bahamas, or even Cuba. The simple effort of running the blockade isn't going well. Revenue from the cotton crop is down ninety-five percent 'cause of so many thousands of bales being confiscated, or burned, by

Union forces.   Ha! Our cotton farmers are getting…what? . . .   one nickel off their crops in Confederate dollars for what they had received one dollar in U.S. Treasury dollars in 1859."

"Well, the more cotton we can stockpile in the Keys, the more cotton can be shuttled to auction in Cuba," offered Thomas Phillips. *Funny how war drags some men into maturity,* thought C.T.

"We'll use Shriver's Bay as the main collection point, then we can bring what we've collected in crops out on four or five sloops via the Little Homosassa or south around Tiger Tail Bay," was M.A. Beck's suggestion.

"If we have one look-out at Crystal Bay reporting back here every two or three days; and one look out at Fillman Bayou—same schedule—we should be able to pick up a pattern of when the Yanks are moving their squadrons," again Johnny Johns, the strategist.

One speaker at a time, no speak-over. So far so good; men I can count on until the war is over and the South has won, C.T. thought, concentrating on the furrowed, thoughtful faces of men he would have to trust with his life and who would have to trust him with theirs.

Each Bay Port man concentrated on the instructions given.   These first few months of war contrasted solemnly to the afternoon at Kildall's when they were all boisterously discussing the outrage of heightened tariffs. The state militia hadn't experienced any skirmishes, but the Union blockade was beginning to starve the families out—regardless of which side of the states' rights and slavery issues they were on. The South was fighting starvation as much as the aggression.

"The sloops will get the bales to the steamers; the steamers will outrun the gunboats, right?" the men grumbled in agreement.

"Only between nightfall and pre-dawn," were the instructions; then the words, "set fire to any bales that are unquestionably going to be confiscated. But, remember how much we are depending on getting the bales to the Keys, and across. Use good judgment."

"Stay in your squads and be responsible for choosing your best shot from your assigned position." were Beck's final words before he lifted the paper weights and rolled the maps up, handing the heavy scrolls back to C.T.

Kildall blew out the lanterns as the men slipped out of the back room and into the reading room one, or two, at a time. Very little light came in through the windows, just a bit of moonlight onto the floor of the saloon. The men lined up along the wall and single file slipped out into the night, some nodding to the darkened room as they left.

Johnny Johns was in front of C.T. He slipped out first.

"My house," he whispered over his shoulder. They would meet M.A. Beck and the other members of their unit at the Johns' home to go over the specifics of their plan.

They would each leave Johns' before dawn to return to their families. Then the men would impatiently wait for bales of cotton to be collected along the shallow backwater channels. The sloops and flat-bottomed barges would be loaded at night. The chore would be finished before dawn, when sloops laden with cotton and crops cargo would be poled through the shallow estuaries out to Cedar Keys. From there, they would make their way down the coast, toward the Caribbean markets upon which the Confederacy depended.

Life On The Homosassa, 1862

Eliza came out to the sun porch with two year old Annie on her hip. Mrs. Colburn was sitting with her embroidery, enjoying the morning sun.

"Good morning, Mother."

"Good morning, darlings."

"Where is C.T.? Is he up?"

Mrs. Colburn reached up to take her grand-daughter. "You're like a sleepy-eyed cuddly little puppy. So soft and warm."

Annie nuzzled the nape of her grandmother's neck while at the same time sucking her thumb. She peered out at the world with expressive brown eyes.

After settling into an embrace that surrounded her granddaughter, Mrs. Colburn replied, "C.T. was already up when I woke. He was dressed and studying maps at his drafting table. He's taking the sloop down river with John Johns and Mr. Beck,"

"Really? Did he say when he would be back? He didn't mention to me that he was going out for the day."

"Three days. He told me he was going out for three days."

"Three days! I don't recall him mentioning that he would be gone for so long."

"Hmm, well, that's what he said yesterday."

"Yesterday? And you couldn't mention it to me? Either of you?

"Eliza, I would think that your husband would have mentioned directly to you how long he was going to be away. I'm not going to come between the two of you. "

Eliza glared at her mother as she took Annie out of her grandmother's arms and walked back into the house. The screen door slammed behind her.

Mrs. Colburn called after her, her voice shooting through the screen door, "I would like to make a point, Eliza. I independently kept up with your father's business. I knew the 'what' and 'why' of every decision he made."

The next three days were chilled by the struggle that continued between Mrs. Colburn and Eliza. Grandmother and mother silently handed their precious package, Annie, back and forth exchanging very few words. Eliza cared for her infant son, who was still at the breast.

Eliza was toweling Annie off her and braiding her daughter's long hair after bath time on the third afternoon of C.T.'s absence. Mrs. Colburn sat with her embroidery hoop on the sun porch, enjoying the soft, comforting warmth of Florida. She observed the tropical fauna along the river's edge and considered her future. The egrets plucked morsels from the muddy banks of the Homosassa and lifted their claws out of the silt, shifting their weight from one delicate leg to the other.

C.T.'s sloop came into sight mid-afternoon. Mrs. Colburn stood up, leaving her embroidery hoop on the rocker, and walked across the sloping lawn to meet her contemporary. Two slaves who worked the Homosassa crops came down from the farm to help pull in the lines and lower the main sail. C.T. jumped from the deck of the sloop to the dock.

"Mrs. Colburn! Are you my welcoming committee?" C.T. greeted his mother-in-law and then, before waiting for a response, finished instructing his men on how the sloop was to be moored.

"How did it go?" Mrs. Colburn whispered once she reached the end of the dock.

"It's hard. Almost impossible. We got through, but I hate this," he growled under his breath.

"After the children go to bed, I need to hear what happened. I've been pacing since you left. Have you heard anything about Richmond, or Yorktown? Anything at all?"

C.T. hugged his friend's shoulders and looked toward his cottage. The property was beginning to show signs of wear. "No, Dear, other than that the siege of

Richmond continues. It is all but impossible to get news of McClellan's movements to the Gulf Coast—or risky to try—let alone get news of your Albert, if that's what you mean. I'm sorry. Not to alarm you, but it's not going well for the Union forces. McClellan was caught off guard in his amphibian assault by Johnston. That's all I know. Unless we can get a copy of a city newspaper, which isn't likely, I'm not sure how we will be able to track Albert's well-being."

The two made their way up the dock toward the cottage in silence.

C.T.'s greeting to Mrs. Colburn had carried to the cottage where Eliza was attending Annie. She gathered her up in a hug, exclaiming "Your father!" Rushing through the cottage, she bustled across the porch and bounded down the steps leading to the dock. C.T. kissed his wife's forehead and took Annie from her as Mrs. Colburn moved closer, cooing at the toddler.

"Darling, you said you were going out to Cedar Keys, but it wasn't clear that your absence would extend three days! You don't mean to cause a strain do you?"

"Eliza, I told your mother that Mr. Johns and I were taking the sloop out to for a few days, surely she told you."

"Oh my goodness, C.T." Stone-faced, she turned and walked back up to the cottage, carrying Annie.

"Mrs. Colburn?"

Mrs. Colburn shrugged her shoulders choosing to stay behind, hoping for additional news about the Union's efforts that might tell her where her son or General McClellan's forces might be ordered once the Peninsula Campaign had ended.

Eliza could hear her mother, whose voice was picked up by a slight breeze. Mrs. Colburn had now turned her attention to inquiries about Davis' Confederate administration.

Eliza fed Annie in the kitchen before supper while the cook set the dining room table for the three adults. A thick, peppered bouillabaisse had been made from the contents of C.T.'s crab pot which had been dragging lazily behind the sloop during his sail out to Cedar Keys and southward.

As they sat down to supper, the two women began discussing the garden. "Shall we begin pulling the carrots tomorrow, Eliza?"

"I don't know, Mother. Shall we?"

Not interested in listening to the beginnings of another squabble, C.T. turned the conversation to the topic of navigating the coast off Bay Port.

Eliza plucked at C.T.'s sleeve, "Darling, are you tired? Would like to retire early this evening?"

"Yes, Eliza. I probably will go to bed early. Why don't you put Annie and John to sleep, and I'll join you in a little bit. I want to show your mother something on the map." C.T. patted Eliza's hand, then lifted it from his sleeve and placing it back on the table, resuming his conversation with Mrs. Colburn.

Eliza pushed away from the dining room table, throwing her napkin to her plate.

"Eliza?" C.T. said.

She did not answer, but went to retrieve Annie from the nanny's watchful eye. The little girl was playing happily on the braided rug in the nursery with her infant brother.

"Hello, my most truest darling." Eliza held Annie close and walked over to the nursery's window. Humming, and rocking her daughter, she watched the egrets continue their specter-like dance as the sun sank heavily toward the horizon. Gauzy cirrus clouds floated across a streaked pink sky, and slowly, the spread of inky blue advanced across the horizon making the clouds invisible.

After kissing and nuzzling her daughter and giving John a reassuring pat, she blew out the candles in the nursery and attended to her bedtime rituals. Slipping out of her clothing and letting her nightgown slide over her lilac-fragranced skin, she pulled back the covers on her side of the bed. She slid into bed, welcomed the comfort of the cool, crisp bedding, and sank immediately into a deep sleep.

C.T. was smoking his pipe on the veranda, staring out to the river after the children had been put to bed and the dishes cleared, when Mrs. Colburn found him, "Well?" The glow of the embers in his pipe as he took each draw brightened. The currents rolled westward toward the gulf catching twigs and moss in little aquatic whorls. "What do you think, C.T.?"

"I think the blockade is tightening around us and the salt mines will continue to serve as the Union's target practice. I think the immediate future looks grim. There was a blockader approaching from Tampa Bay when I left my watch this afternoon. Not one Union steamer in three weeks, and all of a sudden this one appears. Mr. Beck and Mr. Johns are patrolling the shore between the Homosassa spill-out and Tiger Island tonight, and keeping a watch going. It's been a month since we discovered the last dismantled salt mines. One thing is certain. Without the salt, meat cannot be cured. The men fighting in Georgia and northward will soon go on limited rations. That is what I think."

C.T. thought back over the previous three days. A softened version of the situation would have done fine; but he wasn't sure if what he had encountered would reassure or alarm Mrs. Colburn. "Are you sorry you're caught here now, Mrs. Colburn?"

"I don't know, yet, C.T."

No more words were exchanged and C.T.'s thoughts turned back to his watch over the past three days. The marsh grass itched, the sun broiled, his canteen ran dry much too soon on each scouting trip. The shimmer on the water from the blinding sun caused mirages. Maybe a Union steamer was approaching from the horizon; but then again, maybe not. Hour after hour he would pace the stretch of beach, slip back in to the marshes to traverse each inlet.

The boredom was only exceeded by the worry. During those hours he wanted to be back at his farm, enjoying nights such as this one, cooled by breezes that whispered across the river front veranda. He resented the interruption of the war on his new life.

Then he broke the silence, "We saw a trawler coming up over the horizon from Tampa. Had it arrived just twenty-four hours later, we would have already put this months' plan into action. Now we will have to lie low. Wait. The bales will remain in storage at each farm. It's a cat and mouse game. I only see the picture from this small stretch of coast; whatever else is happening in this god-damned war is happening well beyond my awareness. I'm sorry."

Resigned, Mrs. Colburn nodded and went inside to take her worries to bed.

After several hours of fitful sleep Eliza woke to feel C.T. slip into bed. She believed it to be around midnight. But when she woke up the next morning the covers on her husband's side of the bed were pulled up neatly, as though he might not have come to bed after all.

"C.T. the children and I are going to spend a few days with Precious." Eliza stated, finding her husband at his drafting table.

"What, the Ederington's don't have enough children of their own to take care of?" he snorted.

"Annie needs a few days with playmates, and Charlotte and Burilla want to see John. We'll leave before noon. Isum can take us over in the buggy; he'll be back by mid-afternoon."

"Well, Mrs. Jenkins. It would seem you have all the details taken care of. I'll be busy over the next day or so; and I'm sure your Mother would be bored while I'm coming and going."

"It may be the case that Mother would be bored with you not home, if you're suggesting that you have business to attend. But she's not coming with me. I presume *you'll* let her know."

"Your mother's not going with you and the children? Eliza, I don't know what's gotten into you; but taking the children for a visit—no matter how short—without being accompanied by your Mother may not be your best suit."

"Perhaps not, Mr. Jenkins; but it's the suit I'm playing."

"Eliza, let's speak to her. You'll have to talk it over with her."

"I need do no such thing. My things are packed, and I'll be busy this morning getting the children ready. You two can speak to each other all you want."

Eliza retreated as her husband shook his head and turned his attention back to his maps.

That evening dinner dragged on in awkward silence. "Mrs. Colburn, if you would pass the bread, please."

"Of course, of course! What a wonderful meal."

"Well, at least a very quiet meal. How long did Eliza say she and the children would be gone?"

"C.T. I don't know. I thought she would have told you."

"Uhm, no. She didn't, actually. Well, there's the irony, if I understood her argument with me this morning."

"Well! I'm sure Precious will send her home in a day or two. Many times I would bundle Albert and Eliza and get on the train to New York. Oh, my goodness! How exciting it was! To be going someplace. The children would be delighted. It will be good for Eliza and we'll have a chance to catch up with each other."

"Yes, of course, I see. I wasn't sure if you might have tried to talk her out of going."

Oh, my, no! Of course not."

The dishes were cleared by the cook whose lips were pressed in silence, although she looked in anticipation from Mrs. Colburn to C.T. for some word from either of them. C.T. nodded to her and moved his chair back, causing a loud scrape on the pinewood floor.

"I think I'll smoke my pipe out on the dock. Excuse me, Mrs. Colburn."

"Well, then, I think I'll return to my embroidery. You can tell me all about your day when you come in."

At the end of the dock C.T. tapped his pipe and lit the fragrant, tightly packed tobacco which flared on his first deep draw. The smoke curled perfectly against the back of his throat. The ritual was soothing. He stared across the river as two herons swooped into the branches of a lone pine just twenty feet or so from the river's edge. Their smoky grey almost blended with the background of the evening woods.

The male passed a good sized twig to the female who tangled it into the nest, pecking at the mess in an exaggerated manner. He continued to watch the two as the female plucked at the male with her elongated orange beak. Shifting his pipe to his left hand C.T. reached down to retrieve the tumbler of whiskey that he had placed on the dock at his feet. He welcomed the hot sting of alcohol and then turned his attention back to the pair of herons.

There were no fledglings in the nest – yet. Other members of their colony were no doubt engaged in the activity of pecking at a nest, deeper in the woods. These two orange-beaked preeners would stay together until a predator—or an accident—took one of them. Year after year they would stand next to each other in the currents, plucking morsels from the water with their elongated chop sticks. Their fledglings would be nudged and routed until one by one they would tuck their not-yet graceful necks and flutter softly to the grasses at the base of the tree.

Annie would love seeing this.

He slowly turned the empty tumbler in his hand, staring into the emptiness. Sighing, he started to walk back to the cottage. One lantern shone through the windows, glowing like a beacon. He fixed on that glow and walked through the underbrush and onto the porch.

Mrs. Colburn was rocking in her chair, her embroidery hoop lying in her lap, her eyes closed. She looked up expectantly when he came in.

"I'm going over to the Ederington's tomorrow morning. One night away from home should be enough for Eliza."

C.T. Jenkins Journal Entry:

We had been successful in shipping the cotton bales to buyers who had already run the blockade with many thousands of bales, I know not where, but this I do know, of little profit to myself. When I imagined that everything with me was in the most successful operation, I took my sailboat, and two of my men to visit a near encampment of troops down the coast a few miles. I had not proceeded far when I was run down by a fast government patrol steamer, and made a prisoner...When taken aboard I was unceremoniously ordered to be put in the lower forward deck, and a guard placed over me. After much persuasion, and some indignation at the conduct of the deck officer, I was permitted to go aft, and see the Captain. "What is it you want, Sir?" I replied, "Is not your name Semmes?" He said: "Well, yes, what is that to you?" My answer was: "Well sir, you are my cousin; your mother is my Aunt Matilda." (I then related the circumstances of the previous days.) I noticed that Captain Semmes listened very attentively to my statement, and sending for the Officer on duty, said: "Have the two negro prisoners released at once, get them ready for going ashore, give them such rations as you think sufficient for their sustenance if they have far to go." After the Officer left the cabin, Captain Semmes said: "Cousin, take a seat, I will return in a moment," on his returning he handed me one hundred dollars as he said to pay my way home. This offer I positively declined, but with many thanks, stating that it might lead to much trouble in case it should become known, I assured him that I did not need any funds.

   C.T. Jenkins

* * *

20

BETRAYAL

A lone rower pulled his oars toward the steamer anchored three hundred yards from the port. It was that particular moment in the day when the sun dips below the horizon and the shadows lengthen.   Seagulls swooped and screeched from the beach calling the man away from the depths and back to shore. His eyes were hollowed in deprivation, his skin yellowed. He wheezed as he made the final pull toward the Union steamer.

Union sailors lined up on the shore-side of the steamer watching the anguished struggle of the sailor as he made his way across the water to their ship.

"We know this Johnny" observed Captain Boulware, his burly arms crossed. "If you can stand the stench, help him board." The Union sailors grabbed the line tossed up by the lanky, skeletal figure and secured the dingy to the larger vessel.

Two younger men leaned over and lifted the man aboard, then backed away, repulsed by the small of the man as he crumbled to the deck of the ship. The captain shouldered the men out of the way and came up to the unskilled mariner, nudging him with the toe of this boot.

"What do you have for us, Johnny?" greeted Boulware looking down as the puddle of humanity looked up to a ring of faces.

"My wife and I are starving. We have nothing left to eat," began the oarsman.

Captain Boulware laughed dryly, "Well, that's the point. Now, tell us something we don't know." His men chuckled at their Commander's wit.

The sailor started over, "I need to take back food. Something." He coughed spittle and spit onto the deck of the ship.

A lantern was passed forward and hung on the lanyard as it was now nightfall. The vessel rocked gently as the waters off Bay Port lapped against the steamers' port side.

"What if I give you rations to take back to the wife and neighbors back on the farm, but you don't make it? I mean, look at the condition you're in, mate," taunted the Captain.

"I'll make it back," wailed the man, as though the promise meant anything to anyone besides the weary woman waiting for food who now stood in a home next to the shore just within the tree line, peering out the windows.

"Well, Johnny. You know how it works. We're in the trading business; information for rations. What did you row out here to tell us?" Boulware wanted to end the cat and mouse game early and see if the fool had anything better than last time to tell him.

"Don't call me Johnny; that's not my name," was the only assertion made by the farmer-turned-mariner.

"Now, Mister, you know you don't want us to know your name. Why, what if one of your boys overtakes our steamer here with their little skiffs and takes us prisoner? And, what if, under questioning we have to tell them of our association with you. Now who would that work out for?"

The Captain nodded.

Two burlap sacks of rations, sewn shut, were tossed at the man from the back of the cluster of sailors. The sacks landed on the man's foot, eliciting a slight grimace.

"That's yours for the right information, *Johnny Reb*."

"I'm not a Rebel – quite the contrary."

"Well, you are high minded, for a man in your pathetic circumstances, now aren't you? Get on with it then, what do you have to tell us?"

The invalid, bent on surviving his ordeal, began, "There'll be a shallow draft sailboat loaded with cotton bales and four or five men coming from the mouth of the river toward Cedar Keys, the next full moon."

"That's a start. More toward the beginning of early morning or during the night?"

"I don't know," whimpered the man.

"Christ! Who cares, then? Okay then, let's see. Any sugar? How much cotton?"

"I don't know," echoed the man, beginning to lose hope for the rations that lay at his feet.

"Well Johnny, these fine gentlemen are going to put you back on your skiff there. But with only one bag of rations. We'll hold this second bag here for you after we run down your compatriot's little shipment."

The Captain surveyed the amused faces of his men. He nodded to two of them, who lowered the single bag of rations into the skiff, then helped the defeated informant back to his boat. They untied the lines to allow the man to return to a community whose members went to bed hungry and woke up ravenous, day after day.

Cedar Keys, 01 June 1863

Are the children asleep, Eliza?" C.T. looked up from his work table as his wife came in from the children's bedrooms.

"Yes. John-Colburn has been asleep since his sweet little head hit the pillow. Annie still has a fever. Mother's with her now."

"Good."

"You've got to get some sleep yourself, C.T. If you're off—" her voice trailed.

"Yes, I'll be off before dawn."

Through the evening the chirp of crickets formed a wreath around the perimeter of the cottage. Occasionally a bull frog joined in, adding texture to the symphony.

Annie's fever continued through the night. Her grandmother tip-toed across the children's room by candle light A full heavy moon provided shafts of soft light that poured in through the windows. Mrs. Colburn paced her alcove silently until midnight.

Eliza and C.T. whispered to each other between spells of sleep. C.T. held his wife in his arms, their heads resting on the same pillow. At three o'clock in the morning she asked the same question she asked each time he left the house 'for a sail'.

"Cyprian, you promised to tell me. How long will you be gone this time?"

"Not long, Eliza. Don't worry. And if Annie isn't better in a few days have Mae go to Mrs. McKeown's and let her know how you are doing."

An hour later C.T. slipped carefully out of bed, pulled on his clothes and crept into his children's room. He stroked John-Colburn's head, causing the baby to stir slightly. Moving silently to his daughter's bed he noted her flushed cheeks and the lock of dark hair plastered to her forehead. A doll lay next to Annie, legs dangling over the edge of the bed. Its porcelain face suffered cracked glazing, hair was missing from its tufted, nearly-bald head; its body was filled with sand. C.T. straightened the doll, placing it next to Annie's side, then rested his palm against his daughter's cheek before turning to leave the room.

Mrs. Colburn had been watching him from the doorway. She extended her arms for a hug and was taken into a comforting hug.

"I cannot bear another loss, C.T."

"Please don't dwell on the past, Mrs. Colburn."

"Stay safe, then. And come right back to us."

Eliza was waiting for C.T. out on the porch. He found her staring at the slow-moving river currents and the inky blueness that had captivated her four years earlier. He pulled at her crossed arms, untangling her knotted body to bring her in close. They were enclosed together. C.T. rested his chin on the top of her head. The Fourth Florida infantry member was fifty-one years old.

"Eliza, you don't have to say what you're thinking; I know you don't want me to take this risk. But, the children are hungry. We're all hungry. If we don't get through the blockade as often as possible, get as much cotton down to Havana as we can, we will continue to be hungry and the children will be weakened by fever this winter."

"But . . ."

"I know you understand, and I know that you and your mother are strong enough to survive me being gone for a few days. I'll be home before you miss me." With that, C.T. picked up his pack and marched slowly, but decisively, down the steps of his cottage.

Once he established his stride through the brush, C.T.'s tracking instincts took over. The adrenaline surge familiar to him from his scouting days returned, his senses heightened. As he sure-footed toward his destination, he felt as though he could see farther and hear more keenly than he had in years. He moved noiselessly. His second language, Creek, came back to him although the Seminoles and Creeks had completed their migration years earlier. His thoughts were coming to him in a language other than English.

My god, I have constantly been fighting one cause or another for the past thirty years.

It had been a long time since he had left the comfortable, established surroundings of Baltimore Town and his father's home, Huntington Manor.

Suddenly he sensed someone walking parallel to him, about sixty feet away. C.T. stopped and focused his eyes keenly; the hair on the back of his neck was standing up. It was as though sight was the only sense he possessed. He turned his head slightly. His intense focus softened when he realized the person shadowing him was Johnny Johns. He cupped his hands and mimicked the call of a whippoorwill.

The call was returned.

C.T. could see Johns' bright smile and his hand raised in acknowledgement. *Thank God, it's Johns and not someone else. This tension between neighbors is meant to break us.*

C.T. and Johns walked toward each other. Meeting, they grasped hands in a reassuring handshake and continued on through matted, grassy flats to a spot behind a grouping of mangroves where C.T.'s sailboat was hidden. Spanish moss had been flung over the spreader bars, below the shroud to aid in its camouflage. But, anyone who lived on the Homosassa River knew exactly where the Jenkins' sloop was hidden. Johns and C.T. readied the boat, and cast off smoothly toward Monkey Island. They knew exactly where along the river bank the bales of cotton would be waiting. They would be stacked and ready to be moved along to Cedar Keys. The two men poled their way toward the Gulf, past shallow bay inlets and mangroves that, in the pre-dawn light, served as hulking witnesses of their activities.

As Johns and C.T. pulled in at Sam's Bayou, a manatee splashed in the water, the only signal that the sailboat had pulled up to the shore. Three men came out of the groves from different directions

The men swung onto the deck of C.T.'s sloop. As dawn lit the valleys and hammocks, the small farms, and then the waterways, the small militia sailed toward the serene, warm waters of the Gulf of Mexico. Sunrise was at their back. Under any other circumstance it would have been a worry-free, boisterous outing for the five men. However, C.T.'s shallow draft sloop would soon be weighted down with bales of cotton that the men would need to stealthfully load from collection points along the Homosassa River. The cotton would be moved through the Union blockade toward the mercantile center of Cuba. Any mistake that led to detection would spell a prison sentence or death for the men.

Poling the sloop in and out of hidden inlets as though it were a barge, the five used sign language and bird calls to point out the cotton bales that had been hidden under palmetto leaves. As dawn approached, each man furtively surveyed the shallow waters in front of the sailboat, slapping at mosquitoes and wiping their brows as sweat trickled down their faces. The pungent smell of wet bamboo filled their nostrils. Hoping that everything would go as planned, they hedged their bets by turning their sights back often to make sure they were not being watched or followed. No words were spoken. Their brows were furrowed; their stomachs and backs held their pent up tension.

As the sloop floated toward the edge of the protective canopy of weeping cypress and faced the open gulf, the men turned to managing the sails and lines, tightening the sheets leeward. They were gearing up to make their brazen dart across the open waters of the Gulf in an efficient tacking maneuver that they had practiced on many pre-dawn mornings in the recent past. Beck hung onto the shroud and swept his eyes back and forth along the beach as C.T. set the jib. Johns navigated the tiller beside C.T. Wilson and Day stood facing each other mid-sloop, balancing their contraband. Once in open waters they were committed to do nothing but dash and hope to hell they made it to Cedar Keys undetected. As the gulf winds caught and whipped the sail, they were in the all-or-nothing stage of their mission. Being caught now, with their cargo, could mean the gallows.

C.T.'s stomach was sour; his tongue flickered against his lips, tightened over his teeth. His shoulders were burning from holding the lines. His fist, clenched to white knuckles over the line, had stiffened the fingers of his right hand into a claw.

Their overloaded sloop continued its way toward Cedar Keys in spite of the burden. The anomaly in the outline of the key registered with the men, one at a time: a Union steamer. Two Union officers stood on deck of the massive vessel, each holding a telescope trained on the gnat-sized sloop.

They saw us the moment we came out of the inlet, every movement, every hesitation, they have been silently egging us into the open water, C.T. thought. No need to speak. Each of the men would be responsible for talking himself through the terror of the moment.

The hulking steamer chugged toward them, rounding a course that cut the sloop off from any attempt to reverse their course across the open water. Finally, inevitably, the sloop's aft bumped unceremoniously into the windward side of the steamer. The Union soldiers leaned over the side of their vessel, their side arms drawn and pointed at the Confederate Blockade Runners.

One by one they put their hands in the air. The sloop bobbed haplessly. Lines trailed in the water behind the little boat. The jib began to luff; enough of a breeze had sprung up that escape *might* have been possible, had the breeze come but a few moments sooner.

In short order, the five would find themselves prisoners of war, incarcerated at Fort Taylor, praying to get word to their community and their families.

Within ten days they were transferred out of southern waters to New York Harbor's Fort Lafayette.

Journal Entry:

The prison, Fort Lafayette, rises from the depths of New York Harbor like the black specter of Death that it is. We were brought out of the hold by rough hands, up the gang plank, with no consideration for rank; men's shackles clanking, into the sight of the stone cold silhouette of Fort Lafayette looming ominously against a heavy curtain of dark clouds that floated in front of a sweet pale blue Northeast sky.

We were a scuffed lot, some of us wheezing and hacking phlegm. The sickest amongst us raised pitiful seeping eyes and blinked in fear upon a tomb.

Someone at the rear of the line tripped on a plank. The sudden jolt yanked, in secession, on the iron cuffs of each man. Men groaned at the impact; their weakened shoulders jarred by their mates' stumble.

"Step it up Rebs, we don't have all night," was the refrain we heard until all of the men were off the transport. The unmistakable outline of the gallows could be seen to the left of the landing. Each man poked the next, nodding toward the unmistakable frame and the thick rope tied in a hangman's noose swinging at dusk in the chilly evening breeze of the Northeast seaboard.

Our line of pathetic humanity continued to shuffle toward the carved stone entry, back lit by lanterns. We had been down in the ship's hold for days, cramped, jammed next to each other's skin. We were sick of our companions-in-fate and worried into insanity about the welfare of our families.

We had been prosperous men—some of us; and community involved—all of us. We were family men; teachers, merchants, most of us farmers depending on our large families to bring in our yield—At present we are simply men in the hands of the enemy.

Faithfully,
C.T. Jenkins

* * *

21

Capture

Lt. Col. Albert Colburn, US Cavalry, had arranged a letter of transport for his mother at the beginning of the war, in the hopes that she would have used it early on to take flight to Vermont. She hadn't used it for that purpose, and held it aside until immediately after she and Eliza heard of C.T.'s capture. Accompanied on horseback by Mr. Kildall, she rode to Fort Meyer and presented Albert's letter to the commander who was able to arrange an unchallenged journey to New York. She said nothing about her destination being the prison at Fort Lafayette, New York Harbor. Arriving in Atlanta, midway on her trip, she sent a wire to her brother, Israel. Her request was that he accompany her, should she be able to arrange a visit with C.T.

The trip was mapped out within days of her hearing of C.T.'s capture. "Eliza, I may be able to get to C.T., but you realize, until this war is over, I am not at all sure that I will be able to get back to you and the children. I cannot bear the thought of C.T. not knowing whether we know of his plight, or in what manner he can count on us for aid."

Eliza nodded her head, seeing her future through tears, "Ironic, isn't it Mother, that finally, I *am* on my own. With Albert in Pennsylvania, C.T. is God knows where, and you leaving me. This isn't what I had in mind. I'll be totally alone."

"Eliza, you won't be alone. You have the children. What joy that should bring you. And you're not in constant danger. You're safer here than I will be, and surely you're safer than C.T. is right now."

After her mother's departure Eliza could barely bring herself to maintain the property and feed the children. The curtain rod in her bedroom had pulled loose months ago and she had finally taken the curtains down instead of continuing the irritating ritual of patting the rod back into place after opening the curtains each morning. So every day, the room flooded with sunlight at daybreak heralding another miserable day of solitude.

Forcing herself out of bed while the children were still asleep, she stepped across her bedroom and reached for a muslin skirt hanging on a large hook. She gathered the worn fabric and stepped into the skirt, adjusting it over her pantaloons. Next she slipped a pleated white cotton blouse with cap sleeves over her camisole. It was the same skirt and blouse she had worn since the day before, and the day before that.

Any morning in Vermont she would have selected an 'ensemble'. *Ha! Ensemble!* She laughed at the word. Her Paris-inspired hat, purchased from Mme. Spurrier, had been packed away some time ago in one of the matching cedar chests that C.T. had made for her when they returned from their Vermont honeymoon. She had also packed away her silk and taffeta camisoles, shutting the lid on a beautiful range of deep jewel tones. *Ribbons and lace, topaz and emeralds from another time.* Several sets of silk pantaloons and corsets, along with a stack of light textured linen skirts, completed the collection stored in the first chest. The matching cedar chest held the four stacks of neatly folded clothes which Madame Biscay had designed for her upon her arrival to Florida. She remembered how the tailor-made finery replaced the heavy clothing she had packed when she departed Fair Haven. *Such foolish extravagance.*

The silence of each morning, before the children woke, was suffocating Eliza. Having two sleepyheads gave Eliza time to pad down the front steps of the cottage and thrash her way through the brush down to the sloping river bank. She would slip out of her clothing and splash in the murky currents before heading back up the cottage at the sound of John-Colburn's wail. A rusty trough sat on the river bank. She and C.T. had lugged it down to the river after the pump broke the previous year, to clarify river water for the children's baths.

Her only hope was that a messenger would make his way to the cottage, bringing news of her mother or husband. "When is Father coming home?" "Where is Grandmother?" Annie was old enough to comprehend the absence of two central people in her life. Her father and grandmother had been committed to doting on the little brunette's every accomplishment and antic.

"Oh my little miss, play nicely and they will come home soon," her mother advised day after day. Annie's quiet pastime was to drag a stick in the sand leaving a criss-cross trail of her meanderings.

"What's that, Annie?"

"My maps."

"You *are* your father's daughter."

Eliza marveled that there were any yams still growing in the garden, and that the pineapple crop and pecan trees, although struggling, were yielding. So far. But day after day, for months on end, that was all they had to eat. Yams, onions and pecans. That is, unless Eliza caught a turtle. Then turtle soup could be added to Annie and John's menu. So whenever Eliza discovered the children playing with a turtle, or if she discovered a turtle slowly plodding along the river bank she would gather it up and take it to the kitchen. Preparing a fresh turtle for soup wasn't much more difficult than gutting a fish. Cutting the turtle's head off, and simmering it slowly in a cauldron of lemons before splitting it from its shell would produce a delicacy that supplemented the family's diet for at least a few days.

Eliza had been staring absent-mindedly out toward the river while Annie wrapped her tuft-haired doll in a rag that, many years ago, had been one of her father's shirts when prickly feeling and chill overtook Eliza. She became aware of something rustling just beyond the distant tree line. Eliza stood up cautiously. She tightened the swaddling around John and gently placed him in the cradle she kept on the porch. She tipped the little bed to begin the rocking motion that would lull him to sleep. Someone was coming up the dirt lane.

The tall reeds rustled, foretelling an approaching visitor or intruder. And, it was unfathomable to have a visitor in the evening. She stumbled toward Annie, putting her finger to her lips to silence the little girl. Eliza was terrified at the prospect of having to protect the children and the property.

The cottage was so isolated that if trouble was in store for her, it was too late to do anything but face it head on. Why *couldn't* her mother have stayed with her? She shouldn't be here in this cottage alone with two children.

She was short of breath, her heart was pounding heavily. If it was a Union soldier stumbling onto the cottage, he would burn it to the ground. Approaching the property via the river, mooring at the dock was one thing; but how could anyone have found their homestead in the tangle of bushes and overgrowth leading from the south side of the cottage?

"Annie, come here. Right now, to me!" she whispered She held her breath waiting for the intruder to make himself known. Only a moment before her heart nearly burst from beating so wildly, did she recognize the intruder as Mr. Ederington's oldest son, Francis Jr.

The boy was approaching very slowly, dragging each step, eyes on the ground, until he reached the edge of the clearing. He stopped, looked at Eliza, and then looked over his shoulder as though someone were following him. His mother, Precious, was several paces behind, catching up. Her face was flushed; tendrils fell into her eyes, and small beads of sweat jeweled the top of her lip. Mrs. Ederington took a step forward, mis-stepped, and nearly stumbled. Francis caught his mother's elbow and looked to Eliza for assistance. Eliza ran toward them, lessening the distance, lessening the burden of the trek they had made from Snow Hill.

"Mrs. Ederington? Precious?"

"Eliza," the older woman tried to catch her breath. "Eliza," she repeated, "it's about Albert."

"Albert?" She couldn't think of any one named Albert that Precious would know.

Precious started over, pushing the words out, "John just received a wire. Albert died yesterday in St. Louis. He'd been ill." blurted the woman.

"Albert? You mean C.T.? C.T.'s ill?"

Precious shook her head and repeated, "Albert."

"Mrs. Ederington, you don't even know Albert."

"Eliza, I'm trying to tell you. It's your brother, Albert. He's been ill."

Francis took Eliza's hand and pulled her back to the porch step. Eliza sat down, confused, and looked up.

Precious sat down also, wrapping her arms around Eliza.

"Mrs. Ederington. I can't breathe."

Francis went around to the back of the house and ladled water into three chipped cups.

"A message was sent by a Lt. Colonel Thomas meant for your mother. A Union messenger from Fort Myer brought it to the store. John was there," referring to her son-in-law, shopkeeper for the community store and post office.

"No, I don't think so, Mrs. Ederinton."

"Oh, my dear, I am so sorry. All I know is what is in this message." Precious rummaged through the deep skirt pocket and produced the telegram.

Eliza accepted the wire and read,

To: Mrs. John P. Colburn, via Bay Port, Florida
It is with the greatest sadness (stop)
Death of Lieutenant Colonel Albert V. Colburn
On the 17th instant June after short illness (stop)
St. Louis, MO at time of his death. -
My Sincerest Regrets,

On her own terms Eliza came to the realization that Albert was dead. Her grasp of the news came independent of anything Mrs. Ederington had said a few moments earlier. She had to piece the awfulness together on her own. Tears rolled down her cheeks, and the two women held on to each other and rocked in solace for what was to come.

**

FORT LAFAYETTE, NEW YORK HARBOR
TRANSCRIPT of COURT MARTIAL
PROCEEDING

29 August 1863
Special Court Martial Convening Order 63-15.
Court is now in session. All being duly sworn, call the case.
United States of America versus Cyprian Thomas Jenkins.

Please come forward and identify yourself for the record.

Cyprian Thomas Jenkins.

Please state your residence.

Homosassa, Florida.

How long have you resided in Florida?

Twenty-one years.

And, Mr. Jenkins, where were you born?

Baltimore, Maryland.

In June 1860 is it true that you were elected, and served, as a delegate to the Democratic State Convention, meeting at Quincy, Florida?

Yes.

At that convention, is it true that, by unanimous consent, it was resolved that body withdraw from the National Democratic Party?

Yes.

During the June 1860 proceedings in Quincy, Florida was it also unanimously decided that, (word illegible) 'Democracy of Florida'.

Yes.

While a delegate at the convention in Quincy, Florida were you then elected to serve as delegate to a similar Democratic convention held in Richmond, Virginia?

Yes.

At either or both conventions, or proceedings, were the terms 'Democracy of Florida' and 'Democracy of the South' used in the passage of resolutions, or in conducting the general business of any Democratic Party body?

Yes.

At those proceedings or at any time before or after, have you supported the southern states' secession from the United States?

Yes.

Is it true that you are enlisted in the Fourth Florida Regiment?

Yes.

Please state for the court your rank?

Private.

Mr. Jenkins, please state your age for the court.

Fifty-two.

(Chuckles heard in the court room.)

Order! Come to order.

Are you familiar with a certain Captain Alexander Semmes?

Yes, I am.

And, who is he to you, Mr. Jenkins?

He is my second cousin by marriage. His mother, Mary Matilda Jenkins Semmes, is my aunt,.

Did you have an encounter with Captain Semmes in 1861?

Yes, I did.

Can you describe that incident for the court, please?

I was on duty at Wacassa Bay with two of my men.

Please describe for the court who these men were.

They had previously been slaves; at that point they were freedmen working in Bay Port, Florida.

That morning what was 'your duty', as you describe it?

I was in my sailboat; we were on our way to visit an encampment down the coast from Homosassa.

To clarify, you were on your way to visit a Confederate encampment down the coast from Homosassa?

Yes.

Did you have goods on board your sailboat, like, say, cotton?

No.

I see, go on.

On our way we were run down by a patrol steamer.

Would that have been the patrol steamer commanded by your cousin, Alexander A. Semmes?

Yes.

Were you taken prisoner by the crew of the steamer?

Yes.

You heard testimony that this first encounter with Union forces was prompted by suspicion that your men may have had something to do with the murder of three Union soldiers who were coaxed ashore near Wacassa Bay, is that correct?

Yes.

Mr. Jenkins, moving to a different matter: According to a 'Report to the Superintendent' written by A.D. Bache you were involved in an incident in February of 1861 that involved a crew member of the schooner Joseph Henry. Is that correct?

I couldn't be sure.

Let me refresh your memory, reading from Mr. Bache's report, page 54, it states that N.S. Finney, working the northwest coast of Florida encountered a band of armed men, identifying themselves as residents of Bay Port on 11 February 1861. The leader of this armed group identified himself as 'C.T. Jenkins'. Is that you, sir?

Yes, that is my name.

(Chuckles from the Court's gallery.)

I will continue. "At the direction of said, C.T. Jenkins the tents and camp fixtures were confiscated from N.S. Finney and his men at gunpoint." Here, Your Honor, is Mr. Bache's report, Exhibit 15.

Do you now remember such an encounter, Mr. Jenkins?

Yes.

Let the court note that the defendant acknowledges taking up arms against the Union in at least this one documented incident.

Now, moving to the present: On the morning of June 1st of this year you were running cotton through the Union blockade, is that correct?

I had bales of cotton on board my sloop that morning, yes.

And, is it true that thousands of bales of cotton were being slipped though the blockade by members of the Fourth, and other Confederate infantry members?

It's possible.

And, that cotton is being sold in New York for one dollar a pound?

I wouldn't know.

Let the record show that 'a clear profit of $300,000 for a round-trip' shipping cotton through the Union's blockade is 'not uncommon'.

Are you aware of the President's Proclamation of Blockade against Southern Ports which forbids running the legal blockade established to reserve the resources of the United States of America?

You're expecting me to answer that question?

(Chuckles heard in the court room).

Objection.

Sustained.

Who was with you that morning?

I can't recall.

Was co-defendant John P. Johns with you at that time, Mr. Jenkins?

Objection.

(Historical note: several transcription pages are missing from the record at this point.)

All rise. The Court is reconvened in the matter United States versus Cyprian Thomas Jenkins.

Mr. Jenkins, after due consideration of your circumstances and a review of the evidence against you, and this transcript; the court has made a determination in your case.

Would you like to address the Court at this time?

No.

In that case, the Court reminds you that you are charged with the following crimes:

Blockade Running in violation of the United States' proclamation of 19 April 1861, *Proclamation of Blockade Against Southern Ports*;

Treason against the United States of America by virtue of your service to the entity known as the 'Confederate States of America' in that you state, under oath, that you served in the Fourth Infantry of the Florida State Militia.

The Court finds you guilty as charged on both counts.

The Court will address sentencing at this time. Please remain standing.

As to the crime of running the blockade, in violation of the United States' proclamation of 19 April 1861, *Proclamation of Blockade Against Southern Ports*; the court sentences you to two days of solitary confinement to be served here at Fort Lafayette.

On the charge of treason against the United States you are sentenced to death by hanging. That sentence is, however, commuted. You will instead serve a life sentence at Fort Warren, Georges Island in Boston, Massachusetts.

Your will begin serving your sentence for the crime of blockade running immediately. Transfer to Fort Warren, Georges Island in Boston will take place once transport is secured and your sentence for blockade running has been served.

One final note: In reviewing your file, it seems that you have a certain benefactor to thank you for your life: a Baltimore lady, the wife of a Union officer.

You are most fortunate for that, Mr. Jenkins.

Remove the prisoner from this proceeding.

**

In the dim light of his cell block C.T. was barely able to pick his way to his own cot. *Dear God,* he thought. *'Living quarters' might have described my bedroom at Huntington, or my beautiful cottage. But this, this is no place to live. Hell! Give me back the prison of my father's clawing expectations in exchange for this dungeon.* The candles which lit the cell block cast dim shadows on walls caked with grime. The floor under his cot would seep and percolate damp.

C.T. mentally took in the square footage of his prison cell, thirty-one square feet, and sorted out the figures as though the space could be configured to any dimension: *Six feet wide, five feet long; two feet wide, fifteen feet long; four feet wide; eight feet long.*

Having made the walk across the cell block, nodding to anyone who shifted their eyes to glance at him, C.T. would turn around and shuffle back to his cot. He steered around any nest of prisoners huddling around seemingly secretive conversations. He didn't need any more trouble, having already spent two days in solitary confinement in the transit from Florida's Fort Taylor.

Days of monotony and mind-racing worry were broken only by the exercise of a dull trudge across the cell block each day. At five o'clock, the prisoners eyed each other warily and began crowding and jostling for space along the iron grate that served as the egress from their cramped quarters. The clanking of keys would signal that guards were coming. Soon, the grate would swing open onto the muddy yard. The prisoners would lunge forward toward the muddy swatch that stretched along the inside of the prison walls, flailing to distance themselves from the cell block.

After an hour the men would plod back in past the cots that lined the cell block. Four horizontal loopholes sticking out from the wall held the candles that lighted the cavernous space. The prisoners traded whatever they could, extra rations for a month, wraps and capes, in order to be as close to the candle light as possible. The straw on the cots had flattened to a dull grey; no longer the flaxen gold, sweet smelling straw that had been tossed in front of the cell block several months ago.

C.T. dropped to his cot and held his head in his hands, elbows on his knees, staring down at his boots. *Mud's worn into the welt lines; the leather's scarred. Maybe they'll hold out through the winter, I don't see them handing out replacements,* he mused. He was also at a loss as to how he would replace his clothes, which were in need of cleaning and mending.

How the hell can I get a message to Eliza? If I'm to keep my wits, I must put my life in order. If only I can establish some sort of structure, ritual—post mail, write— Maybe then I can get through this Hell.

* * *

22

THE REVEREND'S FOLLY

"Well, Will ya' lookie here," exclaimed the Admiral of the Sapphire Star. "Things just don't seem to change much in these here waters."

Anchored three hundred yards north of Bay Port Harbor, in the same location as six months earlier, a recently promoted Admiral Boulware celebrated his ascension by returning to the spot where his capture of C.T. and members of the Fourth Regiment had taken place.

It was a serene evening as the gulf coast loons sobbed their melancholy cry. A lone man rowed out and to the seaboard side of the frigate.

"Climb aboard, Matey!" laughed Boulware as the old man made every attempt at pulling his boat up to the side of the ship but without throwing a line to tie up.

"I'm not coming aboard! You owe me rations."

"Fine, don't come aboard." Then he added an aside meant to amuse his men, "We'd break his skinny little arms if we pulled him aboard. Hawkins, get a bag of rations while I humor this devil."

Turning back Boulware yelled down, "That was quite a nugget of information you passed on. Surely, I'll grant you, it was worth a second bag of rations."

The man nodded glumly.

"By the way, I hear your son is making a very fine captain for the Union. You have every reason to be proud of him. We certainly are."

The beggar winced.

Nodding to the mate to toss the rations down to the skiff, the Admiral concluded their transaction, laughing, "Good night and much thanks!"

Reverend Moore, aged by his experiences, glared at Boulware as he took up his oars.

**

Letters

Posted: *Fort Lafayette*
New York Harbor

August 27, 1863

Eliza Colburn Jenkins
Homosassa, Florida

My Daughter,

I miss you and the children dearly and hope this letter finds you doing as well as can be expected. We buried Albert in Cedar Grove, next to his father. God tests my faith. I know you are depending on any news I can bring you of Cyprian. Israel and I arrived safely in New York, the details of which I will share with you more fully in subsequent letters. Darling, Cyprian was found guilty of the charge of blockade running. He has received a life sentence, to be served at Fort Warren Prison, Boston Harbor. The trial was so swift it took our breath away. Of course, we praise our good fortune that he did not receive a death sentence. He will be transferred to Fort Warren very soon.

Frederick Jenkins arranged, with the commanding colonel, our visit with C.T. He seemed well enough. He does not have fever, and receives as much food as any of the other prisoners. Frederick is contacting Mary

Jenkins who can arrange that rations be sent him at Fort Warren. Please do not despair.

My visit seemed to cheer him greatly. Although he can hardly bear being separated from Annie and John. And, he sends his affection to you.

In God's Grace,

Mother

--

Posted: C. T. Jenkins
Fort Warren
Georges Island
Boston, Massachusetts

By special courier
Baltimore, Maryland

02 September, 1863

My Dear Lady,
There is no way to ever thank you and your husband for interceding in my behalf.

Were your husband and I fighting for the same cause, on the same side, this missive would be more expansive, but I will not prevail further on him, or you, in long communiqués.

I owe the two of you no less than my life.

With the greatest affection for you both,

Cyprian

--

Cyprian T. Jenkins
Ft. Warren
Georges Island
Boston, Massachusetts

Mrs. Frederick Jenkins
Baltimore Town, Maryland

15 September, 1863

Dearest Aunt,

I will be grateful for the rest of my life for all that you and Frederick have done to relieve the peril of my situation. So many individuals have come to my aid in these past months—but to you and Frederick most of all. The situation at Fort Warren is greatly improved over that of Fort Lafayette and I have you and my Baltimore cousins to thank for that. If I am ever able to step upon the soil of my dear State of Maryland, all of my prayers will have been answered. As winter approaches it is far too cold for one who has grown used to the warmth of southern climes. May I ask that you seek permission from Commandant Dimick to provide me with a coat, or other provisions? Anything you could provide would go far in furnishing me with comfort. We are allowed an hour's turn in the yard each day and some buffer against the cold while I'm out, would do me a world of good.

I know that you realize that you are my lifeline at this time.

Your Nephew,

C.T. Jenkins

--

Posted: *Mrs. Frederick Jenkins*
Baltimore, Maryland

Cyprian T. Jenkins
Fort Warren - Georges Island
Boston, Massachusetts

30 September

Dear Cyprian,

I am in receipt of your letter of 15 September.

Of course, your uncle and I wish you every comfort possible. Your brothers, Enoch and Constantine, are, as you are probably aware, in the tailoring business. They may be able to help you with your needs for clothing.

In the meantime, we will do what more we can to assure you remain as comfortable as possible. To that end, we have engaged the sister of one of our servants, to bring you provisions. Her name is Esther Nells. Her son will be in contact with you shortly, I am confident.

With affection, Your Aunt,
Mary Jenkins

--

Posted: Quinton Estate
Fair Haven, Vermont
03 October, 1863

Eliza Jenkins
Homosassa
Florida

Dearest Daughter,
I send my love and my hopes that you and the children coping. It is only the knowledge that you are surrounded by good and generous neighbors that brought me to the decision that I have made in recent days.
I am unable to return to Homosassa. As much as I miss you and the children, you must know how

impossible it is for me to secure passage comfortably, or safely, in the void left by Albert's death. And, I find the thought of leaving Albert's and John Jr.'s graves unbearable.

There should be little reason for you to need me. So much time has passed since my departure from Florida; you're undoubtedly getting along quite capably. I know that you have dealt with many challenges since C.T.'s capture.

I had expected to always be by your side, so that you would not have to face the difficulties that I faced through life. But that thinking is no longer practical. Who knows how much longer this conflict will continue? Or how long it will be before the family can secure a release for C.T.?

You are from a strong family; there is no reason why you cannot persevere. If God is willing, I will return to you and the children as soon after the war as possible.

Love,

Mother

--

Posted: Constantine Jenkins
North Baltimore
Maryland

14 February 1864

Cyprian T. Jenkins
Georges Island
Boston Harbor
Massachusetts

Dear Brother,

I find myself in a very difficult situation. And, I hope that I might be able to prevail upon you to help me.

As you have no doubt learned, I am incarcerated at Fort Warren prison, torn away from my home in Baltimore and family in Florida.

As winter approaches, I now recall my dislike for the miserable, biting cold of the northeast that, in large measure, drove me out of Baltimore as a youth.

My situation here is meager, although better than most. This letter is not intended to shed light on my misfortunes, save one request.

I understand from Aunt Mary that you and our brother Enoch are tailors. These are difficult times to prevail on others, but, if I could make a request. I have not had a new set of clothes since arriving at Fort Warren. My wife's mother brought two heavy twill suits to me after my transfer to Georges Island, but both were intended to be worn in the climes of Florida.

May I ask you for any coat and cap that you or Enoch might fashion for my use as winter approaches?

It is my hope that this request finds you, your wife and children, in a situation that brings you comfort.

I must admit that while being away from my wife and children, I realize how slowly time passes while waiting for a word from family members. I hope I can hear from you soon.

Your brother,

Cyprian

--

Brother? I don't even know you, Constantine thought as he stared at the handwriting and turned the sheet of paper over in his hand, examining it.

**

Posted: *Magnolia Plantation*
Jacksonville, Florida

April 1864

Eliza Colburn
Bay Port House
Bay Port, Florida

Dear Miss Colburn,
I write this letter with a heavy heart during a very challenging time.
You may possibly know that our son, Taylor, has been serving in the 6th Florida Infantry Battalion for the past year. The 6th came under attack at Olustee this past month. Many fine, brave young men died in the skirmishes between our sons and the enemy. Our beautiful Taylor was among those lost. Taylor fell on the battlefield on 20 February. He died bravely while challenging the rear element of Seymour's formation.
My husband discovered your address in my son's effects several months ago and I feel compelled to contact you, knowing that you shared a fondness for each other.
As you know Taylor was committed to the Confederacy. His father and I have pride in the knowledge that he served this cause with distinction. This, of course, is not the time for a coarse discussion of politics, though, is it?
We had a beautiful sunrise service for our Taylor the first week of March. We can see his marker from the walkway outside our upstairs suite, which gives us great comfort.

I am only now finding the strength to take up a pen to inform you of Taylor's death as I know that you and he were great friends at one point in his short life. Mr. Babcock and I had hoped to make your acquaintance someday. In the future, spending time visiting anyone with a link to Taylor would also be a comfort to us.

If you should ever make your way to Jacksonville, our invitation that you stay with us at our home is extended.

In sorrow,

Mrs. Taylor Abernathy Babcock II

--

Eliza folded the letter into its envelope and placed it on the edge of the dining room table. While the face of the envelope stared up at her, she slowly eased her way into one of the dining room chairs to stare out the window at the still waters of the Homosassa River. A ghost-white egret, nearly translucent, plunged mid-current to snag a trout in its beak. A sudden splash, a struggle, then silence. Eliza sat staring at the river for a very long time.

**

"Are you going, Constantine?"

"I don't know, Father Lahey. I don't think so."

"Well, that's disappointing to hear. You know, I've been the priest of this parish since you were born. It's been a long time and I've seen a lot. I hope to die administering to the families in this parish; but rarely as I am disappointed as I am now, hearing your decision."

"You mean you've been a priest of this parish since my mother died, don't you, Father? No disrespect intended."

"Well, if you'd like to make it one and the same, so be it."

"It's what everyone whose name is Jenkins or Wells thinks when they look at me."

"Is it, Constantine? Is it what they think? Or is it what you remind them of, as you just now did with me? No disrespect intended."

Constantine was silent, staring past the priest who had administered his baptism, his confirmation, his marriage and all of the other sacraments that he had celebrated thus far in his life. His focus of attention was the serene statue of a beautifully robed Mary, holding her child which stood just beyond the nave. The infant was held by his mother, an experience Constantine had never had. But the man who had written to him from Fort Warren prison not only had been held by his mother, but had enjoyed her love and affection.

"Son, look at me and answer this question. If it were *you*, sitting in prison, and the only intellectual escape you could partake in was recollecting every flaw and mis-step of your life, what might you change about how you had carried on toward those the community referred to as your family?"

The wizened priest added, "Confession begins at 9 o'clock this Sunday, Constantine. Why don't you reflect on your brother's needs and the fact that—according to what you learned from your Aunt Mary—Cyprian waited over five months in the cold of prison before approaching you, for what? A winter coat?"

--

Posted: Constantine Jenkins
Biddle St.
Baltimore, Maryland

April 4, 1864

Dear Cyprian,
I am in receipt of your letter of 14 February and appreciate the hardship you must have gone through to have it posted. It is not lost on me that it was penned on our father's birthday.

Not surprisingly to you, I am sure, we have all heard of your plight from Aunt Mary.

These are hard times that try all families whether they are Baltimoreans or Tampa Bay families. It is with interest I note that in your letter you describe your home as Baltimore Town. Isn't that the town you left in 1833?

I sit here and try to think back on how long it has been since you and I corresponded-have we ever? I sent a letter to Bay Port when my son, Frances, was born. He is now four years old and we have just welcomed Mary Melville home to her little bassinette. After Frances was born we did receive a welcome and engaging letter in return from your Eliza, who introduced herself and told us of your busy life in Florida.

You point out in your letter that you have a need for tailored clothing. Dear Cyprian, I am a hatter. My life is humble. However, I will tailor for you what I can from the fabric remnants my wife is able to set aside. Truly, we do not have much and what we have may not meet your standards. But, I will send what I can in the hopes it reaches you without much more delay.

Beyond that, I am sure that your own resourcefulness, I'm sure will prevail over anything that I can provide you.

Respectfully,

Constantine Jenkins

**

What if something goes wrong? Constantine stood on the dock looking across Boston Harbor to Fort Warren. *What if the sentry doesn't let me back out?* He continued tormenting himself remembering stories of visitors held as informants once they disappeared behind the black walls. *Why, it was just last year a woman was hung at Fort Warren—what were the details of that story?* He asked himself. *Damn it! I shouldn't be here,* Constantine chastised himself and began to resent his agreement with Enoch that he be the one to bring the tailored coat and cap to Cyprian. *The guards will have to bring him directly to my side, for how will I even know what he looks like? And, likewise, how will he recognize me! Why I was only seven when he deserted us! He's had his life; and now I have mine,* thought the thirty-seven year old. *We could have sent the coat and cap on. I didn't have to make this trip.* Then he countered his own arguments, *but, maybe it would not have been delivered correctly – or at all.*

The heavy bundle lay at his feet, on the dock, wrapped in thick, brown waxed paper and twine. Constantine expected the package would be unwrapped and inspected several times before he presented it to his brother. Why, Constantine himself had unwrapped and rewrapped the package several times during the journey getting to Fort Warren, just to reassure himself there was nothing in it besides the heavy paisley robe and matching cap that he and Enoch had tailored.

Finally, Constantine saw a skiff coming across the water toward him. He, along with other family members of the prisoners, began shuffling toward the landing plank where they would be cross-examined, and their papers and packages inspected.

A half hour later, nine individuals from various backgrounds stood in a tight cluster, hoping that their return to the Boston side of the waterway would be as uneventful as their trip over to Georges Island had been.

After passing inspection and receiving his papers allowing the visit, Constantine proceeded on with the other visitors. Finding his own spot in the large room they were escorted to, Constantine put the gaping bundle on a heavy wooden table. He waited for Cyprian to be presented to him.

This must be him, my God! A bearded man chatting comfortably with his escorting sentry was led to Constantine.

"Cyprian! Oh dear, is that you?" Constantine clasped his brother's hand.

Thankfully the sentry nodded toward Cyprian and retreated, after eyeing Constantine suspiciously, adding to the younger man's discomfort. *Please say something, Cyprian.* C.T. nodded at the guard who then moved a few feet away.

"Thank you for coming. I know that this trip puts a burden on you and our family. I appreciate your trouble," the man began.

"Our family? You mean Mary, my wife—*my* family?"

"Well, yes. I mean your wife, of course. But, I also mean our brothers. Our family."

"Our brothers are all grown up, as am I. There is no more 'our family'. If you meant to say 'the burden' you place on the Jenkinses, then that's a different matter. Because, I presume their burdens, trouble and worry come to them with little thought of you. I would imagine that like myself, there would be very few of our family who would even recognize you, or be able to pick up a conversation with you based on any correspondence they had shared with you."

"Aunt Mary and I correspond."

"Yes, good choice!" Constantine would have liked to have stopped his words and the damage his blunt honesty was doing, but he couldn't. He and Cyprian were alike in that regard. "I mean, good choice, considering Aunt Mary has the Union contacts and encouraged, in every way imaginable, the woman who interceded on your behalf.

"I mean, good choice, considering you were able to garner the generosity of the one lady, married to a Union officer, who could save your life at your trial. Not that I would wish you direct harm, because I do not." Constantine his brother, rejecting C.T.'s pretty picture of a shared family that, in Constantine's mind, never existed.

"Well, that was a mouthful, wasn't it? I am alone here, Constantine. Truly I have no one other than those who come to see me. So, I thank you for your presence here. My attempt is to recognize that your journey, which I appreciate, is no small endeavor. But, I don't have the means to make your burden any easier."

"Yes, there are relatives who recall that I am part of a large family, which you now describe as fractured. But, it was not always that way. Nor is that the whole of the situation now. It occurs to me that we grew up in entirely different households. The household that I grew up in was a family, with brothers, cousins, aunts and uncles who shared lively visits and wonderful holidays. Our father conducted his affairs in a manner that credited the family."

"Is that how you remember it, Cyprian? Because, unless I'm wrong, you are speaking of the household you chose to leave."

"Dear God, Constantine."

Both men looked around the room, silently observing the other prisoners and visitors. They each measured how *those* encounters might be faring.

Constantine looked back to C.T. He pushed the bundle that lay open at his elbow toward him. Constantine shook his head and muttered, "I hope to hell you are able to get out of here."

"Yes, me too. I need to return to my wife, Eliza, and my children."

Posted: Ft. Warren
Georges Island
Boston, Massachusetts

April 1864

Eliza Colburn Jenkins
Homosassa, Florida

My Dear Eliza,

You and our children are on my mind every moment.

Eliza, I am not going to be with you for who knows how long; so, I am depending on your strength and resourcefulness to see our children through this experience until I can somehow return to our home on the Homosassa. Please do not despair.

There will be a release of prisoners by late spring. I will not be among them. I have managed to save $1.75 to buy a doll for Annie. It will be delivered by one of the men here who *has* taken the oath of allegiance and will return to his family in Florida soon. One does what is necessary, I suppose. Regardless, he has agreed to deliver this precious parcel to Bay Port. I will now begin saving for a toy for John; although I'm not sure yet how it might be delivered.

I weigh constantly the possibility of declaring allegiance in order to return to our family. Being separated from you and our life in Homosassa is my greatest burden.

Life barely exists without you and the children near me. I'm so torn.

With all of my affection,

Your Husband,

C.T. Jenkins

--

Posted: *Mrs. Charles Chadwick*
Malone, New York

Mrs. Cyprian Jenkins
Homosassa River, Florida

June 30, 1864

Dear Eliza,

I hope this letter makes its way to you and finds you coping well. Yes, in answer to your question, Mother is doing fine and has Rufus to thank for her comfort and well-being. Please do not worry about us.

Charles is ministering to the troops, assigned to Major Rowland's regiments. He was able to come home to see me and the children for a little while after the siege at Suffolk, Virginia. The days are very long.

I don't know what to say, frankly. Betsey and Moses are doing fine; although Moses' wife is not well. We should all remember her in our prayers. Betsey is doing all she can, but I expect that Moses will be forced to hire a nurse if Maria's health doesn't improve in the very near future.

One day we will all be together again. I hope it is soon. Please kiss Annie and John-Colburn for me. Don't worry about Mother, as I've said.

In God's Grace,
Your Sister, Susan

* * *

23

Bay Port Shelling

Eliza scrambled out of bed the moment the shelling began. She pulled her clothes on hastily, snatching at a blouse that needed laundering. She clutched at her skirt with clammy palms. Tendrils escaped the upsweep she wore. She rushed through the front room, toward the front porch of the cottage, trying to determine from what direction the intermittent blasts came. Eliza clung to the porch rail and leaned into the rumbling, squinting as she panned the distant hammocks.

Scanning the sky above the tree line she gasped at the sight of the neat spiral of smoke as it rose into the cloudless blue sky. Tears welled then rolled down her cheeks in resignation. *It could be the Hope's plantation. Where is everyone? I'll go mad with worry if I stay here alone with the children.*

The rifle fire stopped for a moment. There was eerie silence before cannon fire rippled across the series of rises that comprised Hernando County.

Not able to manage the children on her own and overcome the terror of being alone, Eliza began planning for a dash to the home of her closest neighbor. It wasn't yet noon and she was exhausted. The shelling sounded like it was coming from the southwest. If that were the case, there was no doubt that the salt works at Bay Port were now destroyed. She had only been out on the porch for a few moments before compulsively returning to the front room of the cottage. She resumed her position in front of the south-facing windows, looking outward toward the distant ridge. It would be only an instant before she was out on the porch again.

Eliza widened her circle, pacing back and forth from the kitchen to the living room. Repeating the morning's compulsive pattern Eliza tiptoed into Annie's room, furtively peeking at the four-year-old who sat terrified in the corner of her room, clutching at the well worn tuft-haired doll. The children had bawled throughout the morning. Two-year old John-Colburn had woken with a startled cry earlier after their one milk pitcher ultimately made its leap from the kitchen counter, crashing heavily to the wood plank floor; the result of a series of little hops toward the counter's edge as each shell hit its mark. The handle had broken off cleanly. Little matter, as for months the pitcher had stood on the counter empty, unused. The likelihood of milk being available any time soon was remote. Like the garden, like their clothing, like the mangy animals that roamed the property listlessly, the neglected milk pitcher was one more item added to the devalued stockpile of household items that collected on the property.

It's too late to leave the cottage now. Oh God, by not acting I've actually made my decision. It's now impossible to leave. By early evening the shelling had ceased, replaced by a haunting silence.

Undergrowth had spread across the rise creeping slowly toward the cottage, choking it off; closing the cottage in. It had been a year since C.T. was captured. Swamp vines silently serpentined the tree trunks, their tentacles strangling the host trees, but avoiding the palmettos. Moss hung from the branches of hickory and cedar trees providing a curtain of camouflage around the property. The garden was in shambles, yielding very little to augment the meager meals that Eliza prepared for Annie and John-Colburn. Eliza and children were constantly hungry. Most garden patches had either dried up or had been destroyed. If any vegetables were harvested, or any fruit picked from the citrus trees, the yield was spread thin among neighbors. Eliza had settled into a lingering depression.

Eliza and the children weren't the only ones suffering. The whole community grew more concerned about starvation as cattle were rounded up in response to the requisition for livestock from General Bragg. Ironically the measly round-up did little to ease the hunger of the Western Army. Eliza relied on figs and pecans to feed the children. To supplement their meals she fed them sparrow eggs in the spring and turtle eggs early in the summer. Some days they had only one meal. Usually she would feed them when they woke, and again just before she put them to bed.

Yield from the land came in cycles. The corn had been picked weeks ago. The chickens were gone, either dead or stolen.

Feeding Annie and John-Colburn, and concern over C.T.'s survival tortured Eliza relentlessly. She was helpless to assist C.T., so she concentrated on feeding the children. Foraging for scraps of food, berries or edible vegetation.

After the children had been sponged off and tucked into their beds one evening Eliza sat in her rocker staring vacantly across the front of the property, listening to the symphony of cicadas. She was lost in time deep in the wish that the war would be over, and imagining that C.T. was once again sitting at his drafting table.

How differently everything has turned out, she thought. *Not just the war, and the irony that both C.T. and mother are gone, but everything. What had happened between her and Taylor? Or, rather, not happened,* she mused. *Had he been fond of me, as his mother suggests. He didn't follow me to Bay Port – not one visit, after he'd promised. How humiliated, after I revealed my interest to Ruth Kildall.* She thought back to how different she was now, compared to the woman she had been when she attended that barbeque six years ago. *Had Mother been right about Taylor back then? He only returned one or two of my letters, then nothing. How had she known?* Tears of self pity collected and threatened to spill onto her cheeks as she continued to rock. She brought out her memories of Jacksonville and lined each one up in the forefront of her mind like little salt crystals to be rubbed into her wounds. Each little crystal dazzling, but filled with a relentless sting. *I shouldn't pity myself, really. How surprising, in the end, that it was C.T. who followed me to Vermont. I just kept hoping...* kept hoping that Taylor would have been the one to show an interest in her; Taylor who would have won her mother over. *Now that I have Annie and John-Colburn I don't regret how it turned out, but what was behind Taylor's dealings with Uncle Harrison, really?* Impossibly she tried to come to terms with the motives of someone she hadn't really known, other than as a dinner party escort. *The terrible truth,* that's what she wanted. *After all, I met Taylor first, before C.T.,* she told herself when she realized that C.T. had an interest in her, and such a strong friendship with her mother. *How unkind, how shallow, to act so ignorantly toward someone trying so hard to find his way into a family. Who was I, then? I deserve this loneliness, I've earned it by my own actions.* And she continued to stare into the darkness.

Suddenly her eyes caught an almost imperceptible movement in the grass at the tree line. She immediately pulled herself back to the present. Eliza eased up from the rocker, edging to the first step of the porch. Her heart pounded. She was startled, but fascinated. Her vision pierced the distance to the edge of the property as she tried to clear her head. The heavy, lumbering opossum that had rustled its way into the pines could have been a hallucination. She made her way cautiously down the porch steps and toward the tree line, moving forward just a little, keeping her eyes intently focused. She wiped her clammy palms down the folds of her skirt.

Thank God the children are sleeping. It took only an instant for Eliza to realize what she must do. Her thoughts repulsed her. There was a roaring in her ears; she couldn't hear anything other than her heart beating. She willed her vision to see through the thickening dusk.

Chills swept over her body. Her mouth began to water, that sickening sweet taste just before retching begins. Eliza tried to keep her teeth from chattering. *The rifle!* She spun around and rushed around to the back of the cottage, pulling the rifle off of its hook above the kitchen door. A light glow from the lantern illuminated the living room, the house was very still. Eliza rushed forward, being careful not to tangle her skirts, or trip in the dark, as she returned back to the front of the house. *Be very still, it will make the first move.* She kept her eyes riveted on the tree line, seemingly hours went by. It was only minutes, in reality, before she knew which tree the creature was climbing, its branches swaying, leaves rustling. The weight of the rifle pulled at her shoulders.

She tried to calm herself, to devise a plan. As long as she had it treed and knew which tree it was in, the prize was hers. It was growing darker, looming. She tested herself by glancing to the right and left of the tree line and then found her way back to where the opossum was nesting. Taking aim at the mid-section of a large hickory tree Eliza fired, once. The shot echoed across the valleys and hammocks, the sound slamming back into the cottage. She looked over her shoulder and listened for the children. The opossum fell heavily to the ground with a thump, stunned. A broken branch caught crosswise as it fell and leaves fluttered to the ground. Eliza was terrified, afraid the rodent-like creature might charge her, its sharp, ugly incisors bared. But logic told her it would not, it would play dead, even if it wasn't.

She knew she only had a few moments. Her hands were shaking as she stepped backwards, keeping her eyes on the large dark scavenger, which now lay at the base of the tree. It was stunned, but not dead, she was sure. She ran toward the house, her heart was racing, her jaws ached from clenching. In the darkness she could see the outline of the pitchfork at the edge of the garden. She yanked it from where it had been struck into the ground and charged back to where the rifle lay among the pine needles.

The opossum was beginning to stir. On its back it clawed the air with its front paws. Eliza could smell its heavy, musky odor. Black eyes glinted wildly in the dark. It was still alive, but she didn't want it to be alive. Somehow she had wanted to skip over what had to happen next. It had to be killed if she and the children were going to have anything to eat.

She was afraid of it, in spite of the fact that she was the one with the rifle, the pitchfork, the wit. Realizing she would lose her nerve if she hesitated too long, she raised the pitchfork over her head. She closed her eyes and brought her full force down on the frantic creature, stabbing it into the ground. The animal screamed, feral and blood-curdling. The sound completely unnerved her.

She scrambled away from the tree line and the mortally wounded creature. She was afraid of what she had just done. She stumbled, tripping on the hem of her dress. She fell, her knee banging against a rock, shooting a bolt of pain into her joint. That's when the retching began. A tendril of hair had fallen loose, her skirt was torn, her shin was bleeding and her knee bruised. On all fours, she glanced at her surroundings. The air was still, the opossum finally dead.

Looking only at the handle of the pitchfork, not at her catch, she pulled the prongs of the pitchfork straight up. She then scooped up the carcass and carried the dead weight toward the house, balancing the corpse as far from her body as possible. She did not want the opossum to fall off the end of the pitchfork. Her shoulder blades hurt from walking back to the house with the over-leveraged weight.

When she reached the backyard she let the dead weight drop heavily to the sand. Eliza dragged a tub away from the house and methodically traversed back and forth, across the backyard to the river's edge, collecting river water in an old pan until the tub was full. She gathered twigs and pine branches and started a fire. Ultimately she had a cauldron of boiling water. Her eyes had adjusted to the dark; she had become a night creature. She looked at her ragged, grimy fingernails; *far from the beautifully manicured hands of a young lady from Vermont,* she thought ruefully.

Finally she stood up. Mechanically, she lifted the pitchfork and, like shoveling dirt, scooped the opossum. Eliza tossed the pronged end of the pitch fork into the boiling water. Dirt and oils from the animal's fur bubbled to the surface of the water as the opossum was blanched. *This is what it's come to, what I've become. Where is the world that included Albert and her mother; Abby and Gerald?* She skimmed the water with the pitchfork and was able to collect the carcass and drop it onto the sand.

Eliza then slipped out of her torn skirt and, after folding it, almost pillow like, opened the door to the back of the house. She laid the skirt on the plank floor of the mud room. Then she went back to the opossum and scooped it up, once again using the pitchfork. It was even heavier now that it was water logged. It rolled off the front of the pitchfork. She was exhausted and her knee throbbed. Overcome, staring down at the animal she had killed, Eliza began to weep. *This is too hard, too much.* She leaned against the cottage sobbing. And finally, she returned to her task, determined to finish it, end it, the whole wretched evening.

Stumbling up the steps with the sopping carcass, balanced on the pitchfork, she dumped it onto what had been, at one time, a lovely skirt. She leaned the pitchfork against the wall, latched the back door, and gently closed the door between the mud room and the kitchen. The house remained incredibly quiet as she crept to the living room, taking in the soft glow of the lantern.

The next morning Eliza bathed, shampooing her hair and wringing it out after reaching for a towel. Her wet hair in a knot, she dressed and went to check on the children. They were beginning to stir. She lifted John-Colburn out of bed and held him on her lap, sitting on Annie's bed as the girl awoke. *Normal, things are normal now.*

Annie caught Eliza's eye, then burrowed into the covers. Eliza patted her daughter's bottom and sung nursery songs, rocking John-Colburn in her lap. For breakfast the three shared an orange. There were two biscuits. The children shared one and Eliza finished the second herself. They would eat well that evening.

It was about nine o'clock that morning when John Kildall pulled his small sloop up to the dock and lashed it to the pilings. The river had been choppy that day; his pant legs were wet and flapping around his ankles as he walked up from the bank of the Homosassa. Eliza was sitting on the steps. The children were playing together on the front porch.

She stood to greet him, "Mr. Kildall."

"Heard a gunshot late last night, maybe early morning," he began, "Thought I'd better check. The Yanks burned the Hopes' place. Yesterday. We're just checking. You alright?"

"Yes, I'm fine. The children are fine." Eliza reassured him. "There's a dead possum in the mud room, blanched, from this morning. If you can help me by skinning it while I watch the children here in the front of the house, we could have stew this evening and for the next few days."

"Oh, Eliza! You *shot* it?" Then, minding his own counsel, he amended, "Well, be careful with those bullets." He tipped his hat and pulled his lips around his teeth to prevent too many words from spilling out. "Round this way?"

Eliza stepped off the porch, toward him, nodding, "Thank you."

Half an hour later he returned to the front of the house. "A nice stew, or baked dish, this evening." He nodded toward the children, indicating that Annie and John-Colburn would eat well. "Took a little for Gwendolyn to do something with," he was already tipping his hat and moving away from the cottage. "Francis, Isaac, and I are going to check on the Hopes. They'll be staying at the Garrisons for a spell. Reckon if we help, there'll be enough food."

* * *

Posted Notice

Lee Surrenders

At Appomattox Courthouse

War for Southern Independence Ends

As General Lee, surrounded by his Army, meets Grant in Northern Virginia, Grant having penned the following:

General R.E. Lee, Commanding C.S.A.:

The results of the last week must convince you of the

Hopelessness of further resistance on the part of

The Army of Northern Virginia in this struggle. April 9, 1865

The Baltimore Sun

Release of Rebel Prisoners from Fort Warren

13 June 1865—On Friday last, orders were received at Fort Warren to release all the rebel prisoners at that place under the rank of Captain, after taking the oath of allegiance. The following parties were accordingly released, and brought up to Boston, to be furnished with transportation: John M. Agler, residence, Madison County, Va; George H. Agre, Loudon County, Va; Thomas R. Baker, do; Mathew A. Beck, Levy, Fla.; Samuel C. Beach, Fairfax County, Va; Thomas Beach,

do; Stephen G. R. Bishop, Loudon County, Va; Richard T. Boarman, Charles County, Md; William H. Bozzell, Loudon County, Va; Isaac Breathed, Washington County, Md; Robert H. C. Colburn, Jefferson County, Va; William S. Coffman, Page County, Va; Henry C. Chamblin, Loudon County, Va; John L. Cornwell, and George Cornwell, Prince William County, Va; Barney Crowley, Fairfax County, Va; William Cromwell, Ann Arundel County, Md; Thomas C. Cropper, Cecil County, Md; Charles E. Davis, Loudon County, Va; Frank W. Dungan, Baltimore, Md; William Gentz, Jefferson County, Texas; Eugene I. Giddings, Bradley County, Tennessee; Mark A. Hardin, Case County, Georgia; Cyprian T. Jenkins, Hernandez, Florida; John P. Johns, do; Philip Key, St Mary's County, Md; John H. Maddox, Fauquier County, Va; John R. Messie, do; David R. P. Pretzman, Washington County, Md; Henry Richards, Loudon County, Va; Philip E. Roach, Alexandria County, Md; George W. Smith, Loudon County, VA; Johns J. Spear, Kent County, Md; John H. Wilson, Loudon County, VA; John Wilson, Levy County, Fla.

The Boston Traveller

The men had more or less baggage. Some had trunks and band-boxes; others had a little bundle, with tooth-brushes dangling from their button-holes. The party, evidently, were mostly Americans. They were a good-natured set of fellows, and readily answered the questions that were put to them. Many of them were of opinion that the government could not have sent them to a stronger fortification than that from which they had just been liberated, or to one where the prisoners were so humanely treated and received such excellent food. Some of them said that they had friends outside of the fort, and were indebted to them for luxuries of different kinds.

The party released were mostly members of Mosby's band. Of the general officers confined at the fort they knew but little. Major Gilmore, some of them thought, was inclined to be "airy", while others, who had been more fortunate in making his acquaintance, considered him of the class of "hale fellow, well met."

"Good bye for now," C.T. threw his arms around Johnny Johns, bidding farewell to the man he had been with every day since their capture off Florida's gulf coast. Only their separate trials and respective sentencing of solitary confinement had kept the two Bay Port men apart after their transport journeys from Fort Taylor, Florida. And that long sad journey to Fort Lafayette, New York Harbor, and on to the Union prison at Fort Warren, Boston.

But this morning, the scene around them was pure bedlam. Each man was heading home, wherever home might be. The Old Colony Depot on Kneeland Street, Boston, was bedlam as wagons filled with scruffy, unshaven men in tattered clothes pulled up to the depot. C.T. watched as scene after scene unfolded as the wagons stopped and the passengers scattered in all directions. Johns held on dearly to his travel scrip, pulling the paper out of his front shirt pocket compulsively every few minutes to stare at it. C.T.'s scrip was in the folder that he had packed that morning in his rucksack. He wasn't taking the chance of pulling it out, should it flutter away in the light breeze.

The scrip would pay for the comparatively short southwesterly train ride out of Boston, to Baltimore, Maryland.

"Thank you for seeing me off, C.T. I'll see you in Bay Port," Mr. Johns said, both looking and sounding much older than his thirty-six years.

"Yes, I won't be long in Baltimore." He gave Johns a warm smile. "There's a lady and her husband I am compelled to see," his voice wavered. "And, my Aunt Mary is waiting."

Both men had outlined for the other their specific intentions after having taken the oath of allegiance to the United States of America, thus securing their release from Fort Warren. And so, Mr. Johns shook C.T.'s hand, and with tears in his eyes, climbed aboard the three o'clock train. He watched his friend from the perch as the train began its slow pull away from the station. And, with a final broad wave, his hand arcing back and forth over his head, Johns began the long journey back to Bay Port.

"I'll see you," Johns called back to C.T. as the distance between them widened.

"I won't be long. Stop in on Eliza!"

**

General Joseph E. Johnston, writing to General Beauregard in 1868:

"We, without the means of purchasing supplies of any kind, or procuring or repairing arms, could continue this war only as robbers or guerillas."

Kildall's wagon tugged heavily along the trail leading to the Jenkins' cottage. At first the two men were silent. It was late in the day and C.T. was exhausted. He knew he looked gaunt; his skin was even more aged and lined than before that fateful day two years earlier. The only compensation was the fresh suit and clean white shirt he wore, a gift from Constantine and Mary. His boots were two years older than when he had entered Fort Warren prison, and their condition contrasted starkly with his new suit of clothes. These thoughts of pride and appearance were interrupted by Kildall's words, "Well C.T., here you are. Suspect your family's waiting for you now, aren't they?"

"Yes, Joseph, I suspect that they are. I'd better be going on in."

"I'm glad you made it through."

"Thank you, Joseph," he said, straightening his shoulders. "So am I. It's good to be home." With that C.T. picked up his bag and stepped off the wagon.

He pulled out his pocket watch and flipped it open with his ragged thumbnail. The crystal was cracked. It was four o'clock in the afternoon when he began his trudge through the tall Florida saw grass. The Homosassa River lay on the far side of his cottage. He thought he saw his sloop bobbing at the end of the dock, but he knew it was a mirage.

A woman edged out of the house. C.T. watched as she closed the screen door, carefully ensuring the latch caught before turning back to him. She was thin, and her thick, braided hair, was grey. She held her hands folded in front of her. He didn't recognize her clothes as anything his memory told him she owned.

"Eliza."

She advanced to the edge of the porch, and then walked down the steps toward him. She nodded, her words choking her.

"Eliza," he said again. "My god, Eliza . . . are you alright?"

The distance closed between them and they were finally in each other's arms.

"No," she began sobbing. "It was too hard. I was alone." She continued, "I didn't ever imagine this moment coming. I could only see you in prison — forever."

"I know, Darling, I know." C.T. drew Eliza close. He could not have held her more closely. He continued rocking her. *I couldn't have imagined this moment either.* He shifted his embrace to reach for his handkerchief as Eliza caught her breath. Before her sobbing began again, C.T. began wiping the tears from her face. First a series of dainty pats across each cheek, then he began blotting her jaw line where tears hung the moment before dropping to the front of her bodice. It had been too long since either of them had received any tenderness. Finally, she began to relax.

C.T. placed his forefinger under her chin and slowly drew her closer again. Their tender, searching kiss sealed every promise, every commitment that they could make to each other. The moment held, for a long time.

Finally they pulled away and C.T. placed his handkerchief in his inside breast pocket. At the same time, still staring into Eliza's eyes he pulled a jewelry box from his inside jacket pocket. "Pink seed pearls, they remind me of you, so sweet, so dainty."

This time Eliza kissed C.T. She brushed her hand through his wiry grey hair, and ran her hand down the length of his beard. C.T. looked over her head at his cottage.

"They're all inside, Cyprian. They are waiting for you."

"The children won't even remember me."

"That might well be true. But in good time what we had will all come back to us." She steered him by the elbow up the steps of his own cottage.

Annie and John-Colburn were standing side by side, cleaned and polished, as though it were Sunday. They remained silent. Annie's hair was divided with one straight perfect part, her braids were pulled back high on her crown. Her wrists extended well past her sleeve cuffs. The hand-me-down ankle boots previously worn by one of the Ederington girls were scuffed, but polished. Four-year-old John was uncharacteristically glum. His thin frame created the illusion that he was tall for his age, but it *was* an illusion, for he wasn't.

C.T.'s eyes drifted to Harrison Moore who stood to the left of the children. *'Good God, he has aged so much more than me.* "Harrison," C.T nodded, acknowledging his antagonist.

Harrison stepped forward. "I'm not staying. I know I don't have any right to be here, considering what I did. I just want to tell you how sorry I am. We were starving; I was overwhelmed watching MaryAnn get progressively weaker. I never thought forward to the outcome of betraying you..."

"Well, we each face our own devils, don't we Harrison? I suppose it hasn't been easy. I'm sorry about MaryAnn. She was a fine and wonderful woman."

"Yes. I didn't deserve her, I guess that's what folks are saying."

C.T. shrugged. "Kildall tells me that Jacob is back at Ms. Harrell's. That's the best place for him now."

"Yes, that's the best place for him. Well, I'd best be getting along, I wanted to pay my respects to your family. I have a horse tied out back, I can leave out the back door. C.T., I know that God will bless you in his own way."

C.T. shook his head back and forth imperceptibly. *I've never known what any of his blessings meant, and now more than ever.* Jenkins noted that Eliza did not walk her uncle to the door or make any move to acknowledge his departure. She picked up John-Colburn and with her free hand steered Annie into the little girl's bedroom.

Closing the screen door carefully behind Harrison Moore, C.T. walked across the living room into the kitchen where his wife faced him.

"She's in Vermont. She couldn't make it back down after Albert was buried."

"I see. Well, we'll carry on."

* * *

25

YULEE'S LANDING

Annie was panting, her little pink tongue licking her salty lips. With eyes darted from side to side she searched out her quarry. The sun was scorching the back of her neck. She knew that she would pounce suddenly, undetected until the very last moment. Bent over, her hands on her knees, she plucked at her long calico skirt, fanning it to cool off her gazelle-length legs. She hated her knobby knees. The heavy itchy stockings she wore kept sliding down into her ankle-high boots, causing them to wrinkle inside her boots. She knew she'd have blisters when she finally unlaced her shoes and kicked them off at bedtime that evening.

She stood erect once she had caught her breath. Pressing herself to the east side of the cottage, she thought through her next move. If she was careful, she would be able to scramble undetected across the lawn and duck behind the overturned canoe that was stored at the water's edge.

She slowly edged forward along the side of the cottage, clinging like a gecko to the cedar shingles. Her long brunette braids swung like pendulums as she leaned forward, peering over the expansive lawn and out toward the Homosassa River that rolled lazily toward the Gulf on the opposite side of the cottage.

She extended her long neck in surveillance; the coast was clear. Sweeping her eyes across the front lawn, she tiptoed out from the cover of the house. She proceeded like a panther across the front of the house, crouching under the living room windows to evade her mother's gaze.

Scratch! Scratch!

Wait! What was that noise? She dropped to all fours, pulling her voluminous skirt out of the way so she could crawl.

Scratch! Scratch!

The noise came from under the porch steps. She turned her head slowly, casting a wicked smile toward her intended captive. A shrill, piercing scream emanated from under the porch, as a little bundle of energy shot out from cover and ran toward the river.

Annie gave chase, clutching at the air as she gained on her little sister. Her reach held! Both girls went down, rolling across the lawn. Tangled in each other's arms and legs, they screamed with laughter. They slapped and rolled down the slope toward the water's edge. In spite of their age difference, the two were inseparable conspirators, and agreed that hide and seek was the best game ever.

"Annie!" A sharp reproach snapped the air like a whip. "Young ladies don't run!" Eliza admonished sharply from the front porch. "They walk, or they stroll. And, I don't want you to encourage Margaret into that rough-housing."

Relentless, Eliza continued her tutelage in the proper behavior of young ladies, "It's not becoming. You'll never have a beau, when the time comes, unless you start showing better manners now. Both of you; cool down and wash up, then come in and set the table. Your father and brother will be in from the groves for dinner soon."

"Yes Momma," Annie answered reluctantly. Eight year old Margaret looked up at her sister with a wrinkled nose and shrugged her shoulders. In response, Annie shrugged her shoulders back at Margaret, covering her mouth with her cupped hands and laughing conspiratorially.

They trudged into the house to clean themselves up properly for setting the table. The Jenkins' cook, Helen Harper, smiled at them over her shoulder, as she washed the pots that had been used to cook supper. Helen soaked a cloth for each of them and they dutifully cleaned up. After the table was set they lollygagged and mugged at each other while waiting for their next assignment.

"Mother" Eliza called to Mrs. Colburn, now seventy-one, "supper will be served as soon as Cyprian and John-Colburn return."

Aged, and subdued from the losses sustained during the war, Mrs. Colburn had returned to the comfort of Florida, bringing her step-daughter, Betsey, with her. She looked up from her embroidery and nodded, looking out the front window before she joined the women in the kitchen. For a moment she thought she could see the Rose Hill arch. She shook her head and realized she was looking out over the calming currents of the Homosassa River across to Yulee's Landing, where the steamer *Mistletoe* was moored.

Washed up and ready to help set the table, Margaret stood at attention. She waited to be noticed by someone. Her Aunt Betsey came into the kitchen, and began stroking Margaret's long hair affectionately.

Margaret smiled up at her aunt as Betsey gathered the little girl's hair and re-tied the ribbon that was sliding down the crown of her locks.

"What are you reading today, darling?"

"Twenty Thousand Leagues under the Sea."

Betsey looked at Eliza, "Isn't that a book more suited for John-Colburn?"

"At least she's reading, Betsey. And, she's happy. She reads everything that's put in front of her. What am I going to do?"

"Couldn't she be reading the Bible?" Betsey pressed on.

"She's read the Bible. She'll be nine in June and she's read the Bible. Twice. She has a book collection that rivals my own." Eliza admitted. "Mr. Jules Verne is the least of my worries."

The sound of boot steps scraping across the front porch was followed by the screen door slamming. A scamper through the front room, alerted the women that John-Colburn and C.T. had returned from Yulee's Landing to collect the mail. C.T. would deliver the letters, packages and periodicals to the Homosassa community over the next week, with the assistance of eleven-year-old John-Colburn.

"Where is everyone?" C.T. called from the living room. When he walked into the kitchen, his sister-in-law was braiding Margaret's hair, carrying on about her niece's reading habits. Mrs. Colburn stood with her arms wrapped around Annie. He ruffled his son's hair and pointed to the sink before crossing the kitchen to plant one kiss on Annie's forehead and one on Mrs. Colburn's cheek.

"C.T."

He winked at his mother-in-law and placed his hand on the top of Annie's head, indicating that his daughter was nearly as tall as her grandmother. Eliza handed the kitchen towel she was holding to Helen, and leaned over to accept C.T.'s buss. John-Colburn returned from the mudroom in a series of hops, and with a grin, realized that he had captured an audience with his larking.

His father suggested, "Shall we sit down? Smells like we are in for a treat, huh, John-Colburn?"

The family took their places around the thick block table.

"Shall we give thanks?" suggested Eliza, as the family sought out each other's hands for grace.

"Betsey?" C.T. suggested.

Eliza's step-sister nodded, both happy and thankful to be included.

"Dear Heavenly Father, we pray," she began. "We give thanks for the generosity of our sustenance, and for this lovely home. We give thanks that we are able to live as one family under your roof, on the beautiful banks of the Homosassa. We acknowledge the mysteries of our respective missions and hope that we each shall flourish under your guidance. We pray for the health of our brother, Moses, and hope that you will allow his ministry to flourish. We ask for a strong family and, in Jesus' name, we thank you for your guidance, goodness and charity. Amen."

C.T., who never closed his eyes during grace, squeezed his wife's hand before placing it gently on the table, winking at Eliza as she turned her head and peeked at him under her eyelashes. A short grace. C.T. and Eliza seemed fine with that.

"Well, what did John and I miss? What is the topic of the day?" C.T. asked, looking around the table.

"Margaret's reading habits, actually," volunteered Mrs. Colburn. "We were discussing whether it's proper for her to be reading *Twenty Thousand Leagues Under the Sea*? She's so young, and it *is* John-Colburn's book, after all," Mrs. Colburn constructed Betsey's argument for her as usual.

"Well, let's ask the subject of this discussion." C.T. turned to his youngest daughter. "Margaret, Maggie-girl," he started, wrinkling his nose to mimic her. "First, I see that you are wearing the pink seed pearl necklace I brought to your mother from Boston. You've dressed up nicely for dinner. You know, Margaret, pink seed pearls *are* your mother's favorite," smiling at his wife.

Margaret nodded, fingering the lustrous gems.

"So! *Are* you reading Twenty Thousand Leagues Under the Sea?" C.T. asked.

"Yes, poppa."

"Hmm. I see. Do you like it?"

"I do!"

"I see. Are you understanding all those big words?"

"Annie is helping me!" Margaret beamed. Annie blanched, caught in the web of her sister's transgression or triumph.

"Well, it sounds like it's a fine collaboration, then. Girls, you must read as much as you can!"

"Well, that's settled." Eliza nodded to C.T. in perfect parental agreement. "Mrs. Colburn, would you please pass me the bread. It looks like Miss Helen has been baking all morning." And the meal continued with C.T. and John-Colburn looking on baffled by the chatter and gossip of five women in the same household.

"C.T. what news do you hear from Bay Port?" quizzed Mrs. Colburn during a momentary lull bridged only by Annie and Margaret's whispers to each other.

"Ah, Mrs. Colburn! I thought you were going to join John-Colburn and me this morning. And don't think I'm teasing. Well, let's see," he gathered his thoughts. "Early Allen is not faring well, I'm afraid. Betsey, let's include him in your next grace. Francis and Precious are doing very well. Indiana Garrison is with child, so let's remember William and Indiana in our prayers also. Judge Mayo seems to have the community under control." He laughed. "Yes, I think everything is fine, Mrs. Colburn. Let's see if there isn't a letter for you from Rufus, or something else nice from Fair Haven, this evening while John and I will prepare our mail route. What do you say, young man?"

John-Colburn nodded his assent.

"Would you like another helping, C.T.?" Eliza asked placing a second helping of blackened trout on her husband's plate.

"I'm not starving, darling," he responded, looking amused. "John-Colburn, would you like to share this second helping with me?"

"Mrs. Colburn? Betsey?" Then C.T. turned to his wife who had placed her napkin at the side of her plate. "Done? Well, that was wonderful! Thank you, Mrs. Harper. Now! Who wants to come with me to see if the fish are biting now that things are cooling off? Mrs. Colburn? Are you joining us?"

"No, dear, I think I'll save the rest of today's energy for the dishes. Betsey will help me."

"I'll go!" "I'll go!" screamed the over-enthusiastic little girls.

Eliza swept her arm around her son and looked down at him quizzically. He nodded, reading her thoughts, and the two took off for their late afternoon walk to check on the hens and ensure the dogs had enough water for the evening.

That night, as Eliza closed their bedroom door and adjusted the shutters to let in the evening breeze. C.T. turned to her, "How do you think it's going to work out, having both Mrs. Colburn and now Betsey join us here?"

"After all?" she began, remembering the long, lonely trudge of years while C.T. was imprisoned. "I think it's going to be fine."

* * *

26

GREENWOOD CEMETERY

"Who's the old lady?" the gravedigger asked; his thick, ebony fingers wrapped around the well worn handle of a pitched-nosed shovel. He was nodding toward a lone woman, dressed in an out-of-fashion, long black dress. Her back was rounded in a dowager's hump, maybe from leaning for too many years on the cane that seemed too short for her.

"I couldn't tell you, Abe" the foreman answered thoughtfully, as he squinted in the direction his charge had pointed. He watched the stooped woman brace herself on one of two matching headstones. "She started showing up last winter. She's here most every day. Same place. Just stands there, for as long as I can watch her. Just stands there," his voice trailing off as the beefy supervisor wiped his brow with a patterned handkerchief, then stuffed the moist, dirt-streaked cloth back into his overalls. He pitched his shovel back into the earth—six more feet and they'd be done for the day.

"Mr. Bobby, she surely seems kind of bony," further observed Abe. He didn't want to leave the subject of the old woman.

"You'll get used to seeing old people wander in and out of here. 'All times of day. Sometimes at night, when you make your last rounds," Bobby counseled. "She's no one special, so far 'as I can tell. She's here most every day. Waiting. If them's her people she's missing, we'll be digging a hole for *her* soon instead of the one we're supposed to be digging today." Bobby gently chided his newest helper back to the task at hand, in an attempt at beating the Florida sun before it settled a searing veil over the scruffy lawn of the Greenwood Cemetery.

The two men went back to work, gouging their shovels into the earth and pitching the dirt over their shoulders, skillfully creating a gentle slope of dirt three feet high on either side of the gaping hole. They dug chest-deep before leaning on their shovels for a break. Bobby pulled a flask out of his back pocket and unscrewed the cap. Dirt clogged the grooves making the maneuver difficult. Holding the battered flask at arm's length he offered a nip to his new partner. The grandson of a Florida slave shook his head, turning down the gesture; but noting the bigheartedness of its intention.

By noon, the only indication that anyone was standing at the bottom of burial site N79 was the pitch of dirt up into the air towards the mounds along each side of the fresh grave. But, no one was watching.

The two men finally finished their work. Abe, younger and certainly the stronger of the two men was able to walk up the sides of the grave as though on stilts, not bothering with the ladder that leaned against the wall of the crevasse. Palms down on either side of the deep hole, he hoisted himself out like a gymnast and over to the other side. He reached down and took his shovel from his supervisor, who extended it up toward the black youth's reach.

Abe extended a hand down to his unsteady supervisor. The senior of the two men grunted and clawed his way out. Clapping the dirt off his hands and uncapping his flask for the last time that afternoon, lapping up the last drop of 'refreshment'. And, with his head back, eyes squinting, he nodded toward the north end of the cemetery.

Abe looked, and watched as the frail old woman moved on, across their line of vision to the west, unaware that she was being observed. Peering intently at the ground, she made her way in slow, individual steps; her gnarled left hand was curled over the top of her carved, hickory cane.

Her right hand clutched at the string of pink seed pearls embellishing the warbled neckline of her dress.

Placing their shovels over their shoulders, the two men ambled toward the spot where they had first seen the old woman earlier that day.

Pausing where she had stood vigil, they read the matching pair of headstones in silence:

Eliza Colburn
Wife of C.T. Jenkins
Born Dec 9, 1831
Died Oct 7, 1904
Saved by Grace

Annie D Jenkins
Born Feb 11, 1860
Died Dec 7, 1931
Asleep in Jesus

THE END

27

Author's Notes

Jenkins Confederate Blockade Runner was written using the name "Eliza" for the character that represents C.T. Jenkins' wife. He was actually married to Lucy Colburn Jenkins; but because Lucy's mother had the same first name – and not to confuse my readers – I used the name "Eliza" for the woman who survived living on the banks of Florida's Homosassa River during the Civil War.

At the time **Jenkins Confederate Blockade Runner**, Edition 1 was published in 2010 many questions remained about the true story of how C.T. Jenkins and his wife, Lucy Colburn Jenkins lived out their post-war years together. This, in spite of the fact that I had spent over a decade researching the 1830s trek C.T. Jenkins made through Georgia into Florida, and his Congressional Record-documented prison term.

Questions such as what was life along the Homosassa River like for the Jenkins family after the Civil War? What were the actual circumstances of Jenkins' release from prison? What had become of the Jenkins' children, Annie, John-Colburn, and Margaret?

In April 2013, nearly three years after publishing this novel I received the most astonishing message from Douglas Parsons of Manchester NH whose ancestors had been Homosassa, Florida neighbors of Lucy C. Jenkins and C.T. Jenkins.

Mr. Parsons is a descendant of Major John Parsons. He contacted me after discovering an historian's jewel: A letter *within a letter* that revealed post-Civil War journeys being arranged with the intention of compelling imprisoned Confederate husbands, sons, and brothers to sign the Oath of Allegiance to the United States and return home to their families.

But for me the letter revealed much more. It revealed the true story of how C.T. Jenkins came to be reunited with his wife and children after the Civil War. The correspondence with its embedded revelations is between Mr. Parsons' two ancestral aunts who are sisters. One sister is relaying to the other the contents of a letter that she had received from "L.C. Colburn" regarding the wife of Major John Parsons.

I owe a debt of gratitude to Mr. Parsons for contacting me after reading the first edition of **Jenkins: Confederate Blockade Runner** and realizing that the "L.C. Jenkins" referred to in his family's historic letter was my ancestral aunt, Lucy Colburn Jenkins.

This is the letter embedded in the correspondence between Abby and Anna, two Parson family sisters:

March~April 1865

From: Lucy Colburn Jenkins
Fair Haven, Vermont

To: Miss Decatur
New York City, New York

My Dear Miss Decatur,
When I parted from your sister's company last, I promised, if possible, to call on you when we arrived in New York; Or, if I could not see you, to write to you at my earliest convenience. We left Bay Port Feb 4th and after a detention of five weeks on the way and a wearing experience of perplexities and seasickness we arrived at New York on the 21st of March. As I had with me my Mother and two little Annie and John I found it impossible to make my visits in New York and took the earliest train for Fray on our way to Vermont.

I regret very much I did not see you. Mrs. Parsons'
account and my own which should have been written to
you some days ago [was] prevented by illness.

I found it very hard to part [from] Mrs. Parsons as I
have become most warmly and gratefully attached to
both the Major and herself. My thoughts go after them
very frequently with a longing anxiety to know how they
are situated, and how they are in these days so fraught
with sorrow to our southern land. I am sorry to say I left
Mrs. Parsons feeble in health and depressed in spirits.
She has missed her home sadly. Major Parsons told me
that he wrote you a full account of their misfortunes and
losses in July last. The experience of those few days
were very painful to us all and especially to your sister.
But she bore it better than I should have thought
possible had I foreseen what was coming upon us - you
are probably aware that a few days after the breaking up
of their home they started for middle Florida where Mrs.
Parsons remained until Dec. Her baby was born in
Monticello two months after the raid.

When I left Florida they were boarding at
Brooksville. Your Brother was there also. You would be
delighted with your sister's children. Little Johnnie is a
bright active boy and [the older daughter] pretty indeed
and little Susie is one of the sweetest of all babies &
fortunately for her mamma unusually good and quiet.
My Mother urged Mrs. Parsons to wean her baby early
and I hope she will not fail to do so. It will be quite as
well for the child as she eats nicely and very much better
for your Sister, who is quite too delicate to nurse her
through the summer months. I should be glad to think
our national matters would become settled so that she
might come north soon. She has a great longing for her
friends and I think the change would be of great
advantage to her health. I am intensely anxious to know
what our southern friends think of their situation and
prospects.

When I came away Major Parsons was very sure he could never take the Oath of Allegiance to the United States. I am greatly indebted to Major Parsons for his constant and unfailing kindness during the last two long years; and to your sister also for many favors and for the earnest sympathy, which has been called forth by our mutual trials. I have not yet seen my husband but have applied for permission to visit him and am anxiously waiting an answer.

Permit me to thank you, my dear Miss Decatur, for every cheering word you have written him during his wearisome captivity. Should I be permitted to visit him ~~in Boston~~ I shall take the opportunity, while in Boston, to call upon Lieutenant Decatur whose address Mrs. Parsons gave me.

As I am not quite certain of your address; will you please let me know immediately if you receive this? And also inform me if you have heard from your Sister since I left Florida? Should you desire any further information, which I can give you, I will gladly answer all inquiries. I should have written more satisfactorily to you and, for myself, I [wish to know] more definitely how much you have heard from Florida during the past year. Hoping to hear from you soon.

I remain, Yours Very Truly
L.C. Jenkins

* *

In this novel I have blended C.T. Jenkins' AOA homestead cottage of 1843 and his post-marriage Homosassa home which he and Lucy C. Jenkins lived in after their December 9, 1859 marriage. It was between December 1859 and CT's capture in June 1863 that they built the Homosassa riverfront home and left Rose Hill.

One summer a couple of years ago I sat on the lawn of Wilma MacRea's riverfront home visiting her in Homosassa. I looked across the water imagining the

Jenkins home that James Randall Ryder had described in his, "Memoirs of a Busy Life."

It was easy to envision the life that C.T. Jenkins and his family would have enjoyed living on the Homosassa River. Crops were barged out, and receipt of supplies arranged through David Yulee's barge company. But I also imagined that the homestead had long since burned down, or had fallen into neglect and finally perished in the harsh Florida landscape and many storms over the past 160 years.

Not so. Only a few weeks ago (April 2015) I learned from Kathy Turner Thompson, curator and historian at the Old Courthouse Historical Museum in Inverness, Florida that an astonishing discovery had been made – the Jenkins home was still standing; and in fact, in good order.

In 1895, after her husband's death, Lucy C. Jenkins sold the Jenkins' Homosassa River property to Mr. H. Y. Castner and his wife, Cora Castner.

In 1903 Mrs. Cora Castner, in turn, sold the property to Mr. Frank Potts, representing the "Atlanta Fishing Club". From that time through to today the slender sliver of riverfront once belonging to C.T. Jenkins and his wife, and across from the what had once been David Yulee's property has been hidden in plain sight as the venerable fishing club and "modest cottage" on West Halls River Road, Homosassa, Florida.

During 2014 and 2015 it was decided by the Homosassa Fishing Club that major improvements were needed. Obtaining building permits for extensive renovations to the cottage required submission of the property's Deed history to the County.

The Deed conveying the property to the Homosassa Fishing Club contains these words [abridged]:

State of Georgia, Fulton County

This indenture, made on this twenty sixth day of March, A.D. one thousand, nine hundred and four (1904) between George S. Lowndes, of the State and County aforesaid, as trustee for the Homosassa Fishing Club, party of the first part. . .

. . . Recited in the deed of Mrs. Cora Castner (party of the first part) to the said George S. Lowndes, as trustee . . . has granted, bargained, and sold to the party of the second part, its successors and assigns . . a parcel of land situated in Citrus County, Florida to wit:

That a certain rectangular piece, parcel or tract of land, fronting seventy feet on the north side of the Homosassa River and extending seven hundred and eleven and one half feet in a northerly direction . . . beginning at a cedar post and on the north bank of the Homosassa River, from which post a certain brick pier situated under the southeast corner to the piazza of the dwelling house now standing on said tract . . . containing one and twelve hundredths acres, more or less the same being the land conveyed to H. Y. Castner by Lucy C. Jenkins by Deed dated January 29th 1895, which is recorded in the Public Records of Citrus County, Florida in Deed book 18, at page 41; and also all the furniture fixtures, household goods and other personal property on said premises (detailed) in a letter of Mrs. Cora M. Castner, dated December 8th 1903 to Mr. Frank M. Potts, Esquire, President of said Homosassa Fishing Club.

[Seal] George S. Lowndes
As Trustee for Homosassa Fishing Club

* * *

28

The Rest of the Story

In 1897 Annie, John-Colburn, and Margaret moved to St. Petersburg, along with their mother, Lucy C. Jenkins. They had lived in Sanford, Florida for a short while after C.T. Jenkins' death.

Annie would have been 38; John-Colburn 36, and Margaret would have been 32 when they arrived St. Petersburg.

In the years following her father's death
Annie Jenkins became a successful St. Petersburg real estate investor. Her income was stated at $25,000 on 1920 Federal census documents. She entertained lavishly and was active in the St. Petersburg First Presbyterian Church. She died in 1938 and is buried in St. Petersburg at the Greenwood Cemetery.

John Colburn Jenkins maintained a career with the U.S. Postal Service throughout his life. He married Elinor Wright and they, like Annie, owned a home in St. Petersburg; although theirs was considerably more modest. John Colburn Jenkins died in 1931 and is buried at Royal Palm Cemetery. Elinor Wright is buried to his right in an unmarked grave.

Margaret Howell Jenkins showed her wit and humor in speeches to ladies guilds and historical societies; the contents of which are found in the archives of St. Petersburg's newspapers.

Her love of books followed her throughout her life as she established the first reading room system in St. Petersburg. She and her sister maintained an expansive library that was bequeathed to Montreat College in North Carolina upon her death.

She died in 1948 and is buried next to her companion, **Elizabeth Talbot**. Miss Talbot was a missionary for the Presbyterian Church who evacuated China during the People's Revolution in China.

* * *

Obituary ~ C.T. Jenkins, December 1893
The Baltimore Sun

Col. Cyprian T. Jenkins
An old Baltimorean Dies in the
State of Florida

His Recollections of this City – *Many Parts Were Woods and Fields When He Was A Lad—Gentlemen With Queues And Pretty Girls Whose Folly was Tight Lacing.*

29 Dec 1893—Col. Cyprian T. Jenkins, an old Baltimorean and the brother of Capt. Wm. W. Jenkins and Constantine D. Jenkins, has just died in Florida where he had resided since 1834. His last visit to Baltimore was four years ago, when he stopped at The Sun office to renew his subscription "for life," as he said.

Colonel Jenkins had a remarkable history and was instrumental as well in making the history of Florida. In an interview on his last visit here he said he remembered well the meteoric showers of 1833.

He saw the first gas lit in Baltimore, saw Charles Carroll of Carrollton lay the corner-stone of the Baltimore and Ohio Railroad, and saw Comet, the first steam locomotive used on it. The cornerstone, he said was laid in Daniel Carroll's field. There were no houses there, but Austin Woodfolk, a slave-trader, lived opposite.

"As a boy," he said, "I attended David McIntyre's school, on Saratoga Street near what is now the Hotel Rennert. There was no street from Washington monument to Jones falls and between the Cathedral and the monument there was a deep hollow, containing no houses except Charles Howard's. Col. Jon Eager Howard's home was in Howard's Park, south of the Cathedral site. Between the monument and Greenmount only two persons lived. George Appold had a tan yard there and Christian Keller had a large flour mill at Belvedere. Charles Street on the east side, from Centre Street to the monument, was called Waterloo Row. There were few houses then east of Broadway and few west of Alsquith Street.

"Baltimore people of those days were primitive, hospitable, and democratic. Only two men in the city were worth a million dollars. They were Charles Carroll and William Patterson. Mr. Patterson lived on South Street, between Lovely land and Water Street. The people loved horse-racing and often assembled at the race track. They attended cotillion parties, the Assembly Rooms on Charles Street, the Old Assembly Rooms at Holliday and Fayette streets, and the Athenrum. They also went to Fairmount and Columbian Gardens, and later to the Vauxhall Gardens, on Broadway, opposite St. Patrick's Church site.

"The beauties of Baltimore had a national reputation then. They dressed plainly but richly. Their greatest folly was tight lacing. A few old men still went about with buckles and knee breeches, among them Christopher Hughes and Grandfather Wells. A great many wore their hair in queues and none wore mustaches. I never saw a mustache until 1840. Boys had their hair cut at home. If my father had caught me in a barber shop he would have licked me."

Colonel Jenkins held many important positions in the service of Florida as a Territory and a State, the first being under a commission from President Jackson. He was the first settler in Hernando County, saw the first wedding and was present when the first child was born in that county. It was Bud Pearson, now a well known resident. Col. Jenkins went into the Seminole war in a company of mounted rangers, commanded by Col. William J. Bailey. He was noted for his conflicts with the Indians and was a government scout when Dade's army was massacred. He fought through the war from 1835 to 1838. In 1832-1833 he served in the legislature.

He was four to eight years a United States timber agent, and was returned to the Legislature in 1861-62. He voted in the body for the first railroad charter given in Florida.

In the Civil War he served as captain and then colonel in the Fourth Florida Regiment. He was captured and remained a prisoner twenty-six months in Forts Lafayette, Taylor and Warren until the close of the war. He was surveyor of his county for ten or fifteen years, and was a farmer on the Homosassa River and had a large orange grove. Colonel Jenkins was eighty-two years old, and was born at the old Jenkins homestead on Jenkins Lane. He married in 1858 at Lake Champlain and had three children. His relatives are numerous in this city and state.

* * *

30

REFERENCES

The map of Gulf Coast: Cedar Key, Florida and the waterways of Cedar Keys to Tampa Bay, Florida Reprinted with permission of Jeff Miller, Historian, New Port Richey, Florida. All Rights Reserved.

A History of the Town of Fair Haven, Vermont. Andrew N. Adams. Leonard & Phelps, Printers, 1870.

Personal Papers. Bobby Snow and Betty Cason-Snow, Brooksville, Florida.

Weekly Herald 26 Dec 1857

Macon Weekly Telegraph 20 Jan 1857

New York Herald 17 July 1857

North American & U.S. Gazette. 06 October 1854

Rose Hill. Pioneer Days. James M. Jones. October 4, 1962

Rose Hill. Bobby Snow September 05, 2002

The Politically Incorrect Guide to the Civil War. H. W. Crocker III. Regnery. 2008

Vermont State Archives and Records Administration. Lydia Mackey.

'Journal Entry' from *Reminisces*, by C. T. Jenkins. *Genealogy of the Jenkins Family of Maryland 1664-1895*, Mary Isabella Plowden Jenkins. Monograph Press, Baltimore, MD. 1895.

Official War Gazette New York, July 11, 1863 http://www.correctionhistory.org/html/chronicl/cw_pow s/html/cwpows3.html

A Confederate Chronicle: The Life of a Civil War Survivor. Pamela Chase Hain. Columbia: University of Missouri Press. 2005

Genealogy of the Jenkins Family of Maryland 1664-1895, Mary Isabella Plowden Jenkins. Monograph Press, Baltimore, MD. , 1895.

The Baltimore Sun, 11 April 1865, The End Approaches, page 2. Reprinted as originally published, reprinted with permission.

Obituary of C.T. Jenkins: *The Baltimore Sun*, 29 December 1893. Reprinted as originally published, with permission

STUDY GUIDE

All of us change our perspectives and change our minds about how we will lead our lives as we grow up; and as we grow older.

In what ways did Eliza change her values from when she is introduced into the story until the end of the Civil War?

Sometimes we practice self-assessment as we face difficult decisions.

At what moments in C.T. Jenkins life did he assessment his values and his dreams in relationship with his circumstances?

We seem to be less dependent on the kindness of strangers, and the generosity of neighbors.

Do you find this statement of to be true? How does the dependence on kindness and generosity affect the lives of the characters in this novel?

Discuss, in terms of women's history, the manner in which Eliza lived her life, and the manner in which her mother lived hers.

What part did being a widow versus being a married woman play in how Mrs. Colburn and Eliza Colburn Jenkins moved about society.

Would you have made the same decision that Jenkins' brother, Constantine, made about coming to visit a brother in prison who had deserted the family?

In your estimation what was the biggest risk that C.T. Jenkins took in his life?

Discuss Reverend Harrison Moore's decision and how it may have contrasted or coincided with his values.

Give a book report to your class about "Jenkins: Confederate Blockade Runner"

* * *

www.ingramcontent.com/pod-product-compliance
Lightning Source LLC
Chambersburg PA
CBHW031554240626
47153CB00002B/508